TWO FOR THE PRICE OF ONE

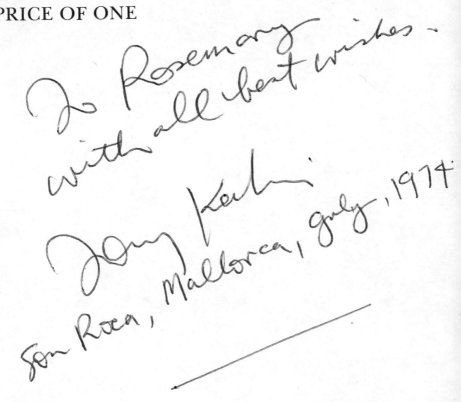

To Rosemary
with all best wishes –

Jony Keti
Son Roca, Mallorca, July, 1974

TWO FOR THE PRICE OF ONE

by Tony Kenrick

The Bobbs-Merrill Company, Inc.
Indianapolis / New York

ISBN 0-672-51888-0
Library of Congress catalog card number 73-10701
Designed by Paula Wiener
Manufactured in the United States of America
First printing

Dedication

For Joan.
And about time, too.

IN A CERTAIN TOWN OF PERSIA a young student, desirous of greater knowledge, asked his tutor to explain the difference between Chance and Kismet. The sage pondered on this and then by way of an answer told this story: "During the reign of the Caliph Haroun al Raschid there lived at Baghdad three honest men whose minds Allah had seen fit to touch. One day, while returning from the house of a physician, they lamed their camel, and although the city was to blame the satraps turned deaf ears to their complaint. Incensed at this injustice the leader of the three devised a bold and curious plan to attain fair compensation. Accompanied by the other two he journeyed forth to acquire a mighty sword, and even though it proved a difficult task he persevered in his endeavor, securing one at length by causing it to fly as if by magic through the air. Then borrowing a trader's sturdy camel, and seizing an opportune time, they loaded the sword upon a dhow and set out for the river palace in which the grand vizier dwelt. Coming upon it they brandished the sword and uttered fearful threats and were quickly paid the monies owing them.

Now at this same time, in another part of the city there lived three thieves, mean and ugly in their ways and unhappy with their meager earnings. And it happened that one of their number, while pausing for refreshment at a watering place, learned of the honest man's plan and acquainted his leader with the scheme. Upon hearing of it the leader thought to turn it to his advantage and, conceiving a plan bolder even than the honest man's, went to spy on the city's treasure house.

With the help of a merchant, a cunning rogue dishonest even unto his own, he enlisted two more assistants, a young man from the country and another, a fierce and violent robber who caused him much disquiet. Together they journeyed to another city where by loathsome means they too acquired a dhow and a mighty sword and sailed it to the treasure house. They dealt the treasure house a dreadful blow and, mounting a winged horse, stole a king's ransom and fled disguised.

And so they thought themselves successful, although their plan, upon examination, was not without surprise or unforeseen events or un-bargained-for occurrences, chief of which was this: the honest men, returning from the palace of the vizier, came quite unknowingly upon the thieves and, through the intervention of a brave but foolish person, recovered the treasure and delivered the robbers, bound tightly hand and foot, to the captain of the vizier's guard. "Thus," said the sage, "they came to rectify and cancel out the evil deed which they themselves had unwittingly begun."

"Chance?" the student asked.

"Kismet," the sage replied. "What will be will be. And what has been is destined to be again."

From 'The Song of Aldebaran.'
The Hazár Afsána Collection.
MS # 472N/6E
British Museum.

chapter 1

". . . three honest men whose minds
Allah had seen fit to touch"

Dibley had a problem.

He knew he didn't have long; when the light turned green he'd be in trouble. He brought a hand up to his face and massaged his brow, then turned the kneading fingers into a fist and thumped it steadily against his temple. None of it did any good. When the light changed he still hadn't remembered. Damn it, it had happened again—he'd forgotten how to drive.

The cars behind started honking and prodded Dibley into experimenting. Gingerly he reached out and pressed a button: the radio came on. He tried another button and started the windshield wipers. He hit every button in sight, but the car stayed firmly where it was. What the hell did you do to make the wheels go round? He spotted a handle underneath the dash and made a grab for it. There was a dull sponk as the hood catch released. The cars behind were starting to pull out and go around him, their drivers rolling down their windows to shout imprecations as they shot by. New Yorkers, happy enough to remain silent in the face of rape or murder or mugging, draw the line at being delayed.

A patrolman ambled over from the curb, taking in the car as he came; the headlights were on, the left indicator was flashing, the wipers were going, the aerial was rising up and down and the radio was blaring a Sousa march. It was an old car, a '62 Studebaker, and it looked to the cop as if years of driving round the streets of Manhattan had sent it off its rocker. But the cop had been around the streets of Manhattan for a long time himself, and he knew that it wasn't the machines that were unstable in New York, it was the people who ran them.

"Let's go. Let's go," he said, slapping the fender. He peered in through the window.

The driver had his eyes shut tight and one hand pressed to his forehead. "You O.K., buddy?"

"What? Oh yeah, sure."

"The car O.K.?"

Dibley nodded, looking round him. "Everything seems to be working."

The patrolman jerked his thumb. "Then how about getting the hell out of here?"

Dibley pointed vaguely at the windshield wipers. "I'm trying to."

"What's stopping you?" the cop asked.

"I've—er—" Dibley coughed, embarrassed. "I've forgotten how to drive."

The policeman, who had been on the force for fifteen years, took the explanation in his stride. "I see," he said. "You drove this thing here, right?"

"That's right," Dibley said.

"Where from?"

"The Village."

"Uh huh," the cop said. That explained a lot. "But you can't drive no further because you've forgotten how, is that right?"

Dibley assured him that it was.

The patrolman looked hard at Dibley. His first reaction was that Dibley was putting him on, but then nobody was stupid enough to try to put a New York cop on. His second reaction was that the car was stolen, but who'd steal a car this old? No, it was pretty clear who he was dealing with; just another of the vast army of nuts that the city teemed with. How come he always got them?

"Well," the policeman said in the softer tone he reserved for special cases, "let's see if we can't give you a refresher course. You see that pedal down there on the floor, the one you've got your foot on?"

Dibley peered down. "This footrest thing?"

"Yeah," the cop said. "That's called the brake. It stops the car."

"Got it," Dibley said.

"Now do you see another pedal down there, right next to it?"

Dibley frowned down at his feet. "No, I don't think I—wait a second, by golly there is one there. A long narrow one."

"That's the one," the cop said. "Now if you take your foot off the brake and put it on the gas pedal the car will go."

"What, like this?" Dibley asked.

The Studebaker leapt forward across the traffic, stripped a wing mirror off a swerving Dodge and zoomed up the avenue. Dibley sat ramrod straight and clutched the steering wheel like a man on his first solo, which, in a way, this was. Ahead of him, cars were backed up at a light. He tried desperately to remember what the cop had told him about stopping the car. With a hundred feet between him and a collision, it came to him. "The footrest!" he yelled. He took his foot off the gas and jammed it onto the brake. The wheels locked and the tires burned black marks on Eighth Avenue. Dibley was thinking of leaving the car and taking a cab, but the light changed and the honking started up behind him again. He thrust his foot down onto the gas pedal and took some more rubber off the tires.

He was wondering what you did to turn a corner—Thirty-fourth was coming up and that was the one he wanted—when he saw the driver next to him turn the steering wheel to the left. Dibley did the same and screeched round the corner on two wheels, swiped a mail truck and continued heading west. Swaboda lived in an old but still good apartment house just east of Tenth Avenue, and Dibley spotted him standing outside. Swaboda spotted him too and watched with some interest as the car tried to stand on its nose, stopping in front of him. He walked up to it, noting the lights and the wipers and the flashing indicator and the aerial rising and falling like a yo-yo. On the radio "The Stars and Stripes Forever" had given way to the "Washington Post March."

"You look like you hit the jackpot," Swaboda said. "Why all the action?"

"I forgot how to drive," Dibley replied.

Swaboda wasn't surprised; he was used to Dibley and his problem and the strange effects it sometimes resulted in. Dibley had the worst memory anybody had ever heard of. It would be fine for a time, as good as anybody else's, but then without any warning it would go on him like a gimpy knee and he'd forget the simplest things, things that for most people would be impossible to forget. Then just as suddenly it would all come back to him and he'd be as normal as anybody else. It made life difficult for him. And for those around him.

"Sorry to keep you waiting, Charlie," Dibley said.

"Don't give it another thought," Swaboda answered, opening the rear door.

Swaboda could afford to be tolerant of Dibley's problem; he had one that dwarfed it. "In you go, Mom," he said to the air beside him. He helped an invisible person into the rear seat, closed the door, then got into the front. Dibley, who was as used to Swaboda's problem as Swaboda was to his, turned and smiled brightly at the empty rear seat. "Good morning, Mrs. Swaboda," he said, overloud. "A little chilly this morning."

Swaboda reached out and jabbed buttons, turning everything off. "I'll leave the heater on for Mom," he said. "You sure you can drive?"

"Positive." To prove it Dibley trod the gas and shot the car away. "I'll get us some nice music," he said. He extended his arm and pressed a button. The glove compartment opened.

Sitting beside each other, Dibley and Swaboda looked like an exaggerated version of Mutt and Jeff. Dibley was tall and

4

slim, angular almost, his arms and legs seeming to go on for a few inches more than they should have. But his body was nicely muscled, and this along with his wide bony shoulders stopped anybody from describing him as skinny. At thirty-five he still had all his own hair, which was dark going on black, thick and fluffy over his head and curly where it stopped low down on his neck. Underneath it was a pleasant face with strong bone structure in the nose and jaw and a firm mouth that showed an abundance of teeth when he smiled, which wasn't 100 percent of the time; Dibley was inclined to be a little mercurial in his moods. When he was up he was on top of the world. When he was down nothing would ever be right again.

Swaboda, on the other hand, standing 5'8" and weighing 180, was blessed with the perpetual good humor of the traditional jolly fat man. Swaboda had been overweight ever since he'd been one year old. "Just baby fat," people had said, pinching the cute little bundle. "That'll soon go." But it never had and Swaboda had been plump all his life. Consequently there was no memory of svelter days, no slim athletic figure to get back to. He always ate seconds and never turned down dessert and had never counted a calorie in his life. He was a happy man; forty, balding, plump and happy.

Making the turn into Eleventh, Dibley took his foot off the gas and braked before he turned the wheel.

"Better," Swaboda said.

Dibley smiled. "It's all coming back to me now."

By the time they pulled up outside the apartment house on West End Avenue Dibley's driving was back to normal.

Walter Byrd came out of the door and over to the car. "Good morning," he said in his squeaky, high-pitched voice. He smiled minutely at the rear seat. "Good morning, Mrs. Swaboda."

"Sorry to keep you waiting, Walter," Dibley said. "I forgot how to drive."

"Think nothing of it," Walter replied.

Walter, like Swaboda, could also afford to be tolerant of Dibley's problem. He had one that put Dibley's in the shade and even outstripped Swaboda's. He got into the car and settled himself on the front seat, making a very small depression in it. Walter was shorter than Swaboda and slimmer than Dibley, having a frame like the guy who gets bullied at the beach. Walter, a few years younger than Dibley, was very quiet and retiring and as timid as a deer. He rarely spoke except for a greeting or in answer to a direct question and then only if he knew the people well. Once, in a rush-hour subway, a man engrossed in his *Evening News* had stood on Walter's foot all the way from Franklin Avenue to Columbus Circle, and Walter had been too reticent to tell him. But his chronic shyness wasn't his problem, merely a result of it.

Walter had a split personality. But instead of being divided neatly down the middle it was split three ways. Being three people in one would have been tough on anybody, but it was especially hard on Walter because his two other personalities were so wildly different.

One of them, who called himself Rocky, was a tough little scrapper who had modeled himself after James Cagney. Whenever Rocky took over, Walter would plant himself firmly on his feet, moving on them slightly, cock his head to one side, hold his hands at half-mast in front of him, do the famous Cagney hitch, and rap out his words in Cagney's staccato delivery, punctuating them with short sharp stabs of both index fingers. Rocky also had Cagney's belligerent approach to the world—a cocky little man with a chip on his shoulder, quick to take umbrage at the slightest provocation. Rocky talked big and tough and backed his words with his fists, all of which was anathema to Walter, but there was nothing he could do about it. Walter was as powerless to prevent Rocky's taking over as he was of his third personality. And, as embarrassing as Rocky was to him, this other personality was even more so.

She was a woman.

Her name was Kitty and she'd also modeled herself on a star of the Silver Screen—Bette Davis at her most vitriolic.

Whenever Kitty would take over, Walter would haughtily draw himself up, whip out a cigaret, light it, blow out smoke noisily, toss his head and deliver his words in Bette Davis' clipped anglicized accent. To add a further complication, not that Walter needed one, Rocky and Kitty couldn't stand each other.

Walter's problem, and Swaboda's problem, and Dibley's problem were what had brought them together. They were all being treated at the same clinic in Westchester, and seeing that the three of them had appointments on the same two days of the week—and seeing that public transportation often proved a little trying for them as well as for the other passengers—they'd each put up fifty dollars and bought a communal car to drive up in. Dibley, who lived farthest south on Manhattan, picked up the other two in the mornings and dropped them off in the afternoons and kept the car in a parking lot round the corner from his apartment. The arrangement worked pretty well as long as Dibley didn't forget where they lived or how to drive.

Right now his memory was working perfectly as he went smoothly across Riverside Drive and up the ramp onto the Henry Hudson Parkway.

He lowered his window an inch. "This isn't too breezy for your mother is it, Charlie?" Dibley couldn't see her any more than Walter could, but each of them respected the others' hang-ups.

"Naw," Swaboda answered, "she loves the fresh air."

They sat back watching the river glide by on their left and up ahead the morning sun backlighting the fine verticals of the George Washington Bridge.

They slowed for the toll gates over the Harlem River, picked up speed again and crossed into the Bronx, just one of ten thousand cars heading north that bright October morning.

They couldn't know it then, of course, but in one of those other ten thousand cars was a man with whom they were due to collide with a resounding crunch.

True it would be at another time and at another place, but

without a doubt at that particular moment the express had been shunted off the siding and was moving onto the tracks.

chapter 2

". . . in another part of the city there lived three thieves . . ."

In the inside lane of the FDR Drive, in the dark green late-model Chev, Frank Mira sat beside his brother Joey. Frank was thirty-two years old, second-generation Spanish, short, compact and with the dark features of the Mediterranean: black eyes, deep olive skin, thick black hair oiled and swept back from a high part to lie neatly in place in broad glossy lines. He looked a lot like the photograph of his father who'd swapped poor lazy days in an almond grove in Málaga for the regular Saturday-night paycheck of a garage in Woodlawn.

Joey, driving the car, was eight years younger than Frank, taller and better built, the Andalusian features not so pronounced, the squat Spanish broadness that was inherent in Frank taking on a more elongated American look in the younger brother. An hour and a half ago, with a jump wire stuffed into the pocket of Joey's windbreaker, they'd taken the subway from 170th Street in the Bronx down to Fifty-ninth Street in Manhattan, to the East Side where people, perhaps remembering an earlier, happier New York, were more inclined to leave their car doors unlocked.

They'd found the Chev at the side of one of the smart hotels, left there, keys and all, by a doorman too busy to garage it right away. The call would go out for it soon enough, but they'd have to be damned unlucky to get picked up in the next forty-five minutes. And that's all they were going to need the car for.

They crept over the Willis Avenue Bridge, slowed by the tight double-lane squeeze, took a right on 138th and pulled up at the Brook Avenue subway entrance.

A man jerked open the curb-side door, talking before he was even in. "You goddamn took your time." The seat squished beneath his weight as he settled himself beside Frank Mira and angrily banged the door closed. Ed Cahill was a big slow-moving man, more fat than muscle, his solidity emphasized by the beer belly that pushed against his belt. Big boned, there was yet a somewhat bloated look to his face and shoulders that took away the first impression of strength. He had thinning, fortyish hair, a small mouth in front of a firm jaw that stopped a little too short at the chin, and a pale lumpy face that a lot of people said had the map of Ireland stamped on it. "Wonder I didn't get picked up for loitering," he growled. The other two, used to his grumbling, ignored him.

Joey took the car away and followed the signs to Bruckner Boulevard, stayed on that for a couple of miles, careful to keep to the speed limit, then switched to the cloverleaf that sprouted at the Bronx River Parkway. Once on the highway and heading north nobody said anything, all three of them nervous. They'd never pulled a job like this before; it was the first time they'd ever stolen a car. They'd never done the kind of job that needed one.

Ahead of them on the side of the road, a sign came up. It said, "Gas ¼ Mile." Frank Mira eased the gun out of his belt and checked it for the second time that day. Cahill, next to him, saw the move and swallowed on a dry throat. "Listen," he said, "if it don't look good when we get there we go on by, O.K.?"

Nobody answered.

"O.K.?" he asked more urgently.

"Quit worrying," Mira said. "We're going to do all right."

Cahill wiped his hands on his pants knees. "If it don't look right we don't go in. No sense bucking the odds. Thing like this could be tricky."

Mira tucked the gun back into his belt and straightened his jacket. "We're almost into it anyway. Just do your job."

They sped past another gasoline sign with a figure in yards printed underneath.

Cahill said sullenly, "Things better go right, that's all."

The inside lane widened, then veered off, leading onto a gas station ramp set in the side of the parkway. The traffic had been light, the lull just after the rush hour, and they were surprised to find two cars getting gas and another just pulling in ahead of them.

"Too many," Cahill said quickly; "let's forget it."

Joey snatched a fast look at his brother, who was leaning forward, his eyes checking the gas jockeys and the other cars on the ramp. Joey let the car roll slowly on past the pumps and pulled up at the air hose. He hopped out, leaving the engine running, walked round, lifted the hose off its bracket and bent down at the front tire.

Mira glanced in the rearview mirror, waited a moment. "Come on," he said and slid across the seat on the driver's side and stepped out onto the ramp.

Cahill stayed where he was, half swiveled round in his seat looking through the rear window. "I don't like it. Too open, too many people."

Mira rested a hand on the door. "All right." His voice was low and hard. "But if Joey and me do it all we keep it all." He straightened and turned towards the office and almost ran into the attendant who had walked up, a sour look on his face.

"You want some gas to go with the free air?" he asked.

Mira asked him a question in return. "You got a fan belt to fit this model?"

The gas jockey shrugged, not interested; accessories weren't his concern. "Check inside." He went away to take care of a new arrival.

Mira started for the office. Behind him he heard the car door slam and knew that Cahill was following.

From the door of the office he saw his brother getting into the car and starting to back towards them.

The man behind the cash desk was reading a football magazine, too fascinated to look up. A door to the right led into a repair shop, the sighing hiss of a machine wrenching a tire off a rim coming from it. There was nobody else in the office. Mira picked up a pack of gum from a display on the counter and put it down with a fifty-cent piece. The man looked away from the magazine long enough to glance at the items and hit a button on the cash register. "Ten cents," he said, reaching for the coin. With the cash drawer open he looked up to see the gun pointing at his mouth. There was a half-second of numb shock, then the whole upper part of his body jerked and he stepped off his stool, backing away.

Mira cocked the gun. "One peep."

Cahill brushed by, thrust his hands into the cash drawer, scooped out money, turned and hurried out to the car that was pulling level with the door.

That would have been it, nice and easy, if the clerk, perhaps reacting to the loss of the money he was in charge of, hadn't taken a bewildered step forward.

"Hey," he said.

Mira didn't hesitate. He reached for him, grabbed a handful of his shirt front and pulled him into the swing of the gun. The man's teeth clacked together and he fell away, bounced against the stool and slid to the floor.

"Come on, come on," Cahill yelled from inside the car.

One of the gas jockeys, the man who'd spoken to Mira before, looked up from inside a car hood and started towards them. Mira let him see the gun as he stood at the door tucking it back into his belt. The man stopped instantly.

11

"Crissake, will you come on!" Cahill yelled again.

Mira stayed where he was, carefully zipping up his jacket, looking at the station man, who was still riveted to the spot. Then very deliberately, taking his time, he got into the car.

Joey gunned the engine, the Chev rocked back on itself, shot out of the ramp and melted into the traffic heading north to Westchester.

chapter 3

". . . returning from the house of a physician, they lamed their camel . . ."

Dibley took the car out of the rush of the Westchester Expressway and onto the suburban quiet of 100-A. A little way along it he turned into a rutted driveway half hidden by the overhanging foliage. The sign across the drive said it was the Sleepy Oaks Country Club. They drove up a road that split the fairways of a golf course, the trees lining the road yellow and brown, the course sparsely populated in spite of the bright fall sunshine, and took a left where the road forked. They went by a row of private houses that bordered the western edge of the course and through large ornate gates into a circular drive that curled in front of a big white rambling frame house. There was a sign here too, newer and more elegantly lettered than the country club sign. It said, "Casa Blanca. For the Study of Advanced Psychiatry." And underneath that, in fine copperplate, "Doctor H. Segal, Resident Psychiatrist."

Doctor Hector Segal thought that calling his clinic Casa Blanca had been a masterstroke of public relations. After all, he'd reasoned, who would want to attend an institution or a mental home? And God forbid if you had to tell somebody that it was your day at the asylum. But nobody minded going to a place called Casa Blanca. Of course the local residents referred to it as Casa Nutter, and when once or twice they'd muttered about a place like that holding down property values, Doctor Segal had been quick to point out that it was a very small clinic with only eighteen patients, all perfectly harmless. Which was perfectly true. And that the other clients, the ones who came for daily treatment, were no more unbalanced than all those people in New York City who went to their shrinks twice a week on their lunch hours. However, this was stretching things a bit, because Doctor Segal only handled the more advanced cases that other psychiatrists passed on to him, in much the same way as an M.D. will pass somebody on to a specialist. Dibley's regular psychiatrist had recommended Casa Blanca after Dibley's sixth session. Swaboda had made it after his first session. And Walter hadn't even got past his doctor's receptionist.

Dibley parked the car in the small black-topped area at the side of the building and they all got out. Swaboda opened the rear door. "Watch your head, Mom." Dibley and Walter glanced at each other as Swaboda helped his phantom mother out of the car.

"I'll see you back here at three," Swaboda said to the space beside him. "And if you go walking on the golf course, watch out for those balls flying around." Dibley, his eyes searching cautiously about, said, "Have a nice day, Mrs. Swaboda." Swaboda waved to what the others assumed was a departing figure. "I hope she stays off the fairways," he said, a little worried. "She's going to get zonked on the head one of these days."

Dibley took a quick look at his watch. "God," he said, "I'd better get moving. I have to drive up to the clinic this morning."

Walter and Swaboda traded glances. "Dibley," Swaboda said kindly, "we just drove up to the clinic."

Dibley looked around him. "Oh yes," he said slowly.

A little way off, on the porch of the house, a staff man was showing a visiting doctor around the grounds. "Ah," he said, "over there, Doctor, by that old Studebaker. Three of our more fascinating cases."

"They look normal enough," replied the doctor, a distinguished-looking man with a sharp-pointed, close-clipped beard.

"Don't they all?" the staff man answered. "The plump one, the one who's waving, has an ever-present doppelgänger, and you'll never guess who he claims it is. . . ."

The visiting doctor thought for a moment. "Large white rabbits were fashionable some years ago."

"It's not a white rabbit," the staff man told him.

The doctor thought some more. "I treated a business man a few months back who claimed Ralph Nader was following him around. . . ."

"No, not Ralph Nader. It's his mother."

"Ralph Nader's mother?"

"No, no," the staff man said. "The patient's mother. Doctor Segal says it's the worst case of parental fixation he's ever come across."

"Ah yes," the doctor said. "Classic. Beckenbridge speaks of it."

"The tall one," the staff man continued, "is also interesting. Chronic recurring amnesia in the downhill stage. Doctor Segal's convinced it's psychiatric in origin, of course."

"Of course." The doctor stroked his beard. "Hoffmier speaks of it. And the third one, the little thin fellow?"

"Ah," his guide said, rubbing his hands together, "Casa Blanca's star patient. A double schizoid, Doctor. That's his natural personality you're seeing now."

"A nebbish," the doctor observed.

"Correct. His second personality is an extremely belligerent type who sees himself in a gangster role as portrayed by James Cagney."

14

"I see," the visitor said, stroking his beard again. "And I would guess that his third personality is somebody correct and well-spoken, somebody the exact opposite to Cagney. A Clifton Webb perhaps."

"Even more opposite than that I'm afraid," the staff man said. "It's Bette Davis."

The doctor raised his eyebrows. "Really? I don't think anybody speaks of that. Does Segal have any theories?"

The staff man raised his shoulders in a fatalistic shrug. "We know the cause but not the cure. The patient was born in the front stalls of the old Roxy during a double bill of *The Public Enemy*, the film you may recall that launched Cagney to fame, and *The Petrified Forest*, Bette Davis' tour de force."

"No kidding?" the doctor said, surprised. "Gee," he said wistfully, "they don't have double bills like that anymore."

Down in the parking lot the man they were discussing was preparing to take his leave. "See you later," Walter said in his thin, barely audible voice, and started to walk away.

"Have a good session, Walter," Dibley called after him.

Walter stopped. When he turned he was a different person. He set himself firmly on feet spaced eighteen inches apart, his hands, bent at the wrists like a dinosaur's, were cocked in front of his body as if he expected a frontal attack. He rolled his neck and shifted his shoulders, hitched at his belt with both hands without touching it and turned his head slightly to one side.

Walter had disappeared.

Rocky had taken over.

"Listen," he snarled in Cagney's soft, menacing voice, "you tell that actress dame"—he set himself more firmly on his feet and stabbed the air in front of him with the forefinger of each hand—"you tell that actress dame to stay away and everything'll be hunky dory."

Dibley and Swaboda swapped glances. "Oh hi, Rocky," Dibley said. "You have a good session too."

"Just tell her to stay out of my hair, that's all." With a last bellicose hitch of his hands Walter turned and strode off like a small express train.

"And don't worry about Kitty," Swaboda called after him. "She's probably with a road company somewhere."

Walter stopped dead. He turned on his heel and they saw that Rocky had gone.

Kitty had taken over.

Walter, with Kitty firmly in control, whipped out a pack of cigarets, nervously stabbed one into his mouth, lit it, took a huge drag on it and folded his arms. "Oh hi, Kitty," Dibley said, trying to keep up with the players, "you just missed Rocky."

Walter exhaled smoke through his nostrils like a Chinese dragon and said in Bette Davis' clipped, theatrical voice, "That cheap hoodlum. He's getting on my nerves, do you hear?" He smoked faster, building up to something. "On my nerves." He blew up and stamped his foot three times for emphasis. "I'm sick! sick! sick! of his paranoic outbursts." He whirled, tossed his head and walked smartly away, his tan $14.99 Florsheims sounding for all the world like an expensive pair of Delmans. Swaboda gazed after him and said to Dibley, "There he goes, a walking matinee." Dibley was watching him go too. "You know," he said, "whenever we pick him up in the mornings I never know whether to say good morning, Walter, or good morning, all."

"I know how you feel," Swaboda answered. "It must be tough on Walter, but still and all, there must be some advantages to being three people in one."

"Like what, for instance?"

Having said it, Swaboda had to think about it. "Well, you only need one more for bridge."

Dibley was unconvinced. "Can you see the three of them playing bridge? Rocky would want to play poker for a start. Kitty would drive everybody crazy slapping down the cards, and Walter would be too shy to trump anyone."

They started walking towards the main entrance, still talking about Walter and his problem. Dibley said, "He wouldn't be in such a fix if only Rocky and Kitty didn't dislike each other so much."

Swaboda agreed.

"Why do you think that is?" Dibley asked.

Swaboda shrugged. "I don't know; two's company, three's a crowd, I guess."

"I mean," Dibley said, continuing his train of thought, "there's no historical basis for it. It's not as if Cagney and Davis fought on the screen like, say, Edward Arnold and Edward G. Robinson."

"Or John Wayne and Randolph Scott," Swaboda added, getting the idea.

Dibley held up a hand. "Please, don't say it. Imagine if Walter's mother had gone to see *The Spoilers* that day. Walter would be spending half the time socking himself in the jaw."

"Or worse," Swaboda said. "*Frankenstein Meets the Wolfman*. That would have been a noisy twosome to share a car with."

They stopped at the entrance to the clinic. "Do you have a morning or afternoon session with Segal?" Dibley asked.

"Afternoon. You?"

"I'm due in now."

Swaboda grunted. "Frankly, I think the whole thing's a waste of time. I don't even know why I come here." He stopped, thinking about something. "I just hope Mom stays off the fairways." He waved and walked off, and Dibley went in the other direction towards Doctor Segal's office.

The daily patients at Casa Blanca divided their time unequally between personal sessions with Doctor Segal and the baths. While the therapeutic value of warm water has long been recognized by the medical profession, Doctor Segal had gone overboard for it, as he liked to say, allowing himself a tiny pun. So the daily patients spent most of their time lying in warm baths, like hippos in the Zambesi, only their eyes showing above the surface. By the time they got to Segal for their sessions they were pink, waterlogged and practically asleep, and also less inclined to talk about themselves, which was the way Doctor Segal liked them. He couldn't stand people telling him about their troubles. "What do they think I am?" he often asked his receptionist. "A bartender?" But, having to ration his time, the doctor was forced to see some patients in the morning before they went in to soak.

Dibley knocked on his door and went in. "Good morning, Doctor," he said amiably.

"Hello there, Dibley. Come in, come in." Doctor Segal was in his mid-fifties, a small birdlike man, nervous and quick in all his movements. "Look at these," he said, excitedly thrusting a package at Dibley. "They just came in."

Dibley peeled away some tissue paper to reveal a pair of black flat-heeled lady's shoes.

"Aren't they beauties?" Segal's eyes danced. "They belonged to a novice Carmelite. Cute little thing, so I hear." He took the nun's shoes back from Dibley and placed them in a rack on a bookcase. There were a dozen pairs of shoes in the rack just like them. "Carmelite," Segal said again. "One thing my collection was a little short of."

"Very nice," Dibley said, for something to say. He was used to Segal and his little excesses; everybody was. The doctor had been treating mental patients for twenty years, and many of their hang-ups had worn off on him. It was just an unusual case of occupational hazard.

"You saw these, did you?" Segal asked, spurred on by what he took as Dibley's interest. He turned round with another pair of shoes in his hands. "They belonged to a Mother Superior from Marymount. You don't come across something like that every day," he said, rubbing them lovingly against his cheek. "Had to give up two fine pairs from Loretto Convent for them though."

"You still came out on top," Dibley assured him.

"You really think so?" Segal was delighted. "Here," he said, picking up another pair, "you'd appreciate these. The gem of my collection. A second-year sister's from St. Mary's." He handed them to Dibley. "See anything different about them?"

Dibley turned them over. "They look about the same as the rest to me."

Segal took them back with a tolerant smile. "You have to know what to look for in this game. These babies cost me a small fortune."

"What makes them so valuable?" Dibley asked, as Segal knew he would.

The doctor carefully placed the shoes back in the rack and leaned forward confidingly. "Excommunicated," he whispered.

"No kidding," Dibley said. "I'd never have guessed."

Segal winked. "Only an expert could tell a thing like that." He went round behind his desk, unbuttoned his jacket, revealing two pairs of suspenders and a belt, and sat down. "Well," he said, "how's the memory coming along?"

Dibley sat down opposite him. "I think we're getting somewhere, Doctor."

"Fine, fine," Segal said quickly. Without the soothing comfort of the nun's shoes he was becoming nervous and irritable. He picked up two little steel balls and began rapidly clicking them together. "Have any trouble with those lines I gave you?"

"Lines?" Dibley asked, puzzled.

"The lines I gave you last week to memorize."

"Oh, yes. I was meaning to ask you about those. What was I supposed to do with them?"

"Memorize them," Segal answered.

Dibley snapped his fingers. "Memorize them, right."

Segal put down the steel balls and picked up a fifteenth-century thumbscrew, wasn't happy with it and discarded it in favor of an old piece of quilted comforter. He put his thumb in his mouth. "So," he said, a little indistinctly, "let's hear them."

"Hear what?"

Segal put the comforter down and picked up a dart and took careful aim at a dart board mounted on the far wall. On the front of the board was pinned a photo of his mother. "The lines I gave you to memorize," Segal said. The dart just missed his mother's left ear.

"Oh, you mean that stuff from Shakespeare. Sure," Dibley said, "I memorized it. Got it down pat too."

Segal reached for a bust of Napoleon and turned it to face him. There were fourteen of them scattered around the office. "Let's hear them then."

Dibley sprang to his feet. "Right." He coughed for a clear voice, threw back his shoulders and set himself like a high-school orator, body one-quarter turned, head held high, hands by his side. "A horse, a horse. My kingdom for a . . . ," he hesitated, ". . . my kingdom for a . . ." Dibley blinked rapidly and frowned.

"Never mind," his psychiatrist said; "that's a hard one. Go on to the next."

"The next, right," Dibley said, full of purpose. He set himself again and paused dramatically before beginning. "To be, or not . . . to . . ." He shook his head and started again. "To be, or not . . . to . . ." He stared at the ceiling.

"Be," Segal said quietly.

"*Be*," Dibley echoed. "Of course." He struck his forehead with the palm of his hand. "To be, or not to be." He thought about it for a moment. "Hey," he said to Segal, "that's a pretty catchy line. Yours?"

In the front seat of the Studebaker, rolling down through the golf course on their way home again, Dibley asked a question. "What kind of a day did you have, Walter?" It wasn't hard to tell when Walter was his old self again; he sat looking straight ahead, as silent and as motionless as a waxworks figure.

"Not very good," Walter squeaked in a voice so tiny they had to lean sideways to hear him.

"What was the problem?"

"The baths," Walter said sadly.

"What about the baths?" Swaboda asked. Walter seldom

offered any information; he had to be coaxed. He surprised them by saying sixteen words in a row.

"I was lying there when Kitty took over and ran screaming for the ladies' changing room."

Dibley and Swaboda exchanged looks. "I'll bet Schenko kicked you out of there in a hurry," Swaboda said, referring to Casa Blanca's head attendant.

"Yes, he did," Walter replied. "He was pretty rough too."

"How did Kitty take that?" Dibley asked.

"She said, 'You coward, pushing a woman.' "

Walter lapsed into silence and Swaboda prodded him again. "So what happened then?"

"Then it got embarrassing."

"Why embarrassing?"

"Because," Walter said, "that's when Schenko whipped off the towel I had round me."

Dibley took a turn at the prodding. "What did he say?"

"He said, 'A woman? You're pretty well hung for a chick.' "

"Hey," Swaboda hissed, "not in front of Mom."

"Excuse me, Mrs. Swaboda," Walter said to the rear seat.

Dibley drove them out of the country club gate, onto the highway for a hundred yards, then down the ramp that joined the expressway. He settled into the traffic and picked up the conversation again. "That Schenko has the manners of a water buffalo."

"Segal's just as bad," Swaboda claimed. "I was having my session with him and Mom came in. Well, do you think he stood up like a gentleman? No sir, he just sat there. And then when I gave him a blast about it he had the gall to suggest that I get away from my mother more. As it is I hardly see her, what with that job he got me."

It was part of Doctor Segal's treatment that all his patients take jobs that would help them with their problems. He'd got Swaboda a three-day-a-week job as a bartender in a men's club, thus excluding his mother. On the theory that Dibley's memory needed all the exercise it could get, he'd talked him into working at the timetable information desk at Grand Central, a job that Dibley had been able to hold only momentarily. When the Penn Central had gone broke, and the newspapers claimed that it was the fault of a grossly negligent management, the directors said that that was nonsense—they'd been sunk by a single employee. Dibley had had a variety of jobs since then, but was between jobs right now. Walter scraped by on a small allowance left to him by an aunt. But then Segal didn't know what kind of a job to suggest for Walter, although Swaboda said he should look for one that required a single man.

"How was your session?" Swaboda asked Dibley.

"Don't even ask. What a frost."

"Did he show you his new plastic raincoat?"

"No, I got the nun's shoes. Do you know what that man's suggesting now?" Dibley braked hard as the car in front decided at the last moment to take the Elmsford turnoff. He accelerated round it and pointed the car towards the thruway sign. He picked up where he left off. "Do you know what he's suggesting? That in addition to my sessions at the clinic he thinks I should take one of those courses. What do you call them again . . . ?"

"A memory course?" Swaboda suggested.

"A memory course, right. Now I ask you, do I need a memory course?"

Walter and Swaboda glanced at each other, then looked quickly away.

"O.K.," Dibley continued, "maybe I don't have total recall, but I hardly think I need to take a . . . what are those courses called again?"

"A memory course."

"A memory course."

"You never know what Segal's going to come out with," Swaboda said. "He's unstable."

"Unstable?" Dibley said. "Do you know what he's suggesting now? That in addition to my sessions at the clinic he thinks I should—"

"You told us already," Swaboda broke in.

"Told you what?" Dibley asked, frowning.

"That Segal wants you to take a memory course."

Dibley's eyebrows climbed. "He does? Funny, he didn't say anything to me about it."

As they got closer to the city the traffic got slower and slower till finally, when the thruway ended at Van Cortland Park, they were reduced to a crawl. Swaboda had his head out of the window. "There must be a lane closed. Grand Concourse is probably our best bet."

"Right," Dibley said, and a slow mile farther he took the turnoff onto the Mosholu Parkway. "I've always been fascinated by the Mosholu Parkway," he said. "As a kid I used to say it over and over again. Indian name, I guess."

"I always thought it was Jewish," Swaboda said. Then a moment later, "Where are you going? You went right by the turnoff."

Dibley thumped the wheel. "I'm sorry, fellas. I was saying Mosholu to myself."

"You'll have to take the Bronx River now, to the Bruckner and down the West Side."

Dibley nodded, but thirty seconds later he disregarded the advice. "Webster Avenue. That'll do, won't it?" He swung the wheel before Swaboda could stop him.

"Terrific," Swaboda said; "now we'll hit every red light in the Bronx."

He was right. They crawled along in stop-start traffic held up by the early end of the southbound rush hour. Dibley was mortified. Like most drivers he was proud of his knowledge of local street geography and liked to think he knew a more efficient way of getting from A to B than his competitors on the road. In an effort to redeem himself he swung off onto a side street that he thought he recognized.

"I know a short cut," he cried.

Swaboda threw up his arms. "Amazing. I didn't think we could do any worse than this."

But they were about to do worse still.

It happened after Dibley got lost in a tangle of back streets just east of Yankee Stadium. They were rolling along a side street that looked exactly the same as the last three, trying to find their way back to the Grand Concourse, when there was a tremendous crash and a jolt that lifted them out of their seats and bounced them against the roof. The car gave a piercing metallic scream that tapered quickly to a low groan as it came to a dragging stop. They climbed out shakily, the front doors resting on the pavement, and took a look.

They were dumbfounded by the sight.

The car's middle was resting on the road, and both ends pointed up in the air, as if it had been stepped on by a giant. They walked back up the road and stared with equal awe at the pothole they'd hit.

Dibley was the first to find his voice, which was half an octave higher than usual. "Will you look at the size of it? A horse couldn't jump over it."

Swaboda marveled at it. "I am waiting for a miner to climb out."

Even Walter was moved to comment. "My, my," he said, which for Walter was a vivid expression of amazement.

They walked back to the car and spent the next thirty seconds looking from the pothole to the Studebaker and back again, trying to make the connection.

Dibley couldn't believe it. "That did that? It's impossible."

"It looks like an air disaster," Swaboda said.

Dibley said, "Buddy, there isn't anything this town hasn't got that isn't the biggest in the world." The surprise was wearing off now and he was starting to get mad. "How can the city leave something like that just lying around?"

Swaboda couldn't imagine. "Maybe the kids swim in it during the summer." He crouched down and tried to look under the car. "Do we have a spare tire?" he asked Dibley.

"Do we have a spare car? This isn't going anywhere without a tow truck in front. One of us better call a garage."

They tossed to see who would go. When Walter lost out they tossed again. It was pointless sending Walter; they knew that whenever he telephoned somebody and the other party said "Hello," Walter was always too shy to answer. This time Swaboda lost.

"I think I saw a call box down that way," Dibley said, pointing. "Do you have any dimes?"

"No, but Mom's got some."

"Just a second," Dibley said. "I think you got a bum call on that last toss. Let's try it again." Dibley made sure he lost this time. "Right," he said, striding off. "I'll go and call a tow truck."

"If he remembers," Swaboda whispered to Walter.

Dibley turned a few yards away and called back to them, "Listen, while I'm there why don't I call a tow truck?"

"Might as well," Swaboda called back.

Dibley had to walk six blocks before he found a call box; then he got on to a garage who promised to send a truck right away. It arrived an hour and a half later, hitched up the Studebaker and took it and the three men to a garage on Westchester Avenue.

They waited outside the repair shop, grouped round the Coke machine, while a mechanic put the car on a hoist.

"What do you figure the repairs'll run us?" Swaboda asked.

"It'd better not be much," Dibley answered. "I'm broke. How about you?"

Swaboda waved his Coke cup. "I spent half my bankroll on this."

Dibley turned to Walter, who dug out his wallet. "Twenty-five dollars," Walter said.

"Anybody got any credit cards?" Dibley asked. The other two shook their heads. "Blue Cross?" Nobody had that either. "Well, hell," Dibley said, "twenty-five bucks should be enough."

"Sure," said Swaboda.

None of them knew anything about cars or mechanics. If they had they would have appreciated the performance they were about to witness, as timeless and classic as a Kabuki play.

The mechanic came out of the repair shop and moved towards them. This one had been in the game some years: his mannerisms were good and his dialogue faultless. He had the correct slow walk and a fine perplexed expression. He was wiping his hands on an oily rag. As he drew level, his head came up and the frown was replaced by a look of bemusement. He began with the standard opener. "Did you *drive* that car in here?" He'd taken it off the tow truck himself.

The question drew the expected response. "Why? What's the matter with it?"

The mechanic let out a lot of breath and combined a tooth suck with a head shake. "That's a mighty sick car you've got there."

"Bad, is it?" Dibley asked, anxious.

The man hesitated a second; this was where he leveled with the customer, who as a mature intelligent person was expected to take it stoically. With consummate timing he stretched the moment with a small cough. "Mister," he said, "you've totaled it."

"Totaled it?" Swaboda echoed back at him. "You mean, totaled it? Like you do in a head-on with a bus?"

"That's what I mean," the mechanic said heavily.

Dibley tried to appeal to him. "But all we did was fall down a hole. . . ."

"You would've been better off hitting the bus," the mechanic said.

"But . . . but it's only done eighty-five thousand. Can't you fix it?"

The mechanic set himself for the painful lecture on automobile economics. "Mister, cars get old just like people. You're driving a twelve-year-old car. In people terms that car's about eighty years old. Now you break a hip when you're eighty, it's tougher than if you break it when you're twenty, right? How much you pay for this car?"

Dibley and Swaboda spoke together. "A hundred and fifty."

The mechanic shook his head. "You couldn't get it back on the road for twice that. I'm sorry, but it's a write-off."

The three men looked at one another with various intensities of shocked dismay. The mechanic's face was dry eyed and tight lipped; he'd delivered news like this many times. It might have sounded callous, but telling the owners straight was the kindest way.

In a last-ditch attempt Dibley said the words the mechanic knew were due round about now. "But surely there must be something you can do?"

This was the part the mechanic always thought of as his "famous brain surgeon who had done everything" bit. At this point he usually held the customer's gaze for a moment, then dropped his eyes and said with a barely disguised catch in his voice, "Nothing. It's gone."

Dibley looked wildly around the circle of faces. "But we didn't take collision insurance, which means we have no claim. Which is ridiculous. We've got to be able to claim against some-body. We didn't put that hole there. The city should have fixed it."

Having passed the high point in his performance, the mechanic was losing interest. "So go sue City Hall," he said.

"Damn right I will," Dibley said loudly. "The city's responsi-ble for wrecking our car. They can just go and buy us a new one."

Swaboda backed him up. "Any court in the country would say the same. It's a clear case of gross negligence."

"Blatant civic indifference," Dibley declared. "Well, they're not getting away with it. I'm going to call my lawyer right now. You got a pay phone inside?"

The mechanic inclined his head. "In the office." He was busy writing out a bill.

"Come on, Charlie," Dibley said, his jaw thrust forward; "the city's going to find out it can't go round wrecking people's cars."

27

"Right on," Swaboda said. They stomped off together towards the office.

The mechanic was still writing. "You owe us for the tow and the inspection," he told Walter.

"Oh dear," Walter said, "I hope it's not more than twenty-five dollars."

The mechanic turned the pencil in his hand, erased the $21.50 he'd just written and changed it to $25.00. "You'll just make it," he said, handing over the bill.

chapter 4

". . . unhappy with their meager earnings"

Mira took the first exit they came to and dumped the Chev in a side street off Gun Hill Road. They hurried into the subway and spent a few nervous minutes waiting for the Lexington Avenue express. Once inside, cloaked by the anonymity of the crowded car—the doors hissing closed and the train picking up speed—they felt safe. They changed at Grand Concourse and went three stops north to 170th, came down the stairs to the street, walked a block and a half and pushed through the doors of the Lucky Shamrock Bar and Grill.

They ordered doubles, knocking them back quickly, letting the liquor flood through them, feeling their bodies relaxing piece by piece. The bar was almost an exact duplicate of the one across the street and the one two blocks up; it was a New York Irish bar interchangeable with ten thousand others: red vinyl-topped stools resting on uneven legs in front of a bar as solid as a ship and running almost the length of the room, a double row of bottles stacked against the gold-flecked mirror behind it. Underneath the mirror was the long dark bank of the beer-filled ice box that opened and closed like a gun shot. Above it, lettered on large board placards, the price of a shot of Carstairs and Fleischmann's and Four Roses and, above these, signed photographs of fighters and ball players of ten years ago. A Shaeffer sign rippled in an electric box near the oversized TV set on a high shelf in the corner. In the window, lit up in faulty neon, Ballantine and Rheingold competed for attention. The Lucky Shamrock, like the majority of its counterparts, was long and narrow, the shape of the bar dictating its dimensions. Three feet away from the stools a row of back-to-back booths lined the wall, and the three men took their second drink over to the one in back.

Cahill drained his immediately, the whiskey working on him and his earlier fright being replaced by a loud truculence. "Twenty-two bucks," he said, spitting the words out. He slammed the glass down onto the table. The bartender looked up from behind his newspaper and gave him a hard stare. "I risk a five-to-ten rap for twenty-two stinking bucks."

"Hey," the bartender called. "Watch the expensive crystal, huh?" He went back to his newspaper again. Cahill, knowing he couldn't see it, gave him a vicious high-sign.

Mira told him to take it easy.

"Screw taking it easy," Cahill said. "We already took it easy. I'd call bringing back sixty-seven bucks taking it real easy. Hey, Syd," he yelled, "another shot over here. Beer chaser."

Mira looked at him and said quietly, "We couldn't know how much was in that cash drawer till we dipped in. It could've been a grand more."

Cahill bit his teeth together. "It friggin' well ought to been, the risk we took. We grab off a car, we go in there, we zap a guy and the take's a fast sixty-seven bucks. Twenty-two apiece and change. It should've been ten times that."

He picked up the glass again and had it halfway to his mouth when he saw that it was empty. "Crissake, what do you got to do to get a drink around here? Hey, Syd, I'm dying over here."

The bartender was on his way carrying two glasses. He put them down in front of Cahill and leaned close, a big, beefy man with thick shoulders. "Buddy, you're making an awful lot of noise. Keep it down or you're out." He stayed there by the table looking down at Cahill, who held his gaze for a moment, then dropped his eyes. When the man moved back to the bar Cahill picked up the shot glass.

"He starts up with me, he'll be sorry." He tossed the drink off and wiped his mouth with the back of his hand. "Twenty-two bucks," he said. "I can do better'n that at the five and ten."

Joey moved his glass in front of him, making small wet circles on the table top. He glanced at his brother, then said to Cahill, "You win some, you lose some."

Cahill didn't even look at him. "Up yours, kid," he said.

Frank Mira leaned across at Cahill and said in a voice with iron at the edges, "I told you to take it easy."

Cahill said nothing. He knew he'd made a mistake talking like that to Joey. He'd found out on a few previous occasions that you couldn't say anything against him without having Mira to deal with. Theirs was very much the big brother-kid brother relationship, with Frank being dominating and over-protective, the way it often is when parents die early. Joey had been a silent child, always letting his older brother do the talking, and that had carried over into later life. Joey still deferred to Frank before he spoke, as if seeking his permission to do so and relying on him for a helping hand if he got stuck. Joey limited himself to a few comments and seldom offered an idea of his own. Frank did the thinking and the talking for both of them, and Joey was content to let it be that way; his brother had always looked out for him and would continue to look out for him.

Cahill drank his beer and gave Mira time to cool off. He'd learned to tread carefully with Mira; he was a strange one. Cahill had never been able to figure him out. He was the most unhumorous guy he'd ever met; he couldn't remember ever once hearing him laugh or tell a joke. The guy didn't seem to get a kick out of anything. He didn't like the booze much and he'd never seen him with a woman; he'd never seen him get a bet down; he didn't go bowling; he didn't seem to do anything except brood like something was gnawing at his insides. For the umpteenth time Cahill wondered what the hell he was doing hitched up to a guy like this. It was getting him nowhere; the guy was a loser, and he was damned if he was going to take orders from a loser. Goddamn it, he was four inches taller and had fifty pounds on him, didn't he? He wasn't going to be buffaloed by a runt like Mira. He had a good mind to belt him one right now. He moved a hand across his mouth, sniffed and shook his head. "Boy," he said sourly, "am I running with a smart outfit."

"You can quit anytime," Mira said. "You didn't sign a contract."

Cahill flared up again. "Don't tell me what I can do. I know what I can do. I can get with a group that knows how to make money. If I had any sense I'd a done it way back before this."

Mira felt his seat bump forward as a man and a woman moved into the booth behind. They were joined by another man who sat down and started to read out the starters from a scratch sheet. Their arrival stopped Mira from saying what he was going to say, and when he spoke again he'd forced himself down.

"O.K., so the take wasn't so big. Maybe we should've hit them in the afternoon, I don't know. We could've got there just before they went to the bank and come away with a couple of grand. Or we could've run into an off-duty cop and ended up in a pool of blood. A lot of things could've happened. You knock over a place, you never know what you've got till you're out of it. It's hard to figure these things."

Cahill said, "If you ask me, we're better off sticking to what we know, laundries, liquor stores, like that. It don't pay much worse than this and it's a hell of a lot simpler. Walk in, grab the dough and beat it down the subway. None of this futzing around with hot cars. We could've been picked up on the road before we even hit that gas station. It was a shitty idea from the start." He was working himself up again, his voice rising. "Look what it got us: peanuts. That's all we ever make is peanuts."

"Shut up! You shut your mouth!" Cahill was surprised at the way Mira flung the words at him, the sudden clenched-teeth anger coming out of nowhere. One of the men in the next booth turned in his seat.

"Keep it down," Cahill mumbled.

Mira started talking rapidly, his voice low and tight, the anger sticking out of it like barbs. His hands gripped the edge of the table and he sat compressed into himself, his eyes rock steady on Cahill. "You think I don't know? You think I figure holding up a deli's going to make us a fortune? What if I told you I'm up to here with the kind of jobs we pull? I want to be a name around this town, get a little respect from people. I ain't going to get it robbing liquor stores."

Cahill spread his hands. "So? That's O.K. too. Maybe we don't go back to the small stuff, maybe we try a big job."

"Like what, for instance? All we'll ever get's what's in the till."

"Then maybe we need a bigger till. A bank or a jewelry store. Something like that."

Mira played with his glass. "You crazy? What are we, three guys and a gun. You need more than that to walk into a bank. You need planning and equipment and rehearsal. Organization. And you need an idea, a new wrinkle. Something they're not protected against. Something they can't do anything about till it's too late."

Cahill spread his hands again. "Then let's get an idea."

"Who's going to come up with it," Mira asked him slowly, "you?"

Cahill's expression changed. His mouth turned surly and mean as he realized that Mira had turned his words against him. The son of a bitch, he never lost a chance to make him look a fool. He'd get his, the bastard, Cahill thought.

Watching the two of them, listening to them rub each other the wrong way, Joey stepped in to stop it from going any further. He never could figure out why his brother liked to ride Cahill the way he did, and he didn't understand why Cahill resented Frank calling the shots. Somebody had to be boss, and Frank was way smarter than Cahill would ever be. "What do we do now, Frank?" he asked.

"We hang in there and we wait. We take home enough to keep us alive and we wait. Sooner or later we'll get a break and have a real payday."

Cahill chuckled, but there was no fun in it. "And just how long before that gets here?"

Mira dropped his eyes to his hands. He said quietly, his voice still a hard growl, "A little while, a long while, who knows? All I know is we'd better be smart enough to spot it when it comes."

chapter 5

". . . a bold and curious plan . . ."

Dibley lived in an apartment on the top floor of a brownstone on Bank Street in Greenwich Village. The building was owned by Mr. Kolynos, who lived below him with his tiny wife and their four colossal sons. Mr. Kolynos had made a lot of money in the chrome-plating business by the simple formula of working seven days a week for twenty-three years. It had been a big day in the Kolynos household when, the Sunday after he'd sold out for a bundle Mr. Kolynos had taken his family to the zoo, Coney Island, Shea Stadium and the Statue of Liberty, trying to make up in one go for all those years of working Sundays. The only other time he'd ever seen his family away from home had been at his father's funeral. He'd bought the house on Bank Street, taken out most of the first floor and knocked down as many walls as he safely could. The result was a room with the proportions of an airplane hangar which he filled with tables and chairs and standard lamps and more tables and chairs. Any parts of the furniture that could possibly be made from metal were made from metal, and all of this was chrome plated. This was called the living room, although the family spent nearly all of its time tumbling over one another in the chrome-plated, gadget-filled kitchen. The bedrooms—for which Mr. Kolynos, perhaps thinking of the little mosques in his native Rhodes, had bought superb oriental rugs, cutting them up with shears and fitting them wall to wall like broadloom—were on the floor above.

Dibley had the apartment on the floor above that.

Mr. Kolynos hadn't been personally interested in this floor, and apart from putting in a half-dozen chrome-plated ashtrays, he had let an interior decorator furnish it. The apartment was done in deep autumn tones, a good-quality beige Acrilan on the floor, stained pine shutters instead of drapes on the windows, big expensively framed pop posters on the warm-colored walls. There was a good-sized bedroom and bathroom on the street side, a little hall leading into a large comfortable living room, with a kitchen running off it big enough to have a breakfast nook. At the back of the living room, French windows led out to a small terrace that overlooked the tiny fenced-off gardens below. The gardens lay in an elongated square bordered by Bank and West Eleventh at the ends, Bleeker to the west and, the Village being the Village, West Fourth to the east. In the summer the enclosed square became a succession of little private parks: kids swinging on swings, people barbecuing steaks, the entire long green enclave a secret from the street.

The apartment should have rented for four or five hundred dollars a month, but Dibley paid only one hundred twenty-five for it, because while Mr. Kolynos knew everything there was to know about the chrome-plating business, he knew nothing about the real estate business. He'd paid sixty-three dollars a month most of his married life for a three-bedroom rent-controlled tenement flat on Henry Street within apple-core distance of the Manhattan Bridge approach. He couldn't conceive of anybody paying four hundred fifty dollars a month rent, as the decorator had estimated the apartment's worth, and when the first applicant, Dibley, had asked how much, Mr. Kolynos had panicked and said one hundred twenty-five dollars and Dibley had said O.K. It was a fantastic bargain and Dibley didn't question it. The front door was painted teal blue and in fine condition, and Dibley reduced its value slightly coming through it that evening. He banged it closed behind him, shook both fists at the ceiling and cried, "They won't get away with it! They will not get away with it!" He stomped round looking for something to karate to death, but everything belonged to Mr. Kolynos, except the girl who came out of the kitchen—she belonged to Dibley.

"Won't get away with what?" she asked. She held a saucepan in her hands.

"Death and destruction," Dibley replied. "They killed the car."

The girl looked at him blankly, then walked back into the kitchen and emerged again without the saucepan. "O.K.," she said, giving Dibley her full attention, "who killed what car?" Her name was Carol Mars. Her grandparents had come from Ludwigshaven, which explained Carol's blue eyes and straw-blond hair and the taller-than-average height. It didn't necessarily explain why it was all put together so beautifully. She wore her hair caught back off her face in a ponytail, which accented the high cheekbones and the wide clear forehead. She didn't need anything to accent her figure. Long and slim and full at the same time, it wasn't the kind men whistled at; it was the kind they gazed after in a longing silence, usually followed by a low moan. Most people assumed that a girl who looked like Carol would be a model or a dancer or a stewardess, but she wasn't any of these; Carol demonstrated stereo equipment at a showroom on the lower concourse at Grand Central, which was where she'd met Dibley.

On her way to her coffee break one morning she'd been riding the escalators up into the Pan Am Building, heading for the Trattoria and their great espresso and Italian cookies, when she'd noticed something different about the main concourse below: The flow and movement of the people down there had changed its pattern radically. Instead of converging on the circular information desk in the center of the floor, asking a question, then striding off purposefully for a particular gate, the people were weaving around in hopeless circles, bumping into one another and looking very lost. Carol had gone back down and over to the desk to find out why. When she'd seen Dibley there and heard the way he was handling the inquiries, forgetting the questions as soon as they were asked, she knew.

She'd been fascinated by this tall, lanky man, gazing up at the ceiling and frowningly trying to remember whether New Haven was in Connecticut or Florida, and when his supervisor had appeared and told him to take a long, long coffee break, Carol had asked Dibley if she could join him. Dibley had taken one look at her and said he guessed it would be O.K. They saw each other every day after that and, a few weeks later when Carol moved in with him, every night too.

"*The* car. Our car," Dibley said, answering her question. "The Studebaker. I drove over a pothole. It might as well have been a land mine." He told her quickly what had happened to them.

"But that's awful," Carol said.

"It's worse than that. I called DeLuca down at the ACLU and you know what he told me? Sure it was the city's fault and sure we could sue, but with the backlog of cases they've got against them we'd be lucky if it came up in six or seven years. And even then the chances of getting a decent settlement are slim. Slim," Dibley said, appealing to a ceiling lamp. "They reduce our car to scrap iron and the chances are only slim. I only hope they don't sue us for hurting their nice pothole."

"I don't understand," Carol said. "It's a wreck and all you did was hit a pothole? What did they say was actually wrong with it?"

Dibley raised his arms and let them fall to his sides. "I don't know. The mechanic said it was eighty years old and had a broken hip."

"I know it's tough, darling, but you have to admit the car was on its last legs."

"Last legs, nothing. How are we supposed to get up to the clinic now? Walter and Charlie don't have the money to go out and buy another car, and I certainly don't."

Carol tried to take the sting out of it for him: "You can always take the train. It's not such a bad trip and you can get a cab to the clinic from White Plains."

Dibley looked pained. "Don't even talk about it. The last time the three of us rode the train to White Plains we'd cleared the car we were riding in by Mount Vernon and were thrown off at Scarsdale."

Being familiar with Walter and Swaboda and their attendant problems, Carol didn't doubt it. "Then we'll have to think of some other way. I'll make us a drink. Maybe that'll spark something."

She went out to the kitchen and Dibley heard her fiddling with bottles and glasses. When she came back in with two Gibsons he was walking round in a circle trying to cool off. "They're not getting away with it, I'll tell you that," he said emphatically, taking a glass from her.

Carol raised her drink to avoid answering him. She knew darned well the city would get away with it; there was nothing they could do. It was a lousy bit of luck, but then a lot of people had lousy luck in New York; it was a tough town and lousy luck came easy in it. She figured that the best thing her boyfriend could do was to accept the inevitable, take the loss and add it to the growing list of reasons why life in New York was becoming impossible.

"Come on," she said, "drink up. How was Doctor Segal today? Did he see any improvement?"

Dibley took a long swig at his drink, which lowered his volume but still left him morose. He slumped down into a chair. "I don't know, Carol, I think my memory's getting worse if anything. Lately I start to say something and before I've even finished the sentence . . ." Dibley stopped, a frown creeping over his face. "I'm sorry, what were we talking about?"

"Us," Carol said, turning his memory lapse to her advantage. She put down her glass and moved over to him and sat in his lap. "I haven't seen you all day." She kissed his chin. "I'm all right demonstrating Beethoven or Stravinsky, but when somebody wants to hear Rachmaninoff I go all to pieces missing you." She kissed his mouth and his eyelids and moved her lips to his ear. "Do you want to eat supper before or after?" she whispered into it.

"Before or after what?" Dibley asked.

Carol wriggled off his lap, got up, bent a hand behind her back, did something with a zipper and pulled the dress over her head. She wasn't wearing any underwear. She dropped the dress onto Dibley's knee and said, "Guess."

Dibley looked down at the dress, his brow furrowed. "The ironing?"

Carol closed her eyes. Sometimes his amnesia could be a little trying.

She took him by the hand, he got up, and she led him towards the bedroom.

A few minutes later, from underneath the bed covers, Carol's voice murmured, "Move forward, darling." There was a moment's pause, then her voice said again, "Move backwards, darling." There was another pause. "Now move forward again."

"Oh yes," Dibley's voice said slowly. "It's all coming back to me now."

It didn't take Carol long to realize that Dibley wasn't going to accept the incident with the car as one of life's little hard knocks. Far from it. For the next few days there were periods of long, extended silences during which he mooned around the apartment with a faraway look in his eye that Carol knew had nothing to do with his faulty memory. Ironically, this was one time when she would have welcomed one of his lapses, but Dibley's memory, being the erratic thing it was, had chosen this particular stretch of time to work perfectly. She knew him well enough to know that he was hatching something, and the following Monday evening she discovered that she was right. They'd strolled down the block to the Jai Alai and shared chuletas and a bottle of rosado, had gone over to the Playhouse and seen a funny movie, then strolled back to the apartment, leisurely undressed each other and got into bed. And it was only a little while after that that she thought his memory had failed him again.

"Darling," she said, "am I mistaken or have we stopped?"

"What?"

Carol said, "We don't seem to be doing what we were just doing."

"I've got it!" Dibley said suddenly. "A foolproof way of getting our money back from the city."

"James," ice cubes tinkled in her voice, "are you thinking about *cars* right now?"

"I'm sorry, Carol, it just popped into my skull."

"Well, you can just pop right out of this bed."

"Don't get mad, sweetie; I couldn't help it. It just came to me. Don't you want to hear it? It's a lulu."

"No, I do not want to hear it. Here I am thinking it was me, your girl, turning you on, and all the time it was a damn Studebaker."

"Oldsmobile," Dibley said. "I figure we'll get an Olds this time."

Carol hit him with a pillow.

Early the following morning Dibley called Walter and Swaboda and arranged to meet them for breakfast before taking the train up to the clinic. None of them had been wild about taking the train, but there didn't seem to be much alternative. Dibley reached the cafeteria across the road from Grand Central before the other two, got himself a cup of coffee and a table and settled down to wait.

Swaboda came in a minute later. "Good morning," he said. "Walter not here yet?"

"I haven't seen him," Dibley said. "I think we should go ahead and have breakfast. You know how Walter is."

"I do indeed." They'd got used to Walter's being unpunctual, but then considering his hang-up they felt it was understandable.

They moved over to the counter, picked up trays and flatware and got their orders. They paid their checks, carried their trays back and unloaded them onto the table. They'd chosen the same things, but while Dibley put down a bowl of cereal, an order of toast, a glass of orange juice and a cup of coffee, Swaboda put down two bowls of cereal, two orders of toast, two glasses of orange juice and two cups of coffee. He set half of the food in front of his own place and half in front of the chair to his right. "Sorry about the toast, Mom," he said to the chair. "They were out of prune Danish."

A man sitting at the next table stopped with a donut halfway to his mouth, lowered it, picked up his coffee and moved to a table farther away.

Dibley and Swaboda started on their breakfast. They were chatting about this and that when a chair scraped back and Walter's thin reedy voice said, "Sorry I'm late."

They looked up. The man sitting down at their table sounded like Walter and was built like Walter but didn't look like Walter. He was wearing a dark double-breasted suit with large notched lapels, white shirt, dark narrow tie tied in a tiny knot and pushed out at the collar by a tie pin, and on his head was a black, high-crown, short-brim felt hat with a four-inch silk headband—Cagney's outfit from *The Public Enemy*.

"Hi, Walter," Swaboda said. "I see Rocky was first out of bed this morning."

40

"I'm afraid so," Walter said sadly. He took off the hat and put it on his lap. The top of the crown still stuck above the table. "By the time he'd gone away I was almost here and it was too late to go home and change."

Two young secretaries sitting within earshot picked up their coffee and moved.

Dibley tried to ease Walter's embarrassment. "Don't worry about it, you look pretty sharp. Like a big-pay ad man from Madison Avenue."

Walter ran the hat around in his hands. The brim snapped up and down with a noise like a stick breaking.

Swaboda was anxious to help too. "Anyway, Walter," he said, "better that Rocky dressed before Kitty, huh?"

Walter said, "There was no danger of that. She was dead to the world."

"How come?"

"She went to a backstage party last night and didn't get home till three." Walter ran a hand over his brow. "I have a terrible hangover."

"If I'm not mistaken," Dibley said, peering at his face, "you also have a bit of a shiner."

Walter touched a gentle hand to his right eye and admitted it. "Halfway through the party Rocky took over and got into a fight with a stage hand."

Dibley said, "Rocky seems to be more trouble to you than Kitty."

"Sometimes," Walter said. "Saturday night, for example." They waited for the example, but Walter appeared to have run out of gas.

Swaboda prodded him. "What happened Saturday night?"

"He cost me twelve dollars." Walter ran out of gas again.

"Twelve dollars, yes . . ." Dibley said, leaning forward, nodding encouragement.

"At Lincoln Center," Walter added.

There was a long moment during which Walter showed no sign of ever opening his mouth again. Swaboda coughed. "Um, you were up to the part where Rocky cost you twelve dollars at Lincoln Center."

Walter took off in a sudden tumble of words. "A friend called and offered me a ticket. They were doing *Bohème*. I took it, naturally."

"What happened?" Dibley asked.

Walter closed his eyes in remembered pain. "Just as the curtain went up, Rocky took over. He went straight to sleep and snored through the entire performance."

"What a philistine," Swaboda said.

"Twelve dollars," Walter said, unprompted.

Dibley jumped into the natural opening. "It's been an expensive week all round. That's why I wanted to talk to you guys. I've been mulling it over, and I've come up with what I think is a pretty foolproof way of getting the city to come across with the money for another car. I just put the finishing touches on it last night and I want to lay it on you now and get your reactions."

As he completed the statement Dibley found himself looking into Walter's blank face and wondering if anything less than a hotfoot would produce a reaction.

He needn't have worried about Swaboda. He was grinning like a Halloween pumpkin. "Fantastic! Let's hear it."

Dibley drank the last of his coffee, dabbed his mouth with a napkin, took a quick look round to make sure he wasn't being overheard and started to talk. "You know what my friend, that lawyer I called, told me: the case might come up in six years if we're lucky and would probably cost us a lot more than we'd get. In other words we're supposed to go out and buy another car and just forget the whole thing ever happened. Well, we all agree that that's not good enough, right?"

"Right," Swaboda said. Walter nodded.

"To put it another way," Dibley went on, "the city owes us one hundred and fifty dollars which it's too busy to pay us.

42

To put it yet another way, the city is holding one hundred and fifty dollars of ours which it might pay us tomorrow if there weren't so many other people waiting in line. Now what I'm proposing is that we jump the line."

"All for it," Swaboda said. "How do we do it?"

"By bypassing the law courts. We simply take the money from the city. It's ours anyway and it'll save everybody a lot of time and trouble."

"Simply? How does anybody simply take money from the city? I mean you can't hold up an entire town," Swaboda said.

Dibley stabbed a finger at him. "Right." This was the beauty part. He leaned back in his chair and delivered it slowly. "But you can hold up a representative of it." He stopped, and when Swaboda didn't get it he said, "I mean the boss, the guy in charge. The man who's responsible for all this mess."

Walter and Swaboda said it together: "The mayor."

"The very man," Dibley said.

Swaboda mulled it over. "I like your thinking. I'm all in favor of taking this thing into our own hands . . ." Walter signified that he held the same view ". . . but the part with the mayor bothers me. For a start, how are we going to get to him? He's always surrounded by newsmen, secretaries, bodyguards. I don't see how we'd even get close."

Dibley was grinning at them; this was another beauty part, even more beautiful than the first one. "We don't have to get close to him. With what I've got in mind we can hold him up right in his own living room from a quarter mile away."

Walter and Swaboda watched their partner closely, both of them wondering if this was a new and unmet phase of his problem. Dibley didn't give them a chance to speculate too long; he launched into a rapid, point-for-point rundown of his idea.

"One," he said, peeling back a finger, "we rip off a cannon."

"A cannon," Swaboda repeated.

"Sure, one of those small army guns they tow behind Jeeps."

"Uh huh."

"Two," Dibley peeled off another finger, "we rip off a boat big enough to take the cannon."

Swaboda was waving his hands. "Hold it. I'm sorry, but at this point I've just got to ask a question."

"What is it?" Dibley asked.

"What are we going to do with a boat and a cannon?"

Dibley hit a third finger. "That's three. We load the cannon onto a boat, sail it up the East River and stand off Gracie Mansion."

"Who's she?" Swaboda asked.

Dibley spread his hands to make his reply all the more obvious. "Gracie Mansion, the official residence of the mayor of New York. It's right on the river at Eighty-ninth Street. We tool up the river, anchor off his back yard, call him up on the ship-to-shore—any fair-sized boat will have one—and tell him that if he doesn't speed up the process of law by handing over the money his city owes us, why then we'll blast him. We'll only be bluffing of course, but he won't know that."

The pumpkin smile was back on Swaboda's face and getting bigger. "I think that's marvelous. Absolutely marvelous. A blue-chip, three-star winner. What do you say, Walter?"

Walter went completely overboard. "I like it."

Dibley made a fist and tapped it smartly on the table top. "Great! I knew you'd go for it. Of course there are one or two details that have to be thought through, but the main thing is we've got a plan that's never been tried before, so they can't possibly be ready for it. They'll be so bewildered they won't know what to do except pay up."

"They'll have to," Swaboda said. "Who wouldn't with an army cannon staring them in the face?"

"Exactly." Dibley was delighted with the reception he was getting.

Swaboda reached over and slapped him on the shoulder. "Beautiful. Super idea. A real two-hundred-watt Mazda."

They talked it over some more and agreed to discuss some of the finer points on the way to the clinic. They were about to start for the station when Walter asked if they could have a fast bite before they left.

"I'm sorry, Walter," Dibley apologized, "I was so wrapped up in this thing I forgot you haven't even had a cup of coffee. And you with a hangover, too."

Walter rose from the table.

"Say, while you're up there would you get me something?" Dibley asked.

"What would you like?"

"Chicken soup, roast beef sandwich and a piece of pie."

"Dibley," Swaboda said, "this is breakfast."

"Breakfast?" Dibley looked puzzled. He shot a long arm out of his sleeve and consulted his watch. "You're right. Well, in that case, Walter, I'll have cereal, orange juice, toast and coffee."

Swaboda and Walter exchanged looks. "Dibley," Swaboda said again, "you just ate that. You just ate breakfast, see?" He pointed to the dishes.

Dibley frowned at them. "Oh. Well, in that case, Walter, nothing for me; I couldn't eat another thing."

"Anything for you, Charlie?" Walter asked.

"No thanks. Unless Mom wants anything more."

Dibley and Walter traded glances. Dibley said loudly to the chair at his left, "You haven't touched your food, Mrs. Swaboda. Not hungry today?"

Swaboda snapped his fingers. "I forgot. She's on a diet."

A fiftyish matron with a fox fur stole picked up her yoghurt and took it to the other side of the room.

Walter went over to the counter, got a tray, put half a grapefruit and a cup of coffee on it and paid for them. He was starting to move towards the table when the checkout girl called him back.

"Hey, you, just a second." She was young and blond and

hard looking and evidently had had a tough morning already. "You didn't pay me for the grapefruit."

"Excuse me," Walter said, crimson with embarrassment, "but I did."

"Listen, you little sneak," she snarled at him, "either pay for that grapefruit you stole or give it back to me."

Walter put the tray down, intending to pay twice rather than argue.

He never got the chance.

As he straightened up, Rocky took over. He turned slowly, spread his feet and set himself. The suit's padded shoulders jerked up and down as he gave a quick double hitch to his belt. His head dropped forward a little and a strand of hair fell down over his forehead. Turning his chin slightly, his eyes boring into the girl, he said in the famous staccato delivery, "You want the grapefruit, sister?" His hand reached down to the tray. "You can have the grapefruit."

And very carefully, and very, very firmly, he pushed it into her face.

chapter 6

". . . mean and ugly in their ways . . ."

The man who'd sold Mira the gun had told him five lies: He'd told him that it was a Colt; that it was brand new and, apart from the test, unfired; that it was untraceable because the serial number had been filed away; and that he'd paid seventy dollars for it and would buy it back anytime for thirty-five.

It wasn't a Colt, it was a Llama, the Spanish copy. The little blue and white button that carried the brand name above the grip had been removed. It still said "España" on the inside of the trigger guard, but who was going to look there?

It wasn't brand new, it was used. And in the worst kind of way. It had been fired three times by a man who'd been aiming at a payroll guard.

And it was far from untraceable. For one thing, the filed-down number would reappear if the gun was dropped into an acid bath. For another, one of those shots had hit the payroll guard, and the slug they'd dug out of his shoulder would have matched the rifling in the barrel.

And finally, the man hadn't paid seventy dollars for it, he'd paid thirty. And since the heat was well and truly on for the payroll job, he wouldn't have bought it back for five dollars.

But Mira believed the gun was everything the man said it was, because he didn't know anything about guns. He'd never been around people who knew about things like that. He'd mainly kept company with people like himself: smalltimers who got their education from other smalltimers; there were no experts anywhere along the way, nobody to teach them anything. Maybe prison was an educational course for some, but it hadn't been for Mira. With its rigid class system, as snobbish in its way as any officers' mess, the specialists—the vault mechanics, the armorers, the explosives experts, men who knew how to handle a thermal lance or rebore a pistol or heat fulminate of mercury safely—kept strictly to themselves in their own little group. The only thing his cellmates were expert in was climbing through a house window or dipping into a handbag. Prison had taught Mira exactly two things: how to run a laundry boiler, and that the main thing you were up against behind walls was not the inmates or the guards or the lack of privacy or losing your identity to a number, but the dull, grinding, day-to-day boredom of institutional life.

He'd served fourteen months of a two-year sentence for Breaking and Entering.

Joey had never been to jail. He'd been on that same job with his brother, but the security men had had time to catch only one of them, and Mira had made sure it had been himself they grabbed and not Joey. Joey didn't know anything about guns either. Like Frank, the people he came into contact with didn't have that kind of knowledge: kids mostly his own age who were either living on the hard stuff or mugging people for money to stay on it.

The kind of things Cahill had picked up weren't much help to them. There was nothing very special about them; they were only what any petty thief knows. When you worked the subways, for example, you always took the local so you could get out in a hurry if you had to. You picked up the shopping bag next to you and made the doors before they closed. Shopping bags were a kind of lucky dip; they could contain anything from cans of spaghetti to old laundry—but sometimes something worthwhile. Or if you were working the ferry you chose a seat near some woman with a small kid. It was two to one that sooner or later the kid would dart off somewhere suddenly and his mother would leave her pocketbook unguarded when she jumped after him. Or at Kennedy you checked to see which of the incoming flights were 747's. There were too many bags to check tabs; you picked a fairly common bag, a Samsonite or one of those big tartan bags from Korvettes. That was another lucky dip. You never worked the same department store more than twice in six weeks. But if you found a good apartment block you hit it again before they fitted a mortise lock. The newer apartments had them built in; they wouldn't keep a pro out—any lock that has a hole for a key has a hole for a pick—but they kept out the amateurs like Cahill.

Cahill had never been to jail either; never been to court, never been arrested. He told people that that was because he was smart and never bucked the odds.

The truth was he didn't have the guts to ever take a chance.

He disliked Mira for the same reason he'd disliked his father and the priests at school and the dispatchers when he'd had a job driving a truck: he hated authority. But being a born follower he needed a leader, and he recognized in Mira a strong confident force which he himself didn't have, although he would never have admitted it in a million years. When he'd joined up with Mira and switched from shoplifting to armed robbery, he felt he'd graduated to the big time, even though the take wasn't much bigger than he was used to. But that didn't bother him in spite of his complaints; the hired help is supposed to complain about the boss. As long as he had money for the rent and money to eat with and pay his bar bill and get him laid when he felt like it, he thought he was doing all right.

On the Friday after they'd robbed the gas station he was standing with Mira in thin morning sunshine outside a shop window on Forty-second Street. It had just turned ten and Dibley, Walter and Swaboda were just emerging from the cafeteria on the same street. However, the cafeteria being east and the shop being west, round the corner from Eighth Avenue, they were five long blocks from each other and not due to meet yet.

They had no reason to meet yet.

The shop window was festooned with South American gear: Indian blankets and bead jewelry, wild-colored ponchos and thick-woven rugs on which red and yellow turkeys strutted. But Cahill and Mira didn't see any of it. Their attention was fixed on a door to their left. High above the door, mixed in with several other signs that climbed the side of the building like ivy, was a white neon that said, "Checks Cashed." It was an old building, the stairway up from the street narrow and worn. On the second floor, opposite the white neon, a door led into a large low-ceilinged room painted a drab hospital green. Two-thirds of it was open space uncluttered by so much as an ashtray. The other third was sealed off by thick safety glass that ran from the ceiling to a counter top, broken only by a small circular voice window with a money slot beneath it. In back of the counter was a steel safe, its heavy flanged door hanging open, dominating the room. There was a battered metal filing cabinet to the side of it with hand-lettered alphabet cards fixed to the drawers. Above the safe, almost as big, from the ceiling hung a sign warning customers that their faces were being recorded on film.

The man behind the counter seemed oblivious of all the security, glancing at the name on a proffered check, hunting it down in the filing cabinet, counting out money from the cash drawer and pushing it through the slot as nonchalantly as if he were selling ice cream in the park.

Strung out in front of the glass was a group of men in a silent line, most of them holding paychecks. At the head of the line was a featureless man in a shabby blue suit who looked as though he might have found the check he was holding. Behind him two construction workers shuffled their feet impatiently. Then there was a thin clerkish-looking man and a man wearing a long white apron under his coat, then a short, dark-haired Greek or Italian in a fur-collared coat. Behind him, at the end of the line, was Joey.

They'd chosen a Friday because 9:30 Friday was payday for a lot of people. And a lot of those people who didn't want to wait in line at a bank, or didn't have a bank account, or wouldn't dream of setting foot in a bank anyway, took their checks to a place like this, which cashed them for a small percentage.

Joey stood a little to the side of the line so he could watch the transactions. The shabby-looking man was paid what looked to be about twenty dollars which he snatched up and counted twice before moving away. The first construction worker stepped up to the window and slid a check through. The counter man riffled cards in the file, found one he liked, then stripped off notes from a pile of tens.

Joey counted twelve of them. He figured that the man's

buddy would probably have a similar check; not bad, but they could maybe do better. That left the clerk, the man in the apron, and the Greek in the expensive coat, who was flashily dressed with gold rings on both hands. He looked to Joey like a bookie, but then he doubted that a bookie would be cashing a check. The clerk looked as though he worked an adding machine all day for some insurance company. Then again, he might be some technical brain with a seven-hundred-dollar paycheck in his hand. You never knew. Joey figured the next man had to be a bartender with a long white apron like that, and there were a lot of bars close by, so it made sense. If so, he could be carrying more than one check; a bar would often cash a paycheck if they knew you—it was worth their while, seeing they got a good chunk of it back across the counter. He could be their man.

The line shuffled forward and Joey patted his pockets, swore softly and moved towards the back of the room, searching in his jacket. The counter man had paid the clerk a little less than two hundred dollars. He wasn't bothering to check the dark man's name but was counting out a pretty sizeable stack of tens. Joey had almost changed his mind when he spotted the barman getting his checks ready. He had three in his hand.

Slowly, still patting his pockets, Joey turned and went down the stairs and out onto the street.

Mira saw him and nudged Cahill.

Joey crossed the road and positioned himself so that he had a good view of the door he'd just come out of.

Cahill coughed and swallowed and ran the palms of his hands down the front of his jacket. He said, "I just hope he picks right." His voice was wobbly. "We don't want nobody giving us an argument midtown broad daylight."

Mira wasn't listening; he was concentrating on Joey, who was watching the door. From where he was standing Joey could see the first half-dozen steps before they disappeared into darkness. He saw the man's shoes first, then dark cuffs, then the bottom of a topcoat. The dark man stopped as he came out onto the street, took a quick look both ways and started walking towards them.

"He looks tough," Cahill said quickly. "That guy could be carrying."

Mira said low, "It's not him." He was watching his brother, who hadn't moved.

Joey was wondering what was holding the bartender up. Then he saw a flutter of white on the stairs and jerked his jacket collar up around his neck.

Mira hit Cahill's arm and moved towards Eighth Avenue. He'd got a good look at the man who'd come out onto the street and had figured the same thing as Joey: the guy was a bartender, probably from the White Rose or the Blarney Stone round the corner. They needed to get in front of him. They nipped between parked cars, crossed the street together and hurried down the other side, overtaking the barman, who was strolling along on the opposite sidewalk. He showed no sign of crossing over himself, so Mira knew he was going to turn right at the avenue. They recrossed the street a good thirty feet ahead of him and moved round the corner.

A short way down the block, flanked by two store fronts, was the doorway of a tenement. Mira darted into it and Cahill continued on a few yards. He stopped and leaned up against the wall and tried to stop breathing so hard; he was supposed to look as though he'd been standing there for a while.

He watched the corner and his pulses jumped when the bartender walked around it. He shifted his bulk and started towards him. He had to time it right; he had to meet the guy right outside that tenement doorway.

But he'd moved too quickly; the distance between them was closing too fast. He slowed and let the man come towards him.

There weren't that many people around: a couple of housewives carrying groceries, a guy looking for a cab, another guy lugging a suitcase towards the bus terminal. He wished there were more people; this left him out in the open, exposed.

He reached the doorway and stopped. He tried to act natural, but his breath was still coming in short little bursts and there was sweat on his forehead.

"Say, buddy . . ." the bartender was almost to him ". . . I'm trying to get to Philly. You couldn't—"

The bartender tried to go round him, but Cahill leaned towards him, forcing him to take a step back. The man started to say something but stopped when he felt something hard pressing into his spine.

"All the way in," Mira said into the man's ear.

The bartender, a young man, didn't get it at first. Then he remembered the money he was carrying. He looked as if he were going to panic, but he did as Mira ordered and stepped into the doorway.

Mira slipped a wallet out of the man's back pocket and stuffed it into his jacket. Over the bartender's shoulder he saw Cahill disappear. "Now turn slow and walk up those stairs."

The man did as he was told, as silent and stiff as a robot. When they reached the first landing out of sight from the street, Mira moved fast and the gun flashed through the air in a quick arc and the man fell on his face on the stairs. Mira put the gun into his belt and went back down to the street. He stopped, took his time zipping up his jacket, then set off slowly towards Forty-second Street.

Joey was waiting for him at the subway entrance. They went down the steps together, dug tokens out of their pockets and pushed through the turnstiles.

They'd just missed an uptown train. Cahill had made sure he'd caught it.

They met up in the Lucky Shamrock. As they came through the doors, Cahill was standing at the bar pouring shots for himself and tossing them back. He splashed another one into his glass and joined them as they walked to the rear booth.

"We do all right?" he asked Mira.

Mira growled at him, "Give me a chance." He continued on past the booth and went into the washroom.

Cahill and Joey sat down facing each other. Cahill drank his drink and made a loud sighing noise in his throat. "Boy," he said, "that guy you picked, what a dummy. I could've taken it from him with a spoon."

Joey, who'd seen Cahill's performance, just nodded.

"You want a drink, kid?"

"I'll take a beer."

"Hey, Syd," Cahill called, "two beers over here. And do this again, huh?" He waved his shot glass. He said to Joey, "I could've handled the whole thing myself. Picked the guy, like what you did, trailed him out, then taken the dough away from him. It didn't need three guys."

Joey was noncommittal. "You figure?"

"Sure, no problem. I'm not saying you two didn't earn your cut; just that a simple job like that don't really take three guys."

The drinks arrived as Mira came out of the washroom. Cahill didn't even wait till the barman had gone. "So?" he said to Mira.

Mira flashed him a hard-eyed look.

"You drinking?" the barman asked Mira.

"In a minute."

The man grunted, slapped the drinks down and went away.

"You want to get us arrested?" Mira asked.

"You don't have to worry about Syd," Cahill said. "Come on, how'd we do?"

"Five hundred twelve."

Cahill's fleshy face, rosy from the liquor, broke into a grin. "Not bad. What's the split on that?"

Joey pulled out a ballpoint and did some fast arithmetic on the table top. "One seventy," he said.

"One seventy. Not bad at all. Hey, Syd," Cahill called again, "three over here. Make it the Powers this time, huh?" He turned back to the table. "One seventy." He drank off some beer. "Not good when you figure what we should be making, but not bad for five minutes' work. Not bad at all."

Mira smacked his hand down on the table. "Will you shove it!"

Cahill looked astounded and his grin turned down at the edges. "What's eating you? It's good American money, ain't it? One seventy apiece. Our best payday yet."

"We mugged a guy," Mira said, disgusted. "Big deal."

Cahill lifted his shoulders. "I don't see nothing wrong with it. One seventy for five minutes' work . . ."

"Christ!" Mira said. He pulled the wallet out and thrust it at his brother. "Give him his cut, Joey." He swung out of the seat and walked out of the bar.

Cahill watched him go. In annoyed surprise he said to Joey, "What's with him?"

chapter 7

". . . while pausing for refreshment at a watering place, learned of the honest man's plan . . ."

At about the time Cahill was wondering what had got into Mira, Carol was picking up the phone in the office next to the stereo room on the Lower Concourse. She was going to call Doctor Segal and wasn't looking forward to it, having called him once or twice in the past. Talking to the doctor in person was unnerving enough, but speaking to him over the telephone was doubly so. Carol wasn't sold on Doctor Segal; she wasn't that sold on psychiatrists in general. Being a normal healthy young woman with pleasant memories of her childhood and her parents, and having no morbid fears or unreasonable doubts or frustrated ambitions that she knew of, and having first come to sex in the back seat of a convertible with a nice boy that she liked rather than being interfered with by a horrid uncle behind the woodshed, she had never felt the need for psychiatric help. She consequently had the outsider's vague resistance to the whole subject, knowing as most people did one or two friends who, after thousands of dollars' worth of treatment, seemed to be no better or worse than they ever were. But then again she knew that it worked for a lot of people. The question uppermost in her mind was whether or not it would work for Dibley. With Doctor Segal running things she doubted it. She hesitated with the phone in her hand, wanting not to make the call, then decided to get it over with. She dialed the number and waited for an answer, then asked for the doctor in a strong, firm voice. Doctor Segal came on a few moments later.

"Hello?" Carol said.

"Goodbye," Doctor Segal said.

Carol knew he wasn't about to hang up on her; Doctor Segal always said that whenever anybody said hello to him on the phone. He'd been giving word association tests for so long that now Doctor Segal often said the first thing that came into his head.

Carol tried it again. "Hello, Doctor?"

"Quack," said Doctor Segal.

"This is Carol Mars."

"Jupiter."

Carol plowed ahead. "James Dibley's girl."

"Breasts."

"Er, Doctor, James asked me to give you a call."

"Girl," said Doctor Segal.

"Breasts," said Carol, trying to get through to him on his own wavelength.

56

"Big," said Segal.

"Um, Doctor . . ."

"Soft," said Segal, not yet finished with the last association.

"Doctor," Carol said in a rush, "he's going to be a little late. His car hit a hole."

"Sex," said Segal, starting to get excited.

Carol persevered. "It was on its last legs."

"Open," the doctor moaned.

Carol spoke faster. "They smashed in the body."

"Naked," he said hoarsely.

"You O.K., Doctor? Your voice is going."

"Coming!" Segal cried.

Carol paused for breath, breathing pretty fast herself. "Doctor?" she said inquiringly. "Did you understand all that?"

There was no answer.

"Doctor?"

From a long way away an exhausted voice said, "Quack."

An hour later Doctor Segal was down on his knees under his desk when he heard a knock on the door. "Come in," he said.

"Sorry to trouble you, Doctor." The man was dressed from head to foot in brilliant starched white that would have been immaculate but for an orange-juice stain running the length of his left sleeve.

"That's all right, Schenko. What is it?"

Instead of answering the question, the man crouched down. "You lose something, Doctor?"

Segal ran his hands over the carpet. "They've been clever this time, Schenko. Damned clever." He was looking for the microphone again.

"Have you looked behind the knives?" Schenko asked, referring to the collection of razors displayed in a glass case in the corner. Schenko had been at Casa Blanca for some years and had always found it a sound policy to go along with the folks in whatever fantasy, dream or delusion they were intent upon. This, of course, included his boss as well. Sometimes most of all.

"I've already checked there," Segal replied.

"How about your certificate?" Schenko indicated the framed document hanging on the wall behind the desk. Visitors to the office naturally assumed that this was Segal's medical degree, but it wasn't. He'd removed it long ago to foil the agents the AMA sent every week to spy on him. Doctor Segal was convinced that by hiding his certificate he'd stopped them from taking his number. To complete the deception, he'd replaced the certificate with one that read in Old English type, "This is to certify that Barry Segal," his name was written in ink, "has this day swum a distance of," and this again was written in ink, "twenty-three yards." It was signed, "Wayne Stewart, Counselor."

"Not there either," Segal told him. He got up from the floor and sat in his chair.

"Did you want to see me about something?"

"It's old Mr. McNulty again, Doctor," Schenko said. "I'm afraid he's kicked in another TV set."

"Damn it, I thought I gave orders he wasn't to watch Frost anymore. That's the third set this month."

"I'm sorry, Doctor. You want I should go buy another one?"

"Oh, very well," Segal said, moodily peering under his desk blotter, "but make sure it's just a reconditioned one. McNulty's costing me a fortune."

Schenko was about to leave when he was stopped by a hissed command.

"Quiet!" Segal had his hand up, his eyes riveted on the door. He slid his chair back silently, rose and tiptoed across the room. He closed a careful hand around the doorknob, turned it slowly, then wrenched the door open.

There was nobody in the outer office, nothing except one of the patients' dogs, a large, fluffy animal curled up in a chair. It lifted its head sleepily and looked at the doctor.

Segal gave a mirthless little chuckle and said to it, a condescending smile on his face, "Did you really think a cheap disguise would fool *me?*"

On his income tax Schenko always listed his occupation as Psychiatric Assistant. He figured that seeing the janitor called himself a Sanitary Engineer he should be allowed to embroider a little too. It was half true at that, when you considered that he did indeed assist a psychiatrist, even if he didn't actually assist him in psychiatry. But Bath Attendant would have been closer to the truth, and General Odd Job Man even closer. It was Schenko's job to supervise the men's baths, which meant he told them to cut out splashing one another when they got bored and stopped them from bringing in any bath toys. It was also his job to run errands, fetch and carry, and look after the new arrivals. He was bell boy, delivery man and sometime-gardener, and also helped the janitor burn trash, a job he felt was a touch menial for somebody with his qualifications. A broad, square-shaped man, he had an easygoing disposition and had a good relationship with the patients, although he was firm with them when the situation called for it.

Leaving Doctor Segal sneering at the dog, he went out of the building, walked round to the garage and got out the clinic's van. He drove it round in front of the house and stopped for a cab that was just pulling up. He saw Dibley, Walter and Swaboda get out and start towards the porch.

"Good morning, Mr. Swaboda," Schenko called. He and Swaboda got on pretty well and would often pass the time of day. Swaboda ambled over and said hello.

Schenko said, "What's with the cab? Isn't that guy from Hartsdale?"

Swaboda affirmed it. "We took the train today."

"You should have got off at White Plains; it's closer."

Swaboda looked down at his feet. "We planned to, only we had a little trouble with the conductor."

"What happened?" Schenko asked. Doctor Segal always encouraged his staff to take an interest in the clients' problems.

"Well," said Swaboda, "it started just before a Hundred and Twenty-fifth Street. You know Dibley has this memory thing . . ."

"Uh huh," Schenko said.

"Well, we'd just left Grand Central and Dibley asks the conductor what time we were due in at Grand Central."

"That got the conductor mad, huh?"

"Sure, but he got madder. Around about Fordham, when he comes by for the tickets, he refuses to punch my mother's ticket. Claims he can't see her anywhere on the train. She was sitting right next to me."

"Guy must have been drunk," Schenko said. He'd met Swaboda's mother, of course. He'd even been sent to get her a glass of water once.

"But the real trouble came later," Swaboda continued. "You know Walter Byrd, don't you?"

"Oh sure," said Schenko. Everybody knew Walter. Visitors to Casa Blanca were always shown two things: the painting in the reception room, said to be an original Remington, and Walter.

"Around about Ardsley, Kitty takes over and starts smoking like a chimney. And us sitting in a No Smoker. By then there were only a couple of people left in the car anyway, but one of them starts complaining, a young guy."

"And," Schenko prompted.

Swaboda sighed. "Rocky took over and made him eat a Marlboro."

"So the conductor put you off the train at Hartsdale."

Swaboda nodded. "Still, we only made Scarsdale last time."

"You guys should take the express. What happened to your car, anyway?"

"We drove it over a cliff in the Bronx." Swaboda told him all about it.

"Gee, that's too bad," Schenko said. "And there's no way you can collect?"

Swaboda dropped his voice and glanced around. "As a matter of fact, there is. Dibley's come up with a wow of an idea." He told him all about that, too.

"Say," Schenko said when he'd heard it all, "that's pretty smart. Yes sir, the mayor won't know what hit him." He put the car into gear. "I guess I'd better get going, Mr. Swaboda. I got to run down to the Bronx myself."

Swaboda stood back. "Watch out for the moon craters."

Schenko took the car down the drive and out onto the golf course. He was a careful driver and he took his eyes off the road only once—to roll them towards the roof as he thought about Dibley's plan.

Without a doubt the most famous borough, section, part or area of any city in the world has still got to be Brooklyn. A lot of people have heard of The Cross, a lot more have heard of Sestière and Soho, and Copacabana's more famous than both. And you'd have to be pretty isolated not to have heard of Montmartre. But there isn't anybody over the age of thirty who hasn't heard of Brooklyn. Because of Hollywood, of course. There was a time in American cinema history when very few films were set anywhere but New York, and practically all of those took place in Brooklyn. The characters were either truculently from there, with excruciating accents to prove it, or happily going there, or, with a deep breath and crossed fingers, passing through there. And seeing that these movies were made before most of the world got television, everybody went to see them. Which is why if you said "Brooklyn" to anybody over thirty in Nepal or Java or Finland they'd know immediately what you were talking about. On the other hand, if you said "Bronx" to them they might possibly think you had a cold.

But, the movies aside, Brooklyn is also better known than the Bronx because there are a lot of famous things named for it. After all, nobody's ever heard of the Bronx Dodgers or the Bronx Bridge or the Bronx Museum or A Tree Grows in the Bronx. Yet the Bronix, as you can call it if you're from there, has its own thing too, and the people who inhabit the borough are very defensive about it. Specially vis-à-vis Brooklyn. They'll tell you that it's more civilized than Brooklyn, safer, quieter, more respectable, a better place to bring up kids, and as far as shops and stores and restaurants go has everything Atlantic Avenue has to offer and then some.

Much of that is debatable, naturally, but they may be right about the shops and stores. Particularly around the area where Schenko finally found a parking spot. Here the IND section of the New York subway was anything but a subway, teetering on elevated iron trestles, which only an Eiffel or a Brunel could have loved, fifty feet above the ground. At the bottom of all the metalwork, tumbling over one another trying to get closer to the commuter, were butchers, laundries, dry cleaners, dress shops, repair shops, bake shops and a thousand other kinds of shops, all talking about themselves in a chaos of electric, plastic, neon and painted signs. The streets were full of cars, people, cardboard boxes and newspapers, and the whole crazy bazaar stretched in four directions as far as the eye could see.

The store that Schenko went into was sandwiched between a Middle Eastern delicatessen and a funeral parlor. It had a bare board floor, nothing on the walls, and was littered with big ugly old-style TV sets and small ugly plastic portables. The store bought up old sets, replaced the tube and a knob or two and resold them for a lot less than a new one would cost. They did a lot of business with people who had lousy credit ratings and couldn't afford to pay cash for the latest Magnavox, or people who wanted a cheap set for the kids' room.

Schenko picked out a fat veneered black-and-white monster resting on spindly metal legs. It would make an all-too-easy target for Mr. McNulty, but it was the lowest priced one they had. The clerk took his money and helped him carry it out and load it into the van. Schenko locked the van up and looked at his watch. No sense hurrying back, he thought; the patients wouldn't drown without him; most of them could dog-paddle anyway. He decided to go and have a beer and relax for half an hour. He looked up and down the street and set off and stopped outside the first bar he came to. To Schenko, not much of a drinker at the best of times, one bar was as good as another as long as it was reasonably clean and wasn't full of a drunken mob. This one seemed all right—it was practically empty and the floor had just been swept. And there was a Ballantine Ale sign in the window; he liked Ballantine Ale on draught. He pushed through the doors, sat down at the bar and ordered a glass. The barman brought it, then reached up and switched on the TV set. Watching it come slowly to life, Schenko thought that up near the ceiling would be a good spot to put Mr. McNulty's set, too.

Somebody in one of the booths called, "Hey, Syd," and the bartender said, "What am I, a waitress? Sit at the bar for crissake." Schenko heard the other man mutter something that was lost as the sound came up on the TV. It was some kind of quiz show and Schenko watched it idly as he sipped his ale. He heard a stool scrape on the tile floor and looked around to see a man sitting down at the bar, apparently the man from the booth going along with the bartender's suggestion. From the sour look on his face Schenko saw that he wasn't too happy about it. He also saw that the guy had had a few drinks. He turned his attention back to the TV. An unctuous young man was asking a housewife from Mineola something about last Sunday's ball game. The housewife was looking sad and dumb, and the audience was groaning. They showed a clip from the game: a hapless quarterback being racked up by the defense.

"Hate to see them get hurt," the man next to Schenko said. "Hate to see it."

They showed a slow-motion replay. The quarterback back-pedaled with short little steps, desperately looking downfield.

The two defensive men slanted in at him, coming on in long lumbering strides, arms and elbows swinging, cleats driving at the turf. The quarterback braked, cocked his arm, stepped forward and brought his arm over in a graceful loop that was never completed. The first man to him drove his shoulder into his middle, buckling him. The other man hit him high. He was lifted clear of the ground, smashed towards it and driven down into it.

The man who hated to see them get hurt cried, "Wow, look at that. They stomped him good." He looked over at Schenko. He was a large man, fleshy and heavy, with a good part of the weight round his stomach. He'd said, "shtomped" for "stomped"; Tenth-Avenue Irish probably, Schenko thought. He certainly looked Irish enough—the nose, the eyes, the pale, freckled complexion; a real spud-face, as his father used to say. Schenko said, "It's a rough game all right."

On the screen a different woman was being asked a question about the Civil War.

The two men lost interest.

"You see the game Sunday?" the man asked.

"The Giants game?"

"Yeah. I took the Browns, eight points. Never did like the Giants nor nothing about them."

Schenko nodded in agreement. "Not my favorite outfit either."

The big man raised his drink. "Which's your team?"

"Nobody now. It used to be the Packers when Lombardi had them."

"No kidding?" The drink came back to the bar. "Me too. Boy, that was a team, wasn't it? I mean who you got today as good as Horning or Taylor or Nietzsche?"

"Right," Schenko said.

"The old Packers, huh?" the man said, smiling. "What are you drinking?"

"Ale."

"Syd," the big man said, "an ale for my friend here, and you can do this again for me." He pulled out a wad of bills and flicked through them slowly as if he were trying to find something smaller than a ten. When he reached the end without success he pulled a bill off the top and slapped it down on the bar.

Schenko said, "You must be doing O.K. What are you, a stockbroker?"

The big man smirked and pocketed the roll. "Plenty of money around if you know how to get your hands on it."

"Never got the knack," Schenko said. The drinks arrived and they started on them.

"What do you do for a crust?" the big man asked.

Schenko told him.

"No kidding? You mean it's a nut house?"

"Well, sort of. No straitjackets or anything though. We have about twenty live-ins and the rest come up to see the shrink a couple of times a week."

"But don't none of them ever get dangerous? I mean, you ever have to bop 'em one?"

"Nah," Schenko said, "they're harmless enough. In fact, some of them are pretty funny. You should hear what one of them came out with this morning." Schenko told the man what Swaboda had told him about getting their money back.

"Jesus," his companion said, "those guys must be crazy."

Schenko finished his ale. "They're all a little crazy where I work," he said.

The little ball shot up the alley, zipped round the metal rim and rebounded against the spring that was waiting in ambush on the opposite side. Surprised by the setback, its confidence shaken, it rolled back to the top of the board and thought about its next move. After a moment of indecision it spotted something at the bottom of the board and made a dive for it. Halfway there it collided with a metal knob which sizzled angrily and lit up in an electric flash and pinged the ball back the way it had come. Rebuffed, the little ball rolled halfway to the top again, then took another stab at it. It went all the way this time, unimpeded, and dropped off the end of the board into a slot.

"You're hitting it too hard. Hit it slower," Mira told his brother.

Joey pumped another ball, pulled the lever back against its spring and released it more gently this time. They watched the ball's crazy progress in silence.

Next to them Cahill was working a similar machine, letting the lever go with a bang. "Hey," he grunted, bored with the game, "you guys want to hear something funny?"

"Try to hang one on the rim," Mira said to Joey.

"Listen," Cahill said, "I'm talking to you. I heard something pretty funny today. You want to hear it?"

"What?" said Mira. "You're hitting it too hard again. Take it easy."

"A guy came into the bar after you guys left and we had a few drinks together. He told me this wild thing." Cahill told them what Schenko had told him. "That's pretty funny, huh?"

Mira was watching another ball shoot round the board. "Hysterical," he said.

chapter 8

". . . journeyed forth to acquire a mighty sword . . ."

"And so," Dibley said, pausing to give a little extra weight to the punchline, "with a cannon staring him in the face he'll have to pay cash on the barrelhead, because he can't risk find-

66

ing out whether or not we mean what we say. He'll hate it, but there's not a darn thing he'll be able to do about it."

"Isn't that the greatest thing you ever heard?" Swaboda asked.

Walter seconded the question by leaning forward in his chair.

Carol said nothing for a moment, looking at each of them in turn sitting around her in the living room. She came back to Dibley. "And you're quite serious about this?" She made it sound like more of a statement than a question.

"Well, of course we're serious." The smile Dibley was wearing lost a little of its bloom. "What makes you think we're not?"

Carol tapped at her teeth with a thumbnail. "Oh dear."

"Oh dear? What's that supposed to mean? We come up with a foolproof way of getting our car back and all you can say is 'Oh dear'?" Dibley was peeved. He'd expected Carol to give him a tickertape parade.

"It's fantastic, right?" Swaboda asked, trying to save the day. He couldn't understand her response either.

Carol sighed, pursed her lips and stared at the carpet. She'd have to tell them sometime. "I agree with you, Charlie, it is fantastic. But not fantastic great, fantastic impossible."

Dibley said, "What do you mean by that?" He knew perfectly well what she meant by that.

"I mean impossible, improbable, implausible. And doomed . . ." she pronounced the word in three syllables ". . . to failure. Utter, complete and total failure."

"You're joking," Dibley said. "It's a terrific idea."

"Darling, it's a terrible idea."

"Tell me one thing that's wrong with it, one thing." He was starting to get a little angry.

"For a start, it'll never work in a million years."

"Why?"

"Oh, darling, come *on*. Steal a cannon, hold up the mayor, and from a boat? It's just so . . ." she searched for a word that wouldn't hurt too much ". . . so illogical, that's all. It's the wildest thing I've ever heard of."

Dibley pounced. "But that's the very thing that gives it a

chance. It's so wild it's got to work. They won't expect it, they won't be ready for it, they won't know how to cope with it. The odds have got to be with us, because nobody's ever tried anything like this before."

"Because nobody's ever been silly enough," Carol said firmly.

Dibley thumped his head back against a cushion. "Do you know what you're doing? You're closing your eyes to it. You're refusing to use the slightest bit of imagination."

Carol leaned towards him, her face set. She was beginning to get a little angry herself. "That's just it, James; it's top heavy with imagination. That's its whole problem."

Swaboda slipped into the strained pause that followed. "I don't get it, Carol. How can imagination be a problem? Look at all the big capers, the hijacks and the train robberies, the warehouse jobs . . . they all had a lot of imagination."

Dibley slapped the arm of his chair. "Exactly."

Carol searched for a way to explain. "Look," she said, "suppose, just suppose, you did pull it off. You know what you'd have besides the money for a new car? A warrant out for your arrest as long as your arm. You're planning to steal a gun and that's a crime. You have to steal a boat and that's a crime. And then you're going to hold up the mayor and that's a crime. You're aiming to turn yourselves into a gang of thieves and extortionists."

"Now, hold on." Dibley sounded extremely righteous. "We wouldn't be doing this if the city hadn't wrecked our car. If anyone's a criminal, it's them."

"They started it," Swaboda chimed in.

Carol opened her mouth to reply, then closed it again. She took another look round their faces thrust forward at her in a determined semicircle. She'd never seen Dibley so resolute before. And Swaboda looked like the portrait of Winston Churchill. Even Walter's tiny jaw looked a little less slack. She saw that she wasn't going to sway them and quickly changed her strategy. She sat back in her chair, recrossed her legs and smoothed her skirt. "No matter what I say you're going to try it, aren't you?"

"You can bet on it," Dibley said.

"You too, Charlie?"

"Me too," Swaboda answered.

"And how about you, Walter?" Carol asked. "Have they convinced you too?"

"Yes," Walter said in a rare outburst.

"And I suppose nothing I could say would sway any of you?"

"Nothing you or anybody could say," Dibley declared.

Carol nodded her head, very businesslike. "Very well, in that case I'm in."

Two voices said, "What?"

"On one condition," she added. "The moment things start looking bad, which should be about five minutes after we start, I have the right to call the whole thing off. Agreed?"

The three men took a silent vote.

"Agreed," Dibley said. His face didn't show it, but he was very relieved that his girl was going along with them. If she hadn't, it would have made for an awfully strained relationship around the apartment. Besides, they had a lot to do and could use the extra pair of hands.

Carol was talking: "I also want you to know that I'm only coming in on this Alice-in-Wonderland thing so I can have some control. Because nothing you've told me has made me feel any different about the outcome, which is as certain as I'm sitting here."

"You wait," Dibley told her; "you'll see."

Carol jumped up from her chair and walked over to the French windows. She clapped her hands and rubbed her palms together briskly. "Right, what do we do first?"

She figured that the sooner they started the sooner the whole thing would collapse by its own weight. What she had to do was make sure that nobody was underneath when it did—especially Dibley.

Dibley got to his feet and moved round the room, equally brisk. "First we get the cannon."

"What kind?"

"It doesn't matter as long as it's big enough to look scary and small enough to tow."

"What do we do, call up the cannon department at Bloomingdale's?"

Dibley refused to get mad. "No, we call up the cannon department at the army. I've been doing some checking." He strode over to the telephone table, picked up a desk calendar, flipped it open and handed it to her. "Call this number and ask to speak to Colonel Brogan, then tell him—"

"Hold it." Carol cut him off. "Whoa back now. What is this number and who is Colonel Brogan?"

"I told you, I've been doing some checking. Colonel Brogan runs the One Hundred and Tenth Regiment Armory, and the One Hundred and Tenth Regiment Armory is bristling with guns."

"And what do I say to him? Hello, Colonel Brogan, how about a gun?"

"Basically, yes," Dibley said. "With a little trimming."

"This is fascinating," Carol said. "What kind of trimming?"

"Easy. You're some general's secretary at the Pentagon and—"

Carol halted him again. "Which general? What's his name?"

"I don't know, make one up. They've got hundreds. Brogan can't have heard of them all." He appealed to Walter and Swaboda. "What's a good name for a general?"

"MacArthur," Walter said.

"Custer," Swaboda said.

"Foods," Carol said.

"We'll call him General Smith," Dibley decided. "You tell Brogan that you haven't had any reply to the letter you wrote him about the gun for the parade the city is planning to give its most decorated soldier. The city has written to the Pentagon asking to borrow a gun, and the Pentagon in turn is passing the request on to the One Hundred and Tenth Regiment Armory."

Carol had her eyes closed and was massaging the bridge of her nose. "This man, New York's most decorated soldier, what's his name?"

Dibley said, "You're a stickler for detail, aren't you? I don't know—we'll think up one for him, too. Let's make him a sergeant; they're always tough. What's a good name for a sergeant?"

"York," Walter said.

"Bilko," Swaboda said.

"Shriver," Carol said.

Dibley decided that Sergeant Jones was just fine. He picked up the phone, dialed the number, waited for an answer and handed the phone to Carol. "You're on."

"Hello," she said into it. "Colonel Brogan please. General Smith calling from Washington." Carol played it straight; she didn't want them to accuse her of sabotaging the plan. She knew they'd try again without her and she wanted to be around when things got out of hand. "Hello? Colonel Brogan?" She gave him the story exactly the way Dibley had told her to.

A deep voice said into her ear, "A letter from General Smith? Nope, if it came across my desk I didn't see it."

Carol said, "It must have gone astray. You can't even get a letter mailed in Washington anymore."

"New York's most decorated soldier, you say?"

"Congressional Medal of Honor winner," Carol said, piling it on.

"What's his name again?"

"Jones. Sergeant Richard Jones."

"What department's he in?" The colonel had thrown her a curve; Carol didn't know anything about the army and she said the first thing that came into her head.

"He's a cook."

"A cook? With a Medal of Honor? I've got to meet this man."

"I'm afraid that would be impossible, Colonel. He's on a very tight schedule."

"I'm only talking about fifteen minutes," the colonel said. "I'd just like to introduce him to my men as an example."

"I'm sorry, Colonel, but I honestly don't think—"

"Look," the colonel broke in—you had to be firm with Pentagon secretaries; the way some of them spoke you'd think they outranked their bosses—"if Jones can't spare me fifteen minutes I can't spare him a gun. That's the deal. Now you think about it and call me back with your decision."

The phone clicked in her ear. Carol hung up too. She was enormously relieved but she was careful not to show it. "You heard. I gave it the old college try."

"What did he say?" Dibley asked. He'd gathered most of it and she only had to fill in a few holes.

"So there goes your ball game," she said. "I'm sorry, gang, but you can't hold up the mayor without a gun, and you can't get a gun without Sergeant Jones."

"Hold it a moment," Dibley said. "We're not giving up that easy. We've hardly started."

"Sure," Swaboda put in, "all we need is Sergeant Jones."

"How's that?" Carol looked perplexed.

"You said it yourself," Dibley told her. "We need Sergeant Jones."

"So? Where are you going to get him?"

Dibley spread his arms. "You're looking at him."

Carol gave them a sickly little smile. She knew it had been too easy.

Twenty minutes after going out of the door Dibley came back through it looking a lot different. He was dressed in the uniform of a sergeant in the United States Army and sporting a stunning collection of ribbons and medals that spread over his chest like a sunrise. Under his arm he carried a box which held his clothes. The lettering on the box said, "Downtown Costume Rental."

He bounded into the room, threw the box onto a chair and snapped smartly to attention. "Sergeant Jones reporting," he said. "How do I look?"

"Very nice," Walter said.

"You look terrific," Swaboda said.

"You look like a Confederate spy," Carol said.

Dibley was a hard man to fit at the best of times but doubly so at a costume rental company that couldn't go in for a big range of sizes. Consequently, the sleeves of the blouse stopped short at his wrists and somebody seemed to have cut a foot off the bottom of the pants. Nevertheless, Dibley was very pleased with the uniform and wasn't at all dismayed by Carol's remark. But then in his present ebullient mood nothing could have dismayed him.

"Just came back to give you all a look and to tell you to call Brogan, Carol. Tell him he's in luck and that Sergeant Jones is on the way." He tugged at his blouse and straightened his cap. "So long, gang, next time you see me it'll be mission accomplished." He threw them a snappy salute, wheeled smartly, marched across the room, pulled open the closet door, which was right next to the front door, stepped briskly in and banged the door closed behind him.

"Not now," Swaboda moaned, "please not now."

"Believe me," Carol said, "he always gets them when you don't want him to."

The closet door opened and Dibley stepped out a lot slower than he'd stepped in. The bubbling confidence of a few moments ago had been replaced by a subdued bewilderment. He stopped, looked back at the closet, then looked at Carol.

"Carol," he said, "didn't we used to have stairs in there?"

"Yes, darling, but we moved them out into the hall."

Dibley was trying to recall the move when he caught sight of himself in a wall mirror. He took a fast step backwards and looked down at his uniform in surprise. "My God! I've been drafted."

Carol said she was going in to lie down.

Swaboda, unwilling to give up yet, came over to Dibley and grasped him by the arms. "Dibley, concentrate. Who are you? Come on, you know."

"Of course I know," Dibley said, annoyed. "I should know who I am, shouldn't I?" He stopped to think. "It's on the tip of my tongue."

"You're New York's most decorated cook," Swaboda told him.

Dibley couldn't believe it. "Craig Claiborne?"

"No, Sergeant Jones."

Dibley snapped his fingers. "Sergeant Jones, of course."

"You sure?" Swaboda asked, looking at him sideways.

"Sure I'm sure. I'm on my way to the One Hundred and Tenth Regiment Armory."

"Who are you going to see?"

"Colonel Brogan," Dibley snapped. "Will you stop treating me like a child?"

"Sorry," Swaboda said. "What are you going to see him about?"

Dibley frowned and blinked hard. "A promotion?"

They decided that Swaboda had better pose as Sergeant Jones.

Dibley went into the bedroom and changed out of the uniform, and Swaboda took it back to the costume company.

The clerk took it out of the box and examined it suspiciously. "Your buddy thought it was fine when he left here—what went wrong?"

"His girl didn't like the fit," Swaboda said.

The clerk grunted. "He's too tall for an army uniform. I'll tell you what, though, I got a Frankenstein costume that'd fit him to a tee."

Swaboda got a fast mental picture of Dibley asking Colonel Brogan for a promotion in a Frankenstein costume. "Thanks, but I think he already has one. Listen, do you think you could fit me in an army uniform?"

The clerk ran a doubtful eye over Swaboda's beachball figure. "We can always try," he said.

When he got back to the apartment Swaboda bounded in through the door in much the same manner that Dibley had. Getting into uniform seemed to have the same stimulating effect on both of them. "How about it," he asked, parading round the room, "do I look like a soldier?"

The uniform didn't fit any better than the one Dibley had worn. The buttons on the blouse looked like champagne corks ready to pop.

"You certainly look like a cook," Dibley said.

"What's in the other box?" Carol asked. Swaboda had brought two boxes back with him.

"Wait till you see," he said, excited. He put both boxes down and opened the top one. He peeled back tissue paper and pulled out a WAC uniform. "Mom's coming too."

They decided that Walter had better pose as Sergeant Jones.

Swaboda gave his uniform, and his mother's, to Walter, who went down to the rental company. He walked up and down outside for five minutes plucking up courage to go in and talk to a stranger. The clerk didn't make it any easier for him. When Walter shyly handed him the two uniforms and asked for one for himself, the clerk gave a tired look and said, "Are you guys auditioning for a war?"

He went away and came back with a uniform and showed Walter the changing room. Like Dibley and Swaboda, Walter was also the wrong shape for off-the-peg clothes and the uniform was way too big for him, the sleeves covering his hands and giving him a kind of Fu Manchu look.

Walter transferred the medals and ribbons from Swaboda's uniform—Swaboda having transferred them from Dibley's—and he was all set. The plan was for him to go straight to the armory; Carol was going to call Colonel Brogan ahead of him.

Now the only problem facing Walter was getting a cab.

Walter was fully aware of the qualities needed to be successful at getting cabs in New York: You had to be virile, fast, rude and cunning—none of which Walter was. His problem was further exacerbated by his reluctance to attract a cab driver's attention. Walter attracted too much attention to want to attract more. He was too timid to call out and had never learned to whistle. His technique was to just stand there on the sidewalk and hope they'd know why he was standing there.

When three cabs had gone by without any of the drivers reading his mind, he forced himself to raise his hand when he saw another one coming.

When the cab driver spotted the movement, Walter dropped his hand to his head and tried to make out he'd just been straightening his hat.

The cab pulled up in front of him. "You want a cab, Sarge?"

Walter shook his head.

The driver shifted the cigar in his mouth. "You were just giving me a friendly wave like . . ."

Walter nodded.

"Come on," the man said, "get in and we'll go somewhere. You army guys can afford it."

Walter allowed himself to be talked into it.

"Where to?" the driver asked. "Times Square, Radio City, the Plaza?"

"The One Hundred and Tenth Regiment Armory," Walter said.

The cabbie considered it. "Yeah, that's good too." He took the cab away from the curb and joined the traffic heading uptown. In his rear vision mirror he watched Walter sitting like a stone statue in the rear seat. "Battle fatigue," he said to his cigar.

The trip didn't take long, just five short minutes. Even in New York nothing much changes in five minutes, and when the cab pulled up in front of the armory the weather was the same, the cab was the same, the driver was the same.

But Walter wasn't.

He hopped out and slammed the door shut with a flick of his wrist. "Here you go, buddy," he slid a folded bill behind the cabbie's ear, "buy yourself a new cigar."

The driver stared at this cocky little guy standing there on firmly planted feet, his shoulders moving and his hands hitching. "Hey," he said, looking round at the back seat, "what happened to my fare? The guy I picked up at Fourteenth. You ain't him."

Walter stabbed two fingers at him, twisted his head to one side, licked his lips and said, "Sure I am."

The driver reexamined Walter. "You seem different somehow."

"Travel's broadening," Walter said. He turned on his heel and strutted up the steps into the armory. He went down a long hall without meeting anybody and then a captain came out of a door and moved to pass him.

Walter shot out a hand and spun him round. "Hey, chief," he said, "where does Brogan hang out when he's not on the golf course?"

"Chief?" the captain said. His eyebrows lowered. When he saw the rows of medals they climbed back up again. "Up the stairs, second on the right."

Walter stepped closer to him. "What does a ship do when it comes into port?"

"Huh?"

Walter reached out and flipped the officer's tie out of his jacket. "Tie's up."

He left the captain staring after him and trotted up the stairs, went down the hall and found a door with the colonel's name on it. A nineteen-year-old corporal was pecking at a typewriter in the outer office.

"Hey, kid," Walter said, "tell your boss Sergeant Jones is here."

The corporal looked up and went goggle eyed. "Wow!" He was looking at the phalanx of decorations. "Washington just called about you, Sergeant. We didn't expect you so . . . Wow!" he said again. "What did you do to get all those?"

Walter gave him a double hitch and a double stab. "Saved up box tops. Where's your boss?"

"I'm afraid Colonel Brogan's stepped out for a moment, Sergeant."

Walter grabbed him by the shirt and pulled him to his feet. "Listen, kid," his eyes narrowed dangerously, "you like these medals, right? You go get your boss and maybe I'll give you one." He shoved him towards the door. "I'll wait in his office, see?"

The corporal didn't hang around. He scampered out of the door and hurried down to the basement, where the colonel was driving golf balls into a practice net.

"Colonel Brogan, sir," he said breathlessly. "He's here, sir. Sergeant Jones."

The colonel, a large bronzed man, paused at the top of his swing. "You mean upstairs?"

"Yes, sir. In your office."

"Splendid," the colonel said, putting his club aside and starting for the stairs. "What's he like?"

The corporal trotted beside him. "A real individualist, sir. He's even had a special uniform tailored."

"Naturally," the colonel said. "He wants to look his best for the parade."

"And talk about tough," the corporal gabbled on. "Wait till you see him, sir. Medals up to here."

"Real fire eater, eh? By God, wait till the Marines hear about this. The army's so tough even our cooks get decorated."

They'd reached the colonel's office. The corporal bounded ahead of him, threw open the outer door, threw open the inner door, stood stiffly to attention and formally announced him. "Colonel Brogan, Sergeant Jones."

The colonel strode in, hand outstretched. "Sergeant, it's an honor."

Walter was perched on the corner of the colonel's desk. He

78

took a huge drag on the cigaret he was smoking, blew smoke out noisily, tossed his head, swung one leg over the other and said with perfect enunciation in a clipped, theatrical voice, "Hello, soldier. Didn't we meet at the Stage Door Canteen?"

chapter 9

". . . thought to turn it to his advantage"

The water churned and boiled up white in huge popping bubbles as if a sea monster were snoring on the bottom of the harbor. The boat quivered and vibrated, wood and metal rattling together as propellers turned in their shafts and pushed the boat, sluggish and heavy, away from its moorings.

The first of the skyscrapers, a stepped, box-shaped pyramid, appeared above the top of the terminal. The vibration lessened, evened out, and the hiss of the water at the stern was replaced by the steady chunking of the engines.

The ferry slipped the end of the dock and the bow came round a few degrees. A second building joined the pyramid, then a third. Then the buildings began to pop up fast, one after another, receding to form a towering vertical solid wall of steel and glass. The boat moved faster and the brown-green of a park appeared and in it the circular gray walls of an old fort. The angle of vision shrank, the perspective grew and the park, the buildings, the dock, the terminal became the tip of an island anchored in the water, a point of land at the conflux of two rivers and the end of a bay.

A cold wind hurtled in from New Jersey and strafed the outside passenger deck. Cahill stuffed his hands into his jacket pockets and stamped his feet up and down. He glanced sullenly at Mira standing beside him and turned his back to the wind and leaned against the rail, hunching his shoulders. "What the hell we going to Staten Island for? I been to Staten Island."

Mira was watching the city get smaller. The wind separated a strand of his dark hair and bent it over his brow, then slid inside his half-zipped jacket and bellowed it out. He didn't seem to notice.

"How about it?" Cahill growled. "It's colder'n a witch's tit out here."

"It's warm inside." Mira snapped out the answer irritably, speaking as somebody does to a whining child. He was concentrating on the candlestick shapes that were starting to define themselves on Manhattan. In a different voice he said to his brother, "Try a couple from here."

Joey fiddled with the camera, an old 120 cassette, brought it up to his eye and took pictures.

"A camera yet," Cahill said. "What are we, tourists? For crissakes will you tell me what we're doing out here?"

"You're the reason we're here," Mira said, watching Joey work the camera.

"Me? What did I do?"

Mira looked at him then. "Remember that idea you told me about, the one that guy at the funny farm thought up?"

"What, you mean what that guy told me? That crazy thing with the gun?"

"Yeah," Mira said. He looked back at the towers of Wall Street glittering in the sun like stacks of coins. "I don't think it's so crazy."

Cahill watched him for a second, decided he was being kidded, swore through his teeth and went inside where it was warm.

chapter 10

". . . even though it proved a difficult task"

While Mira was on his way to Staten Island the next morning, Dibley was on his way to nowhere. He was sitting in the apartment, sunk into an armchair as far down in it as he could get. His physical position reflected his mental state of mind exactly. Dibley was down, low, mired, depressed. He'd gone out and bought a *Times* and a cup of coffee and leafed through the Help Wanted, but he'd been too depressed to look hard, too depressed even to think about going to the movies, which is what a lot of people do after they've been through that particular column. He'd seen everything anyway.

He moped around all morning and he moped around all afternoon till Carol came home from her job at six. They ate dinner and that was better; the sight of her brushing her long blond hair off her face and crossing her long tapered legs, her thighs tightly outlined against her skirt, always made him feel good even if he sometimes couldn't remember why. His spirits rose a little, but later when Walter and Swaboda dropped by to talk things over, he went right back down again. Carol made them coffee, then left them alone to get over their disappointment together.

"Anybody got any ideas?" Dibley asked without much hope.

Nobody had anything to offer.

Dibley stirred his coffee and clanked the spoon down on the saucer. It made a sad despondent sound. "I'm pretty sure there are other armories with guns," he said, "but based on our past experience I'd say the army's too tough a nut to crack. For us anyway," he finished, looking sheepish. Walter and Swaboda looked the same way too.

Swaboda said, "There's nowhere else we could get a cannon?"

"Where for instance?"

"A park, maybe? The things kids play on?" He saw the look on Dibley's face. "Wouldn't do, huh?"

"I already thought of it. The problem is, most of them are nineteen-fourteen vintage and cemented into place. Also they usually take away the breech blocks, so even if we did get one loose the mayor would laugh at us."

Dibley's explanation was good for another two minutes of melancholy silence.

Surprisingly, Walter broke it. "Army surplus," he piped in his paper-thin voice.

Dibley had been miles away. "Pardon?"

Walter remained silent. He seldom said anything once, let alone twice.

Swaboda spoke up. "I think he said, 'Army surplus.'"

Dibley looked doubtful. "I've only seen them selling fatigues and boots and canteens. I don't think they run to field pieces."

"You're thinking of an army and navy store," Swaboda said. "I think Walter's talking about their heavy surplus stuff, like trucks and things. The stuff that's too expensive to junk. He's got a point."

Dibley started to come alive. "You're darn right he's got a point. If they sell off their used trucks they're bound to sell off their used guns, too."

Carol, coming in for the coffee cups, had caught the tail end of the conversation, and what she heard alarmed her. She'd been under the impression that the whole idea was stone dead, knifed by Colonel Brogan, and that this meeting was in the nature of a wake. But here they were on the edge of reviving the silly thing. She thought she'd better give it a final kick.

"But, James," she said, "you can't even afford to buy a used car, let alone a gun. Now can you?"

Dibley subsided again. "You're right. I was getting carried away." He sank back down into his chair. "There's no way of getting a gun. Let's forget it."

The entire scheme would have died and been buried right there and then, just as Carol wanted it, if she hadn't tried to put one last nail in the coffin.

"Besides," she picked up the cups and started towards the kitchen, "they wouldn't sell to individuals anyway. You'd have to be a friendly foreign country."

It was hard to tell who got the idea first, Dibley or Swaboda. They both shot from their chairs and cried, "That's it!" at the same time.

"What's it?" Carol smelled a rat.

"Where we get the gun from," Dibley explained. "A friendly foreign country. We ship guns overseas everyday."

"World's biggest military supplier," Swaboda said with a touch of pride.

"So it follows," Dibley continued, "that the docks around New York are going to be crawling with guns. And that's where we'll get one, from the docks."

"That's impossible. You can't steal a cannon from a dock."

"Why not? Things are always being pilfered from the docks: booze, food, motorcycles . . . we'll simply add a gun to the list."

This was terrible; he was building up a head of steam for another ridiculous idea. She couldn't let that happen; she had to nip it now—she had to think of a real stopper.

She thought of one. "How are you going to find what you're after? There are hundreds of docks. You've got to find the right ship loading the right kind of gun, and nobody's going to make it easy for you."

Dibley looked at Swaboda to see if he had an answer, but Swaboda was looking at him.

It was Walter who came up with it. "An outboard."

"Right!" Dibley chorused. "We'll rent an outboard and tour the docks. Who's going to suspect anything? Just a couple of guys out for a day on the river. We'll do it first thing in the morning." He swung a jubilant fist through the air. "Fellas, we're back in business again."

The four of them had exchanged their earlier positions; the three men were on their feet and now it was Carol who was sitting down, sunk into the upholstery the way Dibley had been. She closed her eyes and allowed her head to flop back. There was nothing she could do about it; the world's most absurd caper was back on the front burner.

chapter 11

". . . went to spy on the city's treasure house . . ."

Joey Mira handed a ticket to a clerk in a drugstore on Lower Broadway around the corner from the Stock Exchange.

"Twenty-four-hour service, was it?" the clerk asked. He got a nod. "What was the name again?"

"Stevens."

The man leafed through a box of yellow folders, matched up the ticket and pulled out a folder. Joey paid him, crossed to the luncheon counter and handed the folder to his brother. Cahill sat beside him gnawing at a donut, crumbs on his mouth and on the counter top in front of him. The place was only a quarter full, the mid-morning coffee break finished, the early lunches not yet started.

Mira put down his coffee cup, opened the folder and pulled out a dozen glossy four-by-two prints. He leafed through them quickly, then went back over them more slowly. He stopped at one and looked at it for a long time.

"Not bad," he said softly, passing it over to Joey.

Cahill was sucking sugar off his fingers. He glanced at the print as Joey handed it back. "I seen better pictures'n that," he said.

Mira told him that he wasn't talking about the snapshot.

The counter man was at the other end topping up syrup flavors. There was nobody near them. Mira said to Cahill, "You wanted to know why we took that ferry ride yesterday." He flicked the print with a finger. "This is why."

Cahill was concentrating on another donut. "I thought you told me you were checking something out."

"I was." The counter man's pad and pencil were lying to his left and Mira reached for the ballpoint. He put the print down on the counter. It was a shot of the Wall Street skyline taken from about one hundred yards out. It was dominated by three buildings, two of them tall slim towers peaked at the top in the florid thirties fashion. The third, a vast, slab-shaped construction higher and broader than anything else, had the flat rectangular look of the sixties. Only the top halves of the buildings were visible, the lower sections obscured by the smaller buildings that clustered around them. Mira moved the pen in a circle over the modern slab; he'd ringed about thirty stories on its eastern side.

"That's what I checked out."

Cahill wiped his fingers on his jacket, picked up the print and examined it. He tossed it back onto the counter and returned to his donut. "A building," he said through a mouthful. "We going into the real estate business?"

Mira was enjoying this: Cahill didn't have the vaguest idea what he was talking about, and that made him feel good. Cahill was dumb. He'd even showed him a picture, practically drawn a diagram for him, and the guy still didn't get it. A million

85

dollars staring him in the face and the dummy couldn't see it.

Cahill stopped chewing and looked up. He knew what Mira was doing: giving him this plan of his in little pieces like a puzzle he was supposed to fit together. Mira wanted him to pant in excitement and ask him to be a sport and tell him all about it. Well, he wasn't going to do that. Screw his idea. It was probably a ball of wax anyway. All the same, it made him mad, Mira doing this. But he wasn't going to let the son of a bitch see it.

"That building," he said, sounding unconcerned, "that a bank?"

"What do you know," Mira said.

Cahill made a lot of noise with his cup and saucer. "And you're saying it looks good to you . . ."

"It looks better than good."

"Bullshit."

Mira signaled the counter man. "You don't believe me, let's go take a look."

They left the drugstore and headed up Broadway. The sun came down in pale little bursts, and the wind was colder than it had a right to be at that time of year. But that was one of the problems with Wall Street: the weather seemed worse there than anywhere else in the city. In summer the buildings, jammed together as they were, trapped the heat and sent it back down into the narrow streets which had too many twists and turns for a cooling breeze to last long. In the winter the wind seemed to have no trouble making the corners, whistling between the East River and the Hudson or blowing in off the bay.

They turned right at Pine, walked a short block to Nassau Street and went up a flight of steps that led onto a raised, parapeted square. On one side a railing circled a huge sunken plaza, the ornamental rock garden laid out at the bottom speared by a fountain of pipes. Opposite, as if a magician had sown seeds, a grove of spiky, red-berried trees sprang out of the cement. Ahead of them the bank that gave the plaza its name reared up eight hundred feet into the sky, as wide and as sheer as a cliff. The vertical cladding that scaled the building in slim aluminum lines did little to break up its million-ton look. For all its acres of glass and long, elegant, thin strips of metal the building was stuck with its shape: a massive, granite-based tombstone, monolithic and impregnable.

Cahill craned his head and looked up at it like a tourist. The place was a fortress; Mira had to be kidding.

They crossed the plaza, entered the building and walked into a cream-colored marble world. The ceiling soared thirty feet above their heads, and beneath their feet, inlaid with a criss-cross of stainless steel ribbing, the crushed-pebble floor was as smooth and as hard as armored glass. In the center of the floor escalators unfolded silently towards a mezzanine, and beyond them, their indicator lights winking like Christmas trees, elevators lined up in six banks carved deep into the wall.

They went down a floor to the concourse level that ran beneath the plaza and found themselves for the first time in something that was very obviously a bank: counters, desks, cashiers, blue-uniformed guards, the click of typewriters, the ring of phones, the sound of bills being counted and change being made and feet shuffling in line.

Nobody took any notice of them, and they melted in with the people spilling in from the street. Behind them, they became aware of a voice ". . . on two and a half acres and at sixty-three stories above street level is the ninth tallest in the world." A young woman was talking to a group of school children. She wore a blue uniform with the bank's emblem, a square with folded corners, embroidered on her lapel. Standing at the back of the group a middle-aged woman, a teacher or a parent, was telling a little girl to stop talking and listen. "Underneath where we're standing now are five lower levels; Miscellaneous Services, Maintenance Shops and Data Processing taking up the first three. On the fourth level is our Check Processing Center, which is the world's biggest. Entirely automated, it handles over two million checks a day. On the fifth level, buried in the actual bedrock of Manhattan ninety feet below us, is our vault, which is also the world's biggest. Almost as long as a football field, it's encased in concrete walls seven feet thick and weighs just on a thousand tons, more than half of that being reinforced steel. The vault contains thirty-two billion dollars' worth of securities and over a billion dollars in cash."

The children oohed and aahed at this, and one little boy asked a question. "Anybody ever rob it?"

The guide glanced up at the older woman and they smiled at each other. "A lot of people ask us that," she said. "No, it's never been robbed. Anybody trying to get in would have a hard time. The vault has seven doors, each built in a series of layers: a layer of copper that's drill-proof, a layer of iron no acetylene torch could ever burn through, and an outer layer of stainless steel. In addition each door is honeycombed with various electronic alarm systems. The doors were specially designed for us and weigh forty-five tons each and, together with the vault, are proof against everything from a tidal wave to nuclear attack." The girl stole a look at her watch. "Now if you'll stay close together and follow me, we'll go up into the lobby and find out more about how New York's biggest bank operates." The girl started off and the children straggled after her, their guardian shepherding them along.

Cahill watched them go, then took a final look at all the chrome and steel and polished granite. He grunted, his mouth set in an unfunny smile. "This place?" he said to Mira. "You're out of your skull."

chapter 12

". . . persevered in his endeavour . . ."

At that particular moment in time, when Mira was walking out onto Nassau Street, Dibley was three miles due south of him and about a dozen feet below him. He and Carol were sitting in a sporty little runabout on the East River opposite the southern section of the Brooklyn docks.

Dibley had made a beautiful discovery: a freighter being loaded with field pieces. The dock was a solid mass of them, lined up in neat orderly rows.

Dibley said, "I can't get over it. I was prepared to look for a week maybe and we find them first time out. Either we're awfully lucky or they must be shipping this kind of stuff out all the time."

It had been just as big a surprise for Carol, too. Right now she was wondering just who it was up there who didn't like her. She pouted and said, "O.K., you've found them. You still have to get one."

"A mere detail."

"James, you're acting as if you already have one tucked in the parking lot. How in heaven's name do you think you're going to get hold of one of those things?"

"Give me a chance, I just got here. I haven't thought about it yet."

"Well, while you're thinking about it, may I draw your attention to the high cyclone fence and what I take to be security guards at that gate? Even if you could get onto the dock, which I doubt, you've got to get off again. And those guns are a little too big to stick under your jacket."

"You know," Dibley said, "up in Tupper Lake, where I grew up, Miss Black always used to say that you could solve any problem if you just thought hard enough."

Carol winced. "Oh, darling, small-town grade-school teachers are notorious for giving bad advice."

"Miss Black wasn't a grade-school teacher," Dibley said; "she was a hustler."

Carol looked at him sharply. "How would you know that? You left there when you were nine."

"I lied about my age."

While they'd been talking, Dibley had been studying the layout. The guns were being loaded by the giant crane that moved up and down the dock on a track. The ship had only one of its derricks working, the one up forward which was loading oil drums in a big rope net. The guns were being swung on board singly. It seemed a slow operation and Dibley wondered if it took a long time to stow them in the hold. The technique was a simple one: Two stevedores laid a wire sling under a gun and attached it to the crane cable. The crane lifted it clear of the dock, swung it over the ship and lowered it into the hold. A minute later the sling came up empty and the process was repeated. Carol had been right about the security guards; he could see their uniforms over against a long double gate. He could also see that the gate seemed to be the only opening in the cyclone fence that sectioned the area off from the outer dock. That meant that there were only two ways a gun could leave the dock—through the gate, the way the guns had come in, or by the river, the way they were going out. Unless, of course, he could think of a third way.

Carol shrugged down deeper into her coat. "Darling, if we're through here, let's take the boat back and trade it in on a bowl of soup. I'm frozen."

"Yeah, O.K. Just give me a minute." Dibley put all the elements into a hat and looked at what he had: a gun, a ship, a dock, a crane, a river, a fence, a gate. At the moment, those guns were getting off the dock by a combination of gun, crane and ship, in that order. He wondered if by changing the combination and/or the order of the elements it would be possible to find another exit. He jumbled them up in his head and pulled them out three at a time. Gun, ship and fence; fence, gun and river; river, gun and dock; dock, gun and crane; crane, gun and fence; fence, gun—he stopped and went back to the previous combination.

"Crane, gun and fence," he said pensively.

Carol bent towards him. "Pardon?"

The idea rose in him like a skyrocket. "Crane, gun and fence!"

"Your lawyers?" Carol asked. She wasn't following.

Dibley whipped his head round to look up at the crane. Way up near the top was a glassed-in cab, the tiny figure of a man just visible inside it. He stabbed an arm at the sky. "If we can get that derrick man to play ball we've got ourselves a gun."

They returned the boat and got a cab back to the dock. To get near the ship they still had to get onto the outer dock, which meant going by a check gate. But the gate man was there more to direct traffic than to play security guard, and he didn't give the cab a second glance. There were still a few passenger-carrying freighters that left from the Brooklyn docks; he was used to seeing cabs go through.

The taxi left them outside the cyclone fence and went away. Dibley had planned somehow to get a message to the derrick man, but when he saw a snack wagon pulled up in front of the gate he figured the derrick man might be coming out anyway. The wagon had one side open, revealing a coffee urn and a counter full of cakes and sandwiches and candy bars. There was a man in a greasy white apron inside moving a fry pan over a gas ring. The name "Angie's" had been painted on the van by somebody who'd never painted a sign before.

They'd timed their arrival perfectly. A siren was just running down and some stevedores were already streaming towards the gate calling out orders for hamburgers and hot dogs while they were still yards away.

Dibley waited till a group had formed around the counter before going over. He gave them all a friendly smile. "Hi, fellas."

"Gimme one with sweet peppers, Angie." They didn't even look at him.

Dibley tried again. "Say, I was wondering if you could help me."

"An' onions. Lots of onions."

Carol walked up to tell Dibley that they were too hungry to talk, and one of the stevedores spotted her. He made a low noise in his throat and nudged the man next to him, who saw what he was looking at and nudged somebody else. Within ten seconds Carol had a very tough-looking bunch of men, all of them thick and heavy set, darkly Italian, leering at her and making growly noises.

Dibley was happy to see that he at last had their attention. "Any of you fellas know the derrick operator?"

"Sure," they said, running their eyes up, down and through Carol. The short-order man was staring too and letting a cheeseburger go up in smoke. Carol drew her coat tighter around her, which only made things worse.

"Does he usually eat lunch here?" Dibley asked.

"Sure," they said.

"When he gets here, will you point him out for me?"

"Sure," they said again. They took a collective half-step towards Carol and might have kept on coming if the short-order man hadn't stopped them. "Ay! I got sausage and peppers getting cold here. Somebody order a burger? Come on, I ain't got all day."

After a long morning's work one appetite proved stronger

than another and the men turned back to the wagon, but all of them doubled their order.

"James," Carol hissed, "let's go. I've been violated five times just standing here."

"Relax, will you? I'll look after you. I'm taller than any of them."

"You're also thinner than any of them. I'm going."

She jumped a foot when a stevedore tapped Dibley on the shoulder. "You looking for me?"

"Are you the derrick man?" Dibley asked.

"That's right. Name's Randall."

Dibley reached for his hand. "Mr. Randall, I'm mighty happy to meet you, mighty happy. This is Miss Mars."

The man nodded at Carol and she relaxed a little. Unlike the others he wasn't built like a Neanderthal. He had a tall, slight frame and wore glasses. There were flecks of gray in his close-cropped hair and his clothes were neater and more conservative. In fact, everything about him was conservative, which was a break for Dibley.

"Mr. Randall," Dibley began, drawing him farther away from the wagon, "sorry to intrude on your lunch hour like this, but I want to speak to you about a matter of vital importance."

Mr. Randall blinked slowly at him. "Uh huh."

Dibley's voice became low and confidential. "It concerns the security of our country."

"Uh huh," Mr. Randall said. The derrick man might not have been the violent type, but it was obvious to Carol that he was no intellectual, either.

"Mr. Randall, would you describe yourself as a patriot?"

Mr. Randall's spine got straighter. "I love my country," he declared. "Been in the Legion twenty years."

"Wonderful," Dibley said. He meant it; things were going to be O.K. "I love my country too, Mr. Randall. That's why they made me president of the GTBTGU."

"The what?"

Dibley looked him straight in the eye. "The GTBTGU is a

patriotic organization formed to safeguard this country against those who would work to subvert it from within. It stands for Get Them Before They Get Us."

The derrick man looked interested. "Yeah?"

Dibley tried to look him even straighter in the eye. "Mr. Randall, are you aware of what's happening in America today?"

"What do you mean?"

"I mean those traitors in Washington who are running the country."

"Oh, them," Randall said. "Sure. Bunch of fruit-fag peaceniks."

Dibley shot a fast glance at Carol; this was going to be easier than he'd thought. He did his sincere bit again. "Mr. Randall, it's up to loyal stevedore Americans like yourself to help combat the menace. What kind of guns are you loading on the freighter?"

"The army stuff? Howitzers. One Oh Twos."

"Are you aware, sir, of the One Oh Two howitzer gap that exists in America today?"

"Bad, is it?"

"Appalling. Why, those fifth columnists in Washington have thousands. The GTBTGU only has three."

Mr. Randall looked concerned. "I didn't know that."

"Mr. Randall, it's your duty," Dibley clutched the man's shoulder, "as a patriot and a loyal stevedore American to help us close that gap."

The derrick man squared his shoulders and drew in his chin as if responding to the distant sound of bugles. He was being called. "Live free or die," he said. "What do you want me to do?"

Dibley looked triumphantly at Carol, who was clearly hating the way things were going, and told the man his plan. Mr. Randall couldn't see any holes in it, and Dibley concluded the business with a warm handclasp. "Sir, Miss Mars and I would like to thank you for what you're doing for America. May God bless you."

Mr. Randall waved away the thanks. "We got to stop those godless fag pinkos. Be in Brooklyn next."

Dibley agreed. "Bunch of Moscow-loving fellow-traveling fairies."

"Long-haired commie dope homos," Randall replied.

"Peking-appeasing pansies," Dibley came back with.

It was Randall's turn, but his vitriol seemed to have run dry. Dibley asked him for a number where he could be reached, told him he'd be in touch when they were all set and said goodbye. They left him standing apart from the lunch wagon, his appetite forgotten, his eyes bright with a far more noble calling.

Walking back through the dock Carol was glum, Dibley on top of the world. He found a call box outside the main gate and went in to phone Swaboda. He told him about his meeting with the derrick man and what he had in mind, and Swaboda thought it all sounded fantastic. But Dibley pointed out that a gun wasn't of much use to them unless they had something to tow it with. He had an idea they could pick up what they needed in Queens and arranged to meet Swaboda there after lunch.

"And listen," he added, "call Walter, or whoever he happens to be, and tell him to meet us there as well."

"Will do," Swaboda answered. "It's all happening, buddy."

"I know it," Dibley said. "What do you think about an Olds this time?"

"I like it," Swaboda said. "See you in Queens."

When he came out Carol said, "Can we eat now? I'm starving."

Dibley took her arm. "Sure. Then we're meeting the boys in Elmhurst."

Carol walked beside him trying to think for what terrible criminal reason they could be going to Elmhurst. She was determined not to ask; she preferred not to know.

"Why are we going to Elmhurst?" she asked.

"We're going to steal a car."

Carol stopped, sighed and closed her eyes. It seemed to her that she was doing a lot of stopping, sighing and eye-closing lately. But then she'd never helped hold up the mayor before.

chapter 13

". . . a cunning rogue dishonest even unto his own"

From the bank they'd gone straight to the subway and had ridden back to the Bronx. Mira hadn't wanted to go to the Lucky Shamrock so they'd picked up a six-pack, mainly at Cahill's insistence, and taken it back home.

Home for the Miras was the top floor of a faded, red-shingled frame house that sat in the middle of a row of identical houses on one of the identical streets west of Claremont Park. The door at the top of the stairs opened into a room furnished with fat, lumpy armchairs, a table, and two lamps standing on black wooden curlicue stems, the yellow paper shades burned brown in patches. Opposite was a good-sized kitchen that had once been a bedroom, and next to it was a room that had been left as a bedroom which they shared. The green linoleum in the kitchen was also down in the other two rooms, unrelieved except in the bedroom by a chenille throw rug that the landlady took away in the summer. The lack of light, the age of the furniture and the general air of drabness combined to give the apartment a murky, clouded look.

As soon as they were inside, Joey had gone out again to the

laundromat with some washing. Mira and Cahill had sat down in the kitchen and started on the beer, and Mira had told him how he planned to rob the bank. He had given it to him in detail from start to finish, then sat back to watch his reaction. He knew Cahill well enough to know what that would be: He'd drain off his beer and get up and get another one to give himself time to shape a reply. And that's exactly what had happened.

Cahill brought the new can back to the table, sat down and tore the tab off with an easy movement. He took a long swig at it. "We're going to do this?" He had a half-smile cemented onto his face and looked faintly embarrassed by what Mira was telling him.

"Sure we're going to do it." Mira could see that Cahill was shaken. He would have been disappointed if he hadn't been.

Cahill moved his feet on the floor and shoved his chair back a little. The half-smile stayed where it was. "Five million bucks. We ain't hardly ever made five hundred."

"So? You're all the time bitching about it."

"Yeah, but five million . . ." He shook his head at the thought, slowly and negatively.

"I thought you wanted a real payday. You're the guy was always talking about it." Mira rubbed it in hard. "Well, this is it. What I'm telling you."

The big man took the beer can quickly up to his mouth.

"Why so silent? You see something wrong with it, a big hole maybe?" Mira was enjoying himself.

"Well, Christ." The can made a bonking noise as Cahill crushed it in his hand. "It's just that we ain't never tried nothing like this before."

"Sure, we have. What do you think we've been doing all along? Stickups, right? That's all this is."

Cahill looked at him. "This, a stickup? What you got in mind? You're crazy."

Mira drew closer to the table. The edge in his words gave

them emphasis. "Sure it's a stickup, the granddaddy of stick-ups. Bigger than anybody ever thought of before. Nobody ever took a bank for five million, but I'm going to do it. People are going to know my name, I tell you that."

Cahill snorted. "The po-leece are going to know your name, that's who's going to know your name."

"They won't be able to touch us. Even when they know all about it they can't stop us. Not when we're grabbing the money or when we split, either. They'll come after us, sure, but with that kind of dough they won't even get close."

The conversation stopped and the loud tinny ticking of a clock took over. The low buzz of traffic from the Cross Bronx Expressway drummed faintly against the window, and down-stairs a TV was turned up too loud.

Cahill made another trip to the refrigerator. "How about the guys we need? If we go with this thing somebody's got to han-dle things down south. Where we supposed to get them from?"

Mira got up from the table. "I'm going to start on them right now." He went downstairs to the pay phone in the hall and made a call. He talked briefly with somebody, hung up and went back upstairs. He picked up his jacket from a kitchen chair and slipped it on.

"You going somewhere?" Cahill asked.

"I told you. I'm going to get those two other guys."

"Wait a second." Cahill looked worried. "We didn't make no decision yet."

Mira hooked the jacket zipper together and slid it closed. "Joey and me have."

"But we ain't hardly talked about it. A thing this big—"

Mira spoke through him. "If Joey and me are going to need three other guys you better say so now."

Cahill didn't say anything.

Mira started for the door. "Tell Joey I'll be back later."

He left the house and took the subway down to 149th Street, switched trains and got off at 72nd. He came out of the subway into a place that was called a square but was shaped more like a triangle. There were some old men sitting around on benches beneath rickety trees that looked as if they'd been set on fire, and a couple of kids trying to get something going with a frisbee.

The man he'd arranged to meet there arrived twenty minutes late. "How's by you," the man said, his eyes sweeping the park, checking it over.

"You want to get coffee and a sandwich?" Mira asked.

"Naw, too many people with big ears in coffee shops. Let's talk here." He hadn't changed much, a little heavier and a lot more prosperous, but otherwise the same man Mira remembered, with the same impatient way of speaking and the habit of not looking at the person he was talking to. He had quick eyes set in a pouchy face that had been carefully shaved and massaged and tanned by a lamp. About forty-five and of medium height, he already had the start of a weight problem. He wore a soft tweed topcoat and a velour hat that looked as though it might have cost as much as the shiny black slip-ons he was wearing. The gloves on his hands were made from a knobby brown leather and had animal fur peeking out at the wrists. He looked richer than he'd looked the last time Mira had seen him six months ago. Before that he'd only seen him in prison denims. That had been when they'd shared a cell for a short time. The man, whose name was Williams, had told him that if he ever needed anything to get in touch. Williams was a supplier; he dealt in equipment and people. If you wanted a gun or a tungsten drill or a stick of dynamite, blueprints, a passport or a clean car he knew where to go to get them. He bought and resold at a profit. Now and then somebody would try to bypass a guy like Williams—they'd try to cut out the middleman and buy direct from the source. It was cheaper that way but, as they found out, very difficult; the manufacturers stayed well hidden. It was easier going through Williams—he was in the phone directory. And you could go to him for more than just hardware; if you had an idea he'd supply the men and the equipment and package the whole deal—for a fat slice off the top. He was also a kind of personnel agency. Pros between jobs would call him and tell him that they were available. When he fixed them up with somebody he got a cut from both ends. Williams traded in everything except the one thing he had more of than just about anybody else in the city—information. As one of the big suppliers he could tell just by reading an account of a job which of his customers had pulled it. But he stayed in business by keeping it to himself. He stayed alive that way, too.

He ran a hand round the brim of the velour hat, smoothing it. "What can I do you for?"

"A couple of things," Mira answered.

"Like what?"

"Two guys. One easy, one a little difficult maybe."

"Start with the easy one."

"Good reliable muscle."

"What's the job?"

Mira hesitated.

Williams said, "If I don't know I can't tell the guy. If he don't know he won't take the job."

"I want him to watch over somebody for a little while."

"A snatch?"

"We're not asking money."

"It's still a snatch. Local job?"

Mira hesitated again. He knew Williams was O.K. but he didn't want to give away any more than he had to. "Out of state," he said.

Williams jingled coins in his pocket, his eyes still covering the park. "Out of how many states?"

"Virginia."

"How long you need him for?"

"A day."

"Percentage or flat fee?"

"Flat fee." Williams didn't reply. "You know a guy?" Mira asked.

"I know lots of guys." Williams looked down at his right shoe and turned it so that the light moved on the top.

The conversation had slowed and Mira knew that this was when they started talking dollars.

"This guy," he said. "What kind of money would he want?"

Williams shrugged. "What kind of guy you want? I got a man'll do it for two hundred."

"Is he good?"

"Not as good as the man I got for two thousand."

"I want the best."

"Then that's him," Williams said. "Name's McNally. He's silent on the job and silent after. He's hard but not dumb. With a gun in his hand nobody's going to screw him around."

"O.K." Mira said.

Williams glanced at him briefly. "How about you, you need a piece? I got a sweet little Brownie, custom job, takes a crimped down thirty-eight. It'll make a hole like a soup plate."

Mira said, "I still got the gun you sold me."

"Still? You been carrying that too long. You used it?"

"That's my business."

"Mister, you need a new piece."

"What I want's two guys."

"You got one, let's work on the other. Same job, same place?"

"Same but different. He goes out of state too, but he comes back to town for the main part of the job."

"You're talking two jobs. What's the second?"

"A bank."

"Then he'll be on percentage," Williams said.

"I figured ten percent."

"No good. Fifteen."

Mira frowned at that. "Listen, we're not knocking over the Good Humor man. This bank's good for two hundred grand."

Williams looked as though he'd heard it all before. "Now it is. When you get there it may not be. You never know with a bank."

"I know with this one."

"This guy," Williams said, "you say he could be tough to find. That mean he's a specialist?"

"Yeah."

Williams waited for him to tell him what kind, but Mira was still holding back.

Williams got tired of waiting; he was getting cold. "So what is he, this guy?"

Mira knew he had to tell him or forget the whole thing. Come to think of it he didn't know why he was hesitating; Williams couldn't possibly figure out what he had in mind.

Mira told him and the supplier looked at him properly for the first time.

Williams was surprised; nobody had ever asked him to find somebody like that before.

"Leave it with me," he said, sounding flat and professional.

Inside he was wondering what the hell kind of caper the punk was planning.

chapter 14

". . . borrowing a trader's sturdy camel"

Dibley was beginning to regret that he hadn't arranged to meet the other two inside somewhere, like the coffee shop opposite where he'd sent Carol to wait out of the chilly wind. He expected Walter to be late, but Swaboda was usually pretty punctual. When he finally did arrive he had an excuse all ready.

102

"I'm sorry I'm late," he said, puffing after his climb up the subway steps; "there was a sale at Klein's and Mom wanted to buy a dress. I left her there walking round in her slip."

"That's all right. Walter's not here yet, anyway."

"You know Walter," Swaboda said, "he'll probably—" He broke off, looking down the subway steps. He said slowly, "I think that's him now."

Dibley turned to look. It was Walter all right; he was wearing a black crepe calf-length dress with an organza frill at the neck, a fox fur and a little black pill box hat perched over one eye.

"Sorry I'm late," he squeaked. "I took a nap after lunch."

"And Kitty woke up first," Dibley and Swaboda said in tandem.

"I'm afraid so." He looked miserable. "I didn't find out till I took over at Jackson Heights. By then it was too late to do anything about it."

Dibley said, "Don't feel bad, Walter; lots of guys wear dresses in this town."

Walter massaged his foot. "It's not the dress so much. It's these pumps."

Swaboda changed the subject fast. "Great news about the gun. You really think we can get one, do you?"

"Positive," Dibley declared. "But we need a car to move it. I think we can rip one off from one of the lots round the corner. We'll simply take something suitable for a test drive and bring it back later than you're supposed to."

"Sounds fine to me."

"Right," Dibley said purposefully. "Then if we're all set, let's go." He turned and marched down the subway stairs.

"Dibley," Swaboda called.

"Mmm?"

"It's this way."

Dibley ascended the stairs with a look on his face that Swaboda recognized as vintage Dibley.

"Hey," Swaboda said, "didn't you tell me on the phone that you'd be here with Carol?"

"Who?"

"Your girl," Swaboda said patiently.

"Oh yes," Dibley said. He linked an arm through Walter's. "Come along, dear."

Swaboda took a fast look around and settled on the coffee shop as the most likely place for Carol to be. He went over to it and dug her out.

"Oh, hi, Charlie," she said. "Did Walter get here too?"

"Yes, indeed. He's across the street with James."

When she got out onto the sidewalk she saw them standing together arm in arm. Swaboda gave her elbow a reassuring squeeze. "It'll never last," he said. "They're living a lie."

They crossed to them and Carol gently disentangled Dibley's arm and the four of them started walking. By the time they'd gone two blocks Dibley had completely recovered from his lapse and was looking like his old self again, which was where he often had the advantage over Walter.

They turned a corner and came out into a street full of used car lots, all of them strung with bunting like a cruise ship in port. The first one promised a cash price for your car beyond the dreams of avarice. The next offered even more money.

They went up one side of the street and down the other and it wasn't till the lots were starting to peter out that they saw what they were after.

The lot was different from the rest in that the stock was different. Instead of late-model Mustangs and Chargers there was a row of camper trucks and a selection of caravans lined up on one side.

They walked in. The place seemed deserted. There was nothing on the front of the lot that appealed to Dibley, so he led them around to the back, and there it was—a long-frame Land Rover with a hefty-looking tow bar bolted neatly into place.

The key was in the ignition.

All four of them looked around. There was still nobody.

Three of them got in. Carol stayed where she was.

"Hop in," Dibley said.

"No."

"You promised."

"I didn't promise to steal a car," Carol said. They were speaking in a shouted undertone.

"You promised to stay with us till something went wrong."

"It's about to."

"It hasn't yet," Dibley said. "Get in."

Carol got in.

The lot was on a corner, the exit ramp ahead of them giving onto a side street. Swaboda, who found himself behind the wheel, started the car, took it out onto the street and missed by an inch the police cruiser that was parked there. He reacted instantly. He turned the wheel, swung the car round in a half circle and drove into the front entrance of the lot. He stopped in front of the office and everybody got excuses ready.

They didn't need them.

A salesman jumped out of the office rubbing his hands and grinning. He was young and nervous and they got the impression that it was his first day on the lot; he certainly wasn't too familiar with the merchandise.

"Folks," he cried, "you've come to the right place, the right place. Nice little car you've got there." He skirted it quickly, making a fast appraisal. "Yes sir, very nice. But I've got six just like it out in back. But you look like nice people, so I'll tell you what I'm going to do. I'm going to offer you fifteen hundred cash, right here and now. I'm taking a beating on it, but what the hell. O.K.?"

Swaboda didn't quibble. "Sold," he said.

The salesman slapped the car. "You'll never regret it. I'll get your money now and come back for the papers. Cash first, ask questions later, that's our motto." He dashed into the office, paused by the cashier's desk and dashed out again. He was counting out fifteen one-hundred-dollar bills into Swaboda's numb hand when somebody called him from the other end of the lot. "Whoops," he said, "the boss. Gotta go. Just take the papers into the office, O.K.?" He dog-trotted away and left them mutely gazing at the money.

They didn't stay that way for long. Another salesman, an older man just back from a late lunch, walked up to them full of sunshine and happiness. Like the previous one he spoke in a form that wasn't designed for replies; a commercial rather than a conversation. "People, you know cars. You picked the best buy on the lot." He slapped the fender affectionately. "Run you for life, this baby. And, because it just happens to be our red ticket special of the week, I can let you have it for just fifteen hundred bucks."

Once again Swaboda didn't quibble. "Sold," he said.

They drove back through Queens in a trance. But by the time they'd reached Manhattan they were chortling with glee, all except Carol, who was still in a trance. Dibley invited everybody back for drinks; he was having a brilliant day. To top things off, there was even a parking space right outside the apartment.

They beat a Cadillac to it by seconds and the other driver got mad. He double-parked alongside them, charged out of his car and started yelling in their faces.

"What the hell do you think you're doing? Just because you're driving a tank don't mean you own the whole goddamn street."

The back door of the Land Rover opened and closed. Walter was on the sidewalk. But by the way he moved towards the Cadillac owner it was clear that Rocky was firmly in control.

"Listen, you dirty rat," he set himself on his high heels, hitched at the dress and tossed the fox fur over his shoulder, "get that heap out of here or I'll eat it."

"O.K., all right," the man said quickly, holding both hands up and backing away.

He jumped into his car and took off up Bank Street, not wasting any time.

"Boy," he said to the windshield, "toughest dike I ever saw."

106

chapter 15

". . . a young man from the country . . ."

"If a guy asks for me, send him over, O.K., Syd?"

"Check."

Mira carried his glass to the end booth and sat down to wait for the man who'd called him half an hour ago. He had to hand it to Williams. He'd contacted McNally for him and McNally was going to call him in a day or two; but he hadn't expected Williams to get hold of the other man so fast—it had taken him only twenty-four hours. The guy must have more connections than a switchboard.

He glanced up at the clock on the wall; the man was late. But then he was coming from midtown. Mira sipped his beer and waited some more.

A man walked through the door, somebody he'd never seen before, and sat down at the bar. But he made it clear by the way he started drinking that he hadn't come for any other reason.

The next man in was the man he was waiting for.

He said something to the bartender, who nodded over at Mira, and Mira watched him come towards him. He couldn't have been much more than twenty-five, a good-looking kid walking loose-jointed and easy as if he were used to treading open fields. He had a fresh, untroubled face, fair hair worn long and full and brushed straight across. He looked relaxed and perfectly at ease with the world.

"Frank Mira?" His voice matched the rest of him, quiet and pleasantly modulated.

"Sit down," Mira said.

"I'm George Austin." He held out a hand. Mira hesitated and shook it briefly; nobody shook hands much in Mira's circle. Austin's grip was firm and friendly, like the smile he wore.

Mira asked him what he was drinking and the man told him that 7up was fine. When the barman brought it he slapped it down on the table. "Let me know if you want a Coke chaser," he said.

"No, that's fine. Thank you," Austin said politely.

The barman went back and said loudly to a man sitting on a stool, "I'm running a soda fountain now."

"Don't mind Syd," Mira said to Austin.

"I don't mind him." Austin seemed surprised, as if it would never have occurred to him to be bothered by a meaningless piece of sarcasm. Mira wondered what it would take to get a guy like this mad.

"You know Williams long?" Mira asked as an opener.

Austin was pouring the pop into his glass with a whack. He brought it quickly to his mouth and gulped at the fizz. "Best part," he said. "I'm sorry, who did you say?"

"Williams. The guy who gave you my name."

"Somebody named Marks gave me your name. An old navy buddy."

Mira nodded. "How long were you in for?"

"Three years."

"See any action?"

"I was in Nam, sure."

"You from New York?"

"No, sir. Not me." He said it as though it were the last place he wanted to be from. "Michigan. My folks run an orchard out there, in the western part of the state."

"But you live in New York now . . ." Mira said, probing.

"That's right."

"You get by all right?"

108

The smile stayed on Austin's face when he answered, but this time his voice didn't reflect it. There was a trace of something in it that Mira couldn't quite identify; a sadness maybe. "There are easier ways of making a buck than picking apples, if that's what you mean." He took a mouthful of his drink. "Can I ask a question now?"

"Go ahead." Mira watched him; there was something different about this guy. He wasn't run of the mill.

Austin checked that nobody was near them. "I understand that this is a bank job."

"That's right."

"Why me?"

"Because of your background," Mira told him.

Austin had been expecting the answer. "I thought so. I've been on a few bank jobs but I'm no expert. What I can't figure out is what kind of bank job needs a guy with my background."

"Doesn't surprise me. Nobody's ever tried anything like this before." Mira picked up his beer and gulped some of it. He was feeling good. He put the glass down, leaned his elbows on the table and started to fill Austin in. He took his time, going over it point for point, explaining exactly what Austin was expected to do. This was the only part he wasn't dead sure of; if Austin said that his part was impossible, the whole thing was impossible.

Mira pulled the Kodak folder from his pocket, chose a print and passed it across.

"See the one I marked? That's it, the bank."

Austin studied the shot. "Where was this taken from?"

"The ferry."

Austin started to chuckle.

Mira didn't understand. "What's up? What's the matter?"

"Nothing," Austin said. "I love it. It's the wildest thing I ever heard of."

"It makes sense? You don't see any problems?"

"Not my end. You figured it perfectly. Except I wouldn't go to Virginia. We can do better up north."

Mira sat back, his heart thumping. The thing was going to work.

Austin laughed again. "And I thought I'd heard of some stickups."

"Stickups are my line," Mira said.

"How much are you going to ask for?"

"Five million."

Austin whistled. "Do you think they'll go for it?"

"If you were them, would you?"

Austin thought about it. "I guess I'd have to." He reached for the folder and started to sort through the rest of the prints.

"They're just the buildings around it," Mira said.

Austin continued sorting through them. He came to one that stopped him and looked at it for a long moment. "Can I keep this one, too?"

"Keep them all."

Mira couldn't figure him; he'd given him a photograph of the bank, a bank that was going to be worth five million to them, and the guy was looking at some cther snap like it was a picture of his girl. He was still looking at it.

He was certainly different all right.

chapter 16

". . . securing one at length by causing it to fly as if by magic . . ."

"We're just not thinking hard enough," Dibley said. "If we're smart enough to figure out how to get it off the dock and how to move it away from the dock we should be able to figure out how to do it without anybody seeing."

Swaboda considered it for the tenth time, hands clasped in front of him, both thumbs tapping against his chin.

Walter had assumed a more classical position of thought, eyes closed, fingers pressed to his temples.

The high spirits brought on by the easy acquisition of the Land Rover had quickly retreated in the face of a detail that hadn't occurred to them before. They'd spent the last forty-five minutes getting nowhere with it.

"This is getting to be a hernia," Swaboda said. "One of those things you think you'll take care of when the time comes, and when the time comes . . ." He left the sentence hanging forlornly in the air.

Dibley started pacing up and down. "I should have thought of this before now—the entire plan hinges on it. If just one man spots us taking that gun we're out of it."

Carol came in and leaned against the kitchen door drying a glass and listening to the conversation.

"How many guys on that dock?" Swaboda asked.

"Dozens of stevedores and four or five security men besides," Dibley replied.

"We need them all to close their eyes for at least three minutes."

"Or something to make them look the other way," Swaboda suggested.

Dibley stopped pacing. "You mean a diversion? That's not bad. Let's work on that. How do we get a bunch of stevedores to look at something else?"

"Good luck with that one," Carol said. "I've seen those guys, and believe me, the only thing that would interest them would be a girl doing a strip."

Two seconds later she could have cut her tongue out.

It was one of those faultless days that make lifetime fans out of visitors to the city and even get the jaundiced residents to stop feeling quite so bad about it. New York gets one now and then in the fall; the cold wind drops and the temperature climbs and there's a pleasant crispness in the air, which has nothing to do with the August dog days or the arctic Februarys that the city's famous for. You'd never think it was the same town; the sky is bright and very high overhead, and the breeze is a kind one, sucking exhaust fumes away and opening up the avenues for miles. The flags whip and crack above the stores on Fifth and the merchandise in the windows seems even more desirable and, somehow, even a little more obtainable. New York, probably the harshest, most abrasive city in the world, takes on an unfamiliar softness and seems to be designed for people again.

Walter and Swaboda could feel the change in the atmosphere as they walked down Charles Street together. Everything was set up: Yesterday, when Carol had unwittingly solved their problem for them, Dibley had called the derrick man, told him that they'd be there today and explained exactly what he wanted him to do. Walter and Swaboda were on their way to the parking lot; it was their job to drive the Land Rover.

The lot was on Greenwich Street in a nothing area given over mainly to trucks and tenements just south of the Washington Synagogue. It was an open, asphalted lot backed by a building and fenced in on three sides. The nearby residents parked there on a permanent basis and had their own keys. There was a man on duty through the day, but at nights and on weekends you locked the gate behind you and hoped for the best.

Dibley had parked the Land Rover at the back of the lot the night before, up against the wall where it was almost hidden from the street. Swaboda backed it out, Walter climbed in and they headed for the Brooklyn Battery tunnel. As they intended to give the car back within a few days, neither of them regarded it as stolen, and so they weren't worried by any thought of the police. It was a beautiful day, they were part of a beautiful plan, and everything was going to come up roses. Both men hummed to themselves.

Swaboda, perhaps unconsciously reflecting his mental hang-up, was crooning "Me and My Shadow," while Walter, who had probably chosen his song for the same reason, was humming "That Old Gang Of Mine."

When they were through the tunnel and into Brooklyn they took the Fourth Avenue turnoff, drove down as far as Thirty-ninth Street and followed Dibley's directions from there. As they came up to the gate of the outer dock Swaboda stopped the car and leaned out of the window, doing his best to look tough.

"Local four-sixteen," he said, trying to say the words without moving his mouth. "We got a report you got agitators on Twenty-eight."

"News to me," the gate man said.

Swaboda shoved the car into gear with a vicious crunch. "O.K. we look around?" The gate man flicked his eyes over them. Walter tried to look like a labor goon.

The man waved them through.

They drove past an Egyptian ship loading sewing machines and powdered milk. Alongside the next dock was a tiny freighter not much bigger than a tug, with a Union Jack fluttering at its masthead. It was struggling with a crate bound for Brazil.

The next dock had a high cyclone fence and guards at the gate.

Swaboda ran the Land Rover along the side of the fence and stopped when they were opposite the derrick. They watched it move through the sky, dip down, pluck up one of the guns and swing it over and into the ship.

Swaboda got out, lifted the hood and pretended to poke around with the engine. He saw by his watch that they'd cut it pretty fine; it was almost time.

High above him in the derrick's cab Mr. Randall was checking his watch too.

He was nervous and his mouth was dry. A minute later when he saw the outboard coming into view his mouth got dryer. He'd never done anything like this before, and now that he was coming to the crunch he wondered whether or not he was doing the right thing.

It was only a momentary lapse. He thought of those traitors in Washington who were running the country and his jaw tightened. "Dirty red radical chick nances," he said.

In the boat on the river Dibley was also checking his watch. "Are you ready?" he asked.

Carol was sitting in the bow of the boat clutching a topcoat around her. "I'm too cold to tell," she said. Underneath the coat, she was wearing a bikini bra and pants studded with sequins that Dibley had stuck on with Elmer's glue. Dibley had designed the costume and Carol had very reluctantly gone along with it, although she'd drawn the line at tassels.

"No tassels," she'd said firmly.

"You're kidding," Dibley had replied. "No stripper goes on without tassels."

"No stripper goes on in her underwear, either."

That seemed to settle it, although Dibley was still piqued. "You might have told me," he said, "before I ruined a perfectly good dressing-gown cord."

Dibley put the engine into neutral and allowed the boat to drift. They were level with the freighter now and about a hundred feet out from it.

He watched the derrick come up empty from the hold, swing back and drop onto the dock. He was too low to see it but he knew that another gun, their gun, was being hitched up. He kept his eyes riveted on the cab, the tiny figure of Randall vaguely visible.

Then he saw it: The window slid back and an arm appeared, waving up and down.

Dibley clicked a button on the piece of equipment that was

set up on the seat in front of him. It was a portable public-address system that ran off a six-volt battery; he'd rented it, and the tape deck that was plugged into it, the day before.

He snatched up the mike. "Yessir, fellas, tonight and every night this week, the Snowball Club, on Broadway at Forty-second, presents non-stop Striporama." Every stevedore on the dock stopped what he was doing.

"Fifteen beautiful girls, fifteen, in the year's most sensational show. And here to give you a little preview, the Blond Bomber from Cleveland, Miss Shaker Hites." Dibley clicked a switch that cut out the mike and brought in the tape deck.

The music blasted out at a million decibels, a low-down dirty saxophone accompanied by a drummer with a heavy foot.

"O.K." Dibley yelled.

Carol jumped to her feet.

The stevedores streamed towards the river like lemmings.

Carol's coat was held closed by a full-length zipper that ran from collar to hem. It had worked perfectly two or three hundred times previously, but, with the incredibly bad sense of timing peculiar to zippers, it refused to work now. Carol tugged at it gently at first, then harder and harder.

"Come on Carol, take it off," Dibley yelled above the music.

The stevedores felt the same way. "Take it off," they called.

"Carol, will you take it off!" Dibley shouted.

"I'm trying to take it off. The damned thing's stuck."

The side of the ship was now lined with dockers, and the security people from the gate had joined them. The dockers, never overly famous for their patience or understanding, had changed their cry somewhat. "Ya dumb hooker, get the friggin' thing off."

Dibley was yelling at her too. "Will you come on? They're going to be asking for their money back."

Carol was close to tears. "I can't come on. I'm locked into this thing." Dibley was getting close to tears himself. He thought the whole thing was about to go down the drain because of a stuck zipper. What he didn't realize is that a young

lady taking off her clothes is only second in eye-stopping interest to a young lady *about* to take off her clothes. Consequently,
the only man on the entire dock whose attention Carol didn't
have was Mr. Randall high up in his aerie. Mr. Randall was
pulling on a lever and lifting a gun into the air. But instead
of swinging it towards the ship as he'd done with a few
thousand others, he swung it the other way towards the fence.

It cleared the top like a home run ball and dropped gently
down behind the Land Rover.

Mr. Randall was an expert operator and he held the gun
a few inches off the roadway so that all Swaboda had to do
was swing the gun train over the Land Rover's tow bar and
lock it on. The gun came down the rest of the way, Swaboda
unhooked the cradle, waved an arm and the derrick swung up
and away.

Dibley had watched it all. He cut the music, pulled Carol
down, opened the throttle and took the boat roaring away
upriver.

Behind him the freighter rocked under a hat-stamping rage.

Two hundred yards later Carol was still struggling with the
zipper; she didn't like to let a thing beat her. Dibley grasped
the hem and held the coat straight, Carol tugged mightily and
the zipper sprang open.

The coat billowed back, and Dibley became the only man in
Brooklyn to get a look at the Blond Bomber from Cleveland.
Carol whipped the coat around her, but not before he'd seen
what was underneath: very little costume and just about all of
Carol. A lecherous grin appeared on his mouth, and his eyelids
drooped.

"Say, Carol," he said, "as soon as we get the boat back let's
go straight home."

Maybe it's New York or maybe it's just human nature, but
let a man hurry along concealing something under his jacket,
or even run along the sidewalk and not be clearly chasing a

bus or a cab, and he's bound to make some cop suspicious. But there's nothing furtive about a Land Rover towing a howitzer, which was probably why they got it back to the parking lot without being challenged.

They parked against the wall again and covered the gun with a tarpaulin they'd picked up the day before. They got back to the apartment at about the same time Carol and Dibley did.

There were handshakes and big smiles all around.

"We did it, Carol," Dibley called into the bedroom. "Come on out here and take a bow."

"I can't," Carol's voice came back. "The son of a bitch zipper's stuck again."

Dibley paced the room excited, flexing his fingers like a pianist about to play. "This is great. Great. All we need now is the boat and we're all set."

"How about that?" Swaboda asked. "Where do we get it from?"

"I've got it all figured out. Tomorrow we get over to the boat basin at Seventy-ninth Street. We grab a boat, a big Chris-Craft with a ship-to-shore. We sneak on board, hot-wire it, take it downriver to a ship, load the gun on, sail up to Gracie Mansion, hold up the mayor, get our money, sail the boat back, unload the gun and leave it and the Land Rover on a back lot somewhere. Everybody'll get their property back, so nobody's out except the mayor."

"Faultless," Swaboda said. "Not a chink, not a crack."

"Very nice," Walter said.

"It's a lot of hogwash," Carol said, coming out in a dressing gown. "The only part that makes any sense was what you said about the mayor being out."

She held up a copy of that morning's *Times*. There was a picture of the mayor standing on a beach in a swimsuit.

He was on vacation in Puerto Rico.

chapter 17

". . . a fierce and violent robber . . ."

By all rights the mayor's unavailability should have put Mira's schedule way ahead of Dibley's. But because the moving finger had writ concerning the date and circumstance of their eventual meeting, and because as everybody knows not even the piety of a Billy Graham nor the wit of a Bill Buckley shall lure it back to cancel half a line, Mira ran into a snag himself and was thus also delayed.

It started on the evening of the day that Dibley had stolen the gun. Joey came into the kitchen and told his brother that there was a call for him. Mira forked up the last of the chicken from the foil tray on the table, pushed his chair back and went downstairs to the phone.

"Frank Mira?" The voice was heavy and accusatory.

"That's right."

"McNally."

"You're a friend of Williams, right?"

There was no answer, and Mira knew he'd made a mistake mentioning a name that didn't need to be mentioned. He cursed silently; this guy McNally was a top pro, used to working with some big names. It was important to stay on top of people like that, to let them see you knew what you were doing so they'd have confidence in you. And have respect for you.

The voice said, "You got a job for me?"

"We'd better talk. You want to come up here? I'll give you—"

McNally was speaking. "Take a room at the Ambrose on Forty-third. I'll be there in an hour." The phone clicked and the dial tone came on.

Mira hung up too and found Cahill standing at his elbow. "What are you doing here?"

Cahill had the nail of his little finger between his front teeth. He dug something out, examined it and flicked it away. "Thought we might go for beers," he said.

Mira told him that he had to meet a guy.

Cahill inclined his head towards the phone. "That guy?"

"Yeah."

Cahill watched him, waiting for more.

"McNally," Mira said. "I told you about him."

Cahill was smiling slightly. "Oh sure, the muscle. I'll come with you."

"Why?"

"No special reason. Maybe I like to know the guys I'm working with."

Mira didn't want him to come but didn't know how to keep him away. Irritated, he went upstairs and got his jacket.

"You going out?" Joey asked.

"What's it look like?"

Mira and Cahill rode downtown to Times Square, then walked east. The Ambrose was one of those slightly faded Broadway hotels that was used by out-of-towners on a budget. It was dull and respectable, had a good location and didn't charge the earth. Like a lot of similar hotels, it broke a little better than even on accommodations and made a bundle on its bar, a large brassy affair with a canopied entrance extending over the sidewalk.

They went in and had a fast drink, then Mira went through into the lobby. The desk clerk, polite and busy, rented him a room, took his money and didn't comment on the lack of baggage. Mira waved away a bellboy, rode the elevator to the sixth floor and let himself into a room filled with twin beds and too much furniture.

Cahill arrived with a pint bottle in a paper bag and found two glasses in the bathroom; they sat down to wait.

By the time McNally arrived, Cahill had killed half the bottle. He got up to answer the door.

"Mira?" the man outside asked.

Cahill told him to come in.

When Williams had described McNally as hard he'd chosen the right word. The man had a flat solidness about him that started in the stony features of his face and extended into a body that looked as trim and inflexible as a paving stone. He moved into the room, tall and tight-shouldered. His hands hung perfectly still by his sides and he seemed coiled within himself, the way a slugger looks when he's waiting on the fast ball.

Mira spoke from the bed where he was sitting. "I'm Mira."

McNally jerked his head. "Who's he?"

"He's in on it."

Cahill held out the bottle. "You want a snort?"

McNally ignored the offer and sat down in a chair. He sat on the edge of it, his weight forward.

Cahill said to him, "What are we doing in a hotel anyway? You got ladies coming later?"

McNally gave him an overlong look and took his time replying. "A hotel room's quiet, it's private. This one's got thick walls so you say what you want and nobody hears. It's out of the cold and it's cheap. Satisfied?"

"Cheap for you," Cahill said, drinking. "We picked up the tab." He sat down on the other bed just to the right of McNally, who turned to Mira.

"This job, I hear it's someplace in Virginia. Where and when?"

"Late this week or early the next. And we changed it from Virginia." He told him where they were going.

"Who do we grab?"

"I got a man working on that now."

"You don't know? I don't get it."

120

"We're hitting a bank on Wall Street. To make it work we have to grab some people. Some housewife. She'll probably have kids too."

Cahill snickered. "We'll try to pick a good-looker for you, so's you won't get bored."

McNally said over his shoulder, "Fat man, I don't want to hear another word out of your mouth." He said to Mira, "Then what?"

"You see they stay put."

"For how long?"

"You pick them up, say, eight in the morning; we'll have the money and be out of it round five."

McNally's next question was fractionally slower coming. "A bank job that takes eight hours, daytime?"

Mira took a long time over the words. "It's kind of special."

"What's the matter," Cahill said, "you can't make out with a broad in eight hours?" Almost lazily McNally leaned back and brought his left arm swinging round. The back of his hand caught Cahill flat in the face, shocking him and knocking his glass away from his mouth. It landed on the carpet unbroken. "You're not listening," McNally said.

Mira had risen from the bed as surprised by the move as his partner. "Take it easy," he said, looking back and forth between the two men.

McNally said, "I don't like clowns. Then what?"

Cahill's face was an all-over crimson, his eyes blinking fast and irregularly. Mira was still on his feet waiting for Cahill's reaction, but Cahill just touched his mouth and looked at the little red smear on his fingers, almost as if he didn't know how it had come to be there. Mira slowly subsided back onto the bed, not quite convinced it was going to end that fast.

McNally apparently was. "Then what?" he asked a second time.

"Then you leave them go and get out of there," Mira answered, his eyes still on Cahill.

"You got a place lined up where I hold them?"

"The guy's checking that too," Mira said.

"Have him look for someplace out of the way. No phone. And no motel. That's the first place they'll look."

Mira said, "The way I got it planned they're not going to be looking. They're not going to know."

"You hope." McNally got up from the chair. "O.K., I'll take it now."

"What?"

"Don't get cute."

Mira frowned. "What are you talking about?"

"Money." McNally's voice was flatter than before. "You owe me a grand."

It stopped Mira and he almost let it show. "You're not making sense. You get paid when we get paid. After the heist."

McNally said, "You don't know anything, do you? If you get paid it's the whole pot. But what if you don't make it and there ain't a pot? That's why I work on salary. And that's why you owe me half now." McNally had risen and, it seemed to Mira, had come a touch closer to him, although he hadn't seen him move forward. Mira tried to keep his voice steady. "Williams didn't say anything about that. He didn't say nothing about paying half now."

"Maybe he figured you'd know a thing like that."

Mira swallowed. "All I'm saying is it's news to me."

McNally said, "Mister, we both been surprised. I didn't know I was going to be working with a greenhorn. If I'd known I wouldn't of took the job. But I'm in this now, otherwise I wasted my time coming here, which means you owe me a grand like I said." He brought his hand up fast and leveled a finger. "You don't have it to pay me tomorrow night, it's your ass." He turned abruptly, crossed the room and went out of the door.

Mira stared into the empty hallway, then dropped his head and rubbed a knuckle over his mouth.

Cahill got up and slammed the door closed. "The bastard. If we didn't need him I'd of taken him apart."

Mira said, "We've got to find a thousand bucks by tomorrow night."

Cahill bent and picked the glass up off the carpet. "Forget that scumbag. I can do his job."

Mira said, "We've got twenty-four hours to get a grand up."

"I'm telling you, forget that bastard. Let him come after us. I can handle him."

Mira looked up at him and said very deliberately, "You couldn't even park his car."

Cahill, furious, took a step towards him, stopped, then turned and hurled the glass across the room. It shattered against a radiator. "Stinkin' job! I wish I'd never heard of it."

Mira got up and walked towards the door. "Come on, we're through here."

They left the hotel and took a subway uptown. Cahill had quieted and sat next to Mira, running his tongue over the lump on the side of his mouth.

"If we knock over three stores, say, bing, bang, like that. If we get lucky we'll get the grand up."

Mira didn't think so. "We'd be asking for trouble, three in one day. Son of a bitch, I know we can get out with five million. I don't want to screw it up going after a lousy grand."

The train stopped at a station and they left off talking as the doors hissed open. A group of kids carrying skates spilled into the car, laughing hysterically at something. The doors closed and the train picked up speed and the roaring metal-against-metal noise masked their conversation again.

"What do we do?" Cahill asked.

"Throw it back in Williams' lap. He got us into it."

As soon as he got back to his rooming house Mira called Austin and asked him when he was planning to leave. When Austin said that he was catching a Greyhound in a few hours' time

Mira told him that they'd run into a snag and to hold off till he heard from him. Then he called Williams and asked him what the hell he thought he was doing. "You didn't tell me the guy would want half the bread now. You didn't tell me a goddamn thing about it."

"I didn't figure you for a rookie," Williams said.

"You should have told me," Mira shouted into the phone. "A thing like that? Now I got to find a grand by tomorrow night."

"I can see your problem," Williams said. "I'd hate to owe a guy like McNally and not come through."

"Yeah, well it's your funeral. You should've said something. You got to find me a grand."

"I don't have to find you nothing. I'll give you a number's all I'm going to do. Then you're on your own."

Mira dialed the number that Williams gave him and spoke briefly to the answering voice. It told him to be on a street corner in Washington Heights in thirty minutes. It wasn't far for Mira and he got there a quarter hour ahead of the long blue Eldorado that pulled up at the curb.

The interior light flicked on and somebody leaned across to the window and said, "Frank? Hop in."

The door opened and Mira slid into the passenger seat. The man was holding out a hand and smiling. "Hi there. Sorry if I'm a few minutes late. It's a little chilly to hang around street corners, eh? My name's Wetzel, Ralph Wetzel." He was a young man, expensively dressed in a beautifully tailored dark blue suit, cream silk shirt, pale blue silk tie. He could have been the top salesman for an electronics or an aerospace firm, some business that dealt in million-dollar orders. He had the salesman's instant chumminess, the happy-to-meet-you smile and the firm handshake. He turned off the interior light and flicked a switch somewhere and a map light winked on under the dash. There was just enough light to see each other's faces.

"Well," he said. "What'll it be?"

"I need money," Mira said.

"That's why I'm here. How much?"

"A thousand."

"Fine," the young man said. "That shouldn't be too difficult." He clicked open the glove compartment and reached for a fat brown envelope. There was a cloth duster next to it and next to that a gun. Wetzel saw Mira looking at it. "Can't stand the things," he said. "But I've got to have one carrying money around, you know?" He dug his hand into the envelope and brought out a bunch of bills, counted some off and held them out like a fan. "Ten, right?"

Mira took the money and Wetzel made a note on a slip of paper he took from his pocket.

"So," he said, "just so everything's clear. We're lending you a thousand dollars at an interest rate of twenty-five percent a week."

"Twenty-five? I thought the rate was twenty."

"It is on big sums with long-term repayments. On something like this it's twenty-five. That's standard."

Mira merely grunted. It wouldn't be long before he'd be able to pay the debt off ten times over and not even notice it.

Wetzel thrust out a hand, the smile still on his face. "Frank, nice doing business with you."

Mira shook his hand limply and got out of the car. Wetzel leaned over to close the door. "And Frank," he said, winking, "go straight home with that money now." He waved and drove off. Mira watched him go. He patted the money in his jacket.

"Hell," he said to himself, "that wasn't so tough."

Mira met McNally the next evening and paid him. When he got back to his place the phone was ringing.

"Frank? Ralph Wetzel. How are you keeping, O.K.?"

"Sure." Mira wondered why the guy was calling.

"Listen, Frank, I've run into a little problem. That transaction last night, we're going to have to conclude sooner than expected."

Mira's stomach started to ice up. "I don't follow."

"I'm sorry, Frank, but head office just phoned. We're going to have to call the loan in."

"What are you talking about? We had a deal." Mira gripped the phone tighter. "There was no time limit."

"It's out of my hands, Frank; I'm just a messenger boy. Money's tight or something, I don't know, but head office wants all this week's loans in by the day after tomorrow."

"But I won't have it then. I'm waiting on something. You can't do this to me."

"It's not just you, Frank. And it's not me doing it to you. They're calling in loans from all over. It's tough on a lot of people."

"Listen," Mira said. He ran his tongue around his lips. "Tell them this. Tell them that if they give me ten days, just ten days, I'll give them five times what they lent me. Five times."

"No can do, Frank. They want the money now."

"That money's long gone now. Why do you think I borrowed it, to keep in a sock?" He bit his teeth together and slammed his fist against the wall. "I don't *have* a grand to give 'em."

Wetzel sounded very understanding, quietly sympathetic. "Frank, you've got to realize something. It's not just a grand. It's twelve-fifty, Frank. You owe the interest too."

"You're joking. One day—that's all I've had that money. They can't expect that kind of interest for one day . . ."

"You haven't got the picture, Frank. These people don't expect. They don't hope and they don't wish. They tell. You don't say no to them. I've got to go now, Frank. I'm sorry things have worked out this way. The day after tomorrow." He hung up quickly.

Mira hung up a lot more slowly. He leaned his head against the cool plastic of the phone and tried to think. Digging up a thousand had seemed impossible; finding twelve fifty was insanely out of the question. He'd been crazy to get in this deep. McNally would have been tough to handle, but he was still only one man; these other people . . . he was in deep trouble.

He called Williams again and told him he had to see him right away. Williams said he couldn't make it right away, and couldn't it wait? Mira insisted and Williams finally gave him a time two hours away.

Mira killed it by lying on his bed and worrying. He didn't tell Joey anything and was relieved that Cahill hadn't shown up. That at least was a break; he didn't relish the thought of having to tell Cahill what he'd gotten them into. He left the house early, even though he knew Williams would probably be late, rode down to Grand Central, then walked up the slope of Forty-first as far as he could go. The temperature had dropped again and the wind blew in off the river like a message from the North Pole. It whipped through him as he came around the corner of the tiny park at Tudor City. He cursed Williams and his love of open spaces; he cursed him for getting him into this mess in the first place.

When Williams arrived late again he acted as though he were the one who'd been kept waiting. "Let's have it, I'm in a hurry."

"So am I," Mira said bitterly. "I'm in a hurry for twelve hundred fifty bucks."

Williams said, "That number I gave you, didn't he come through?"

"Oh sure. Nice, polite guy. Clean cut. Handed me ten bills just like that. It cost me more than I'd heard, but I figured what the hell. So I hand it to McNally and get him off my back. Then I get a call tonight they want the grand plus interest the day after tomorrow. I won't even be close the day after tomorrow."

Williams sucked at his teeth. "Yeah, that can happen. They use a lot of their shark money to bankroll their big operations. They need cash up front quick sometimes. You got a bad break."

"I don't need a bad break. Let somebody else have a bad break."

"I know how you feel, but you'd better get them their money. You don't want to lose your security."

"What security, what are you talking about? They didn't ask for security."

Williams turned away with a short laugh. "Boy, are you from Missouri. These people ain't dumb. They don't go around handing out dough without checking on you. A bank don't, they don't. They know if you got a wife and kids, a girl or whatever." He shot him a sidelong look. "Didn't you tell me once you had a kid brother?"

Mira stood very still.

Williams said, "You would've been better off holding out on McNally. With him you would've gone home with a pain in your gut and a sore head. But with these guys—Jesus, you don't come through and they'll put the kid in a wheelchair for life."

Mira lunged at him, grabbed at his coat, jerked him towards him. "I'll kill 'em! They touch him and I'll kill 'em!"

"Hey now." Williams closed his hands over Mira's. "Hey." He looked down distastefully at the crease they were putting in the lapels. "It ain't me that's doing it. Don't get mad at me." He waited a beat, then took Mira's hands away. "I just gave you a number. It ain't my fault if you hit them at a bad time."

Mira stepped back, breathing loudly through his mouth. He sucked in air, kept it bottled up inside him, then let his chest collapse. He said drably, "What am I going to do?"

Williams didn't have much to offer. "I could give you another number, but you could run into the same problem right now."

"It's crazy. I've got a foolproof way to walk off with the biggest haul you ever heard of. In a week I could tip a cabbie what I owe."

Glancing at his watch Williams said, "I could maybe find you an angel, if you want to do it that way."

"A what?"

"A guy who buys in. It comes high though."

"How high?"

"Sixty percent of the take."

"Sixty?"

"They run a big risk. A job comes up empty and there goes their dough."

"But sixty percent . . . that's a fortune."

"Look," Williams said, "I know a guy bought into three jobs. Cost him over eight thou. You know how much he made? Nothing. Not a bean. All three jobs went belly up. It's a big gamble they take."

Mira was shaking his head. "I couldn't do it, not that high. That's giving it away."

Williams tugged at his gloves and looked around him. "Up to you," he said. "Listen, I got to see a guy. I'll see you round, huh?" He turned and started off.

Mira called after him and Williams stopped and waited impatiently as Mira came up to him. "Say you did look for a guy. Would you find him before the day after tomorrow?"

"Probably," Williams answered. "They go for bank jobs. When they work they pay good. You want I should try?"

Mira looked at the sidewalk. He said, as much to himself as to Williams, "What else can I do?"

"I'll call you tomorrow." Williams crossed the street and made for the steps that led down to First Avenue. He went halfway down them, stopped, walked back to the top again and watched Mira rounding the corner of the park and moving down Forty-first. Williams waited there till the car pulled up for him. It was a long blue Eldorado.

"He go for it?" Wetzel asked.

"Lapped it up."

Wetzel laughed. "Williams, you're a bad man."

"Real bad," McNally said from the back seat.

Wetzel asked a second question. "What do you think his chances are?"

"You never know with a punk. It's a bank job and they ain't easy," Williams replied. "But he's got some kind of new wrinkle, so who knows? If it works he's got to come out of a bank with fifty grand minimum."

"Thirty of it ours," Wetzel said.

"If he don't get pinched," McNally added.

"Just make sure you don't get pinched."

"I'm O.K. I'm out of it up north."

"Come on," Williams said, "let's go eat."

Mira got a call late the next day. "Mira? Williams. Listen, I found a guy for you. He put up the whole twelve fifty. I got it on me."

"We'd better meet then."

"I'm going to be tough to find today. But I tell you what, I got to see Wetzel myself about something else. I'll give him the money for you."

Mira thought it over for a moment. "Just make sure he gets it. I can't afford a slip-up on this thing."

"He'll get it, don't worry. I'll get him to call you so you'll know."

Wetzel didn't call that evening, and when he hadn't called by five the next day Mira called Williams but couldn't get him. After dinner he dissuaded Joey from going out and waited downstairs next to the phone, watching the front door, his gun tucked into his belt. When the phone rang about eight he jumped for it.

"Frank? Ralph. I just called to say thanks for the money."

"You got it O.K.? The twelve fifty?"

"Twelve fifty. I'm sorry I had to rush you on this, but you understand."

"Then we're all square," Mira said.

"Yep, even-steven. If you ever need the service again, Frank, I'll try to do better by you next time, all right?"

Mira said sure and hung up, a floodtide of relief washing over him. He sat down on the stairs and dropped his head back and let his insides unwind. He felt as if he'd just been released from forty-eight hours in an airless box.

Gradually, his feeling of relief was supplanted by a growing depression. He'd got Joey out from under, and that was the main thing. But now that he was safe he began to wonder if he hadn't given up more than he needed to. In fact, now that he had time to think about it, he'd got himself a fantastically bad deal: He'd agreed to pay a man three million dollars for lending him twelve fifty.

That'd be the day.

The first thing Austin did when he arrived was to rent a car. He could have got a better deal on one in New York, but he didn't want to drive around with out-of-state plates; people noticed things like that. He used a license that said his name was Vernon Howe.

The second thing he did was to check into a motel, the Howard Johnson's on West Main Road; it was only about two miles from where he was going to be operating.

The third thing he did was to change into tennis gear. He figured that going over there and playing tennis would be a good safe way of getting the information he was after. He knew that he could have got it faster by doing it more directly, but this way nobody was going to get suspicious. On the way there he stopped off at a sports store and bought some tennis balls. He hoped his game wouldn't be too rusty; he also hoped the gate man wouldn't look too closely at the date on his pass. But he found that he had nothing to worry about on that score; the man just glanced at it and waved him through.

He drove down a road that curled past a succession of one-story buildings and branched off towards two baseball diamonds that butted onto each other. The tennis courts were set in back of the first cage.

They were all empty. He wasn't surprised; it was still on the far edge of lunchtime, and it wasn't the best tennis weather anyway. He parked the car, went onto a court and put his gear down at the net post. He dug the can of balls out of his bag and opened it with the metal key. The can hissed as the key lifted the sealing strip and he held it to his nose and sniffed. It reminded him of summers at the lake; the big black inner-tubes they used as floats would get the same fresh-baked rubber smell, the sun pounding down on them making them so hot you had to kick them into the water before you could touch them. They'd swim all day and play tennis till it was too dark to see the ball, then barbecue steaks and drink too much of the cider his dad always made. Real summers. But that kind of life had stopped very suddenly for him one day five years ago. Although it seemed to Austin to be more like fifty.

He tried a couple of serves and was thankful for the warm-up time; the balls banged into the net or sailed over the line. He worked at getting his toss right and at swinging his racket across his body on the follow-through. The serves started going in, not much pace to them but a nice slice that kicked left. He tried a few ground strokes, but it was too hard without some-body hitting them back. He put his jacket on and waited in the car.

Shortly after that two men arrived and started warming up on a far court. Two was no good to him; he wanted one or three.

A quarter hour later he got his wish. A third man joined them and one of them took a rest; it didn't look as though they were expecting a fourth. He went over to them.

"Hi, you want to play a little doubles or are you happy?"

They asked him in, rallied together for a few minutes, then started a game. They weren't that good and Austin held his own. Between sets, chatting amiably with them, he found that none of the men had the information he was after, and he was glad when the game ended.

He returned to the car, toweled off and sat down to wait again. A brisk wind had got up and was coming in sharp off the bay. He watched a group of seagulls fighting in the sky for a piece of garbage one of them had been bold enough to come down and grab. They played a kind of keep-the-ball with it, one bird snatching it from another, the rest wheeling round and screeching, waiting for their turn. A crazy bird, the seagull.

He got tired of watching them and tired of sitting there and he began to wonder as the courts stayed empty if this had been such a hot idea. He gave it another half-hour and got another game but didn't learn anything that helped him any. He drove back to the motel, showered and changed and went into the bar for a drink. He toyed with the idea of going back there for dinner; if they were still keeping to the old schedule there'd be a buffet supper and a dance tonight; he could meet a lot of people. He decided against it, remembering how the barmen would sometimes ask to see your pass if they didn't know you. No, he'd stay with his original plan; go back there tomorrow and try the tennis bit again. All he needed was to find the right guy and it shouldn't really be that hard. But it had to happen soon; for one thing, he couldn't get by on that pass forever. For another, he wanted to get the show on the road. This was a great idea that guy had come up with, but like all great ideas the longer you left it the more risk there was of something going wrong. And they'd already had one holdup.

He finished his drink and went into the restaurant and ordered dinner. When he was through it was too early to go back to his room so he drove downtown and went to a movie, then drove back to the motel. He felt pleasantly tired as he undressed, his muscles stretched and a little sore, and he knew he'd have no trouble sleeping. Before he turned his light off he got out the folder of photographs that Mira had given him. He leafed through them, picked one out and studied it. It was the same one that had interested him the first time he'd seen it. He'd looked at it a lot since then.

It was a different man on the gate but he was waved through just as he had been the day before. He wondered again if he'd be so lucky tomorrow.

There were three courts being used when he got there, the better weather pulling a few more people out. It was still chilly but without the cold wind, and the sun was bright behind thin clouds. There were a singles and a doubles going on and, over on a back court, a man by himself taking the cover off his racket. He told Austin that he was waiting for his buddy to arrive but that he'd be happy to rally with him till he came.

The man's partner stayed away long enough for Austin to learn that he wouldn't have to worry about getting by the gate man the next day.

When he got back to the motel he made straight for the telephone. "Hello? Do you have a number for Burgess, Charles M. Burgess?" He heard the sound of pages flicking. The woman's voice said, "I have a Chester Burgess, no Charles."

He asked her to check the new numbers, and she found it there and gave it to him. "Is that on Green End Avenue?"

"Eighty-nine Shortlands," she replied.

Austin thanked her and hung up. He opened his suitcase and pulled out a clipboard and jotted the address down. Then he took a fast shower and changed into a suit. He picked up the clipboard, put the pen in his pocket and went out to the car. From the glove compartment he took a street guide of the town, checked the address and drove there.

Shortlands Road was in the center of what looked to be a fairly new, upper-income development. The houses were modern Cape Codders, retaining the traditional steep gables but doubling the height and the width of the cottages they'd been modeled after. There was plenty of room between them, and they were all set well back from the elms that lined the edge of the street. Number eighty-nine was painted a brick red, a handsome house, the clipped lawn raked clean of leaves. There was a white Volkswagen parked in the drive. Austin could see by the blue and white bumper sticker that this was the Charles Burgess the man at the tennis court had told him about.

A pretty, smiling woman answered his ring. She was wearing a smock over some slacks and had a stream of dark hair falling to her shoulders. She was petite, with fine bones in her face and hands, a clear white skin. When she spoke there was a trace of a Scots or North of England accent in some of her words.

"Oh, good morning. I thought you were the dry cleaner."

Austin smiled at her. "No, I'm not delivering anything, but then again I'm not selling anything, either."

She laughed. "Well, that's a relief."

Austin said, "I'm with Consumer Answer Index. Maybe you've heard of us?"

"I'm afraid not."

"You're in the majority; we're pretty new. I just wanted to ask you a couple of fast questions. It'll only take a few minutes and I'd be awfully grateful." The woman took her hand off the doorknob. "I guess I can spare a few minutes."

"Fine." He brought the clipboard up and nestled it in the crook of his arm.

He reached for the pen and clicked the button down. "We're conducting some research into consumer patterns in the area, where they shop, when and how often, that kind of thing. Now if I could get a little background on you and your family . . . how long have you lived here?" She told him and he wrote it down. "And your husband's occupation?" He was already writing when she told him that.

"Children?"

"Yes, one."

"Good," he said softly.

The woman said, "Good? Sometimes I wonder."

Austin laughed with her. "I know what you mean. I've got a couple myself." He kicked himself for relaxing. This woman wasn't stupid; she'd know it if he didn't sound right. He tightened up. "You have one car, two?"

"Two. My husband drives an Electra. The VW's mine."

"You happy with it?"

"Love it. It's great for running around town and doing the marketing and things."

"How about that marketing—that's what we're particularly interested in. Which days do you shop?"

"Mondays and Thursdays as a rule."

135

Austin wrote it down. "And do you stay pretty much with the same supermarket?"

"Pretty much, yes."

"How about weekends? Let's take this Friday, for example. Say you were going out of town, would you shop at your regular store before you went or buy when you got where you were going?"

"If it was a long weekend I guess I'd shop when I got there."

"Uh huh," Austin said, scribbling. "But seeing you'll be home you'll shop the day before at your regular supermarket . . ."

"That's right," the woman said.

"One last question and I'll let you go. In the last two weeks have you bought any Birds Eye, S&W, Nestle's or Betty Crocker brand products?"

"Yes I have."

"Right." Austin made a final note on the clipboard and put it under his arm. "Then that's it. I want to thank you, ma'am, for your cooperation. Believe me, in this job I run into people who won't even give you the time of day."

The woman started to step back. "You're very welcome. Goodbye now."

"Bye," Austin said. He started off down the path. Behind him he heard the door close.

Mira hung up the phone, then called Williams. The person who answered told him that Williams wasn't there right now but that he could leave a message.

"My name's Mira. Tell him it's Friday. Tell him to get McNally to call me tomorrow; you got that?"

"Mira," the voice repeated. "It's Friday. McNally should call you tomorrow."

"Check." He hung up and called the Lucky Shamrock. "Syd, is Ed Cahill there?"

Cahill came on a minute later sounding annoyed. "Yeah?"

"You going to be there long?"

"Who wants to know?"

"We're going up Thursday. If you want to be a rich man get here early." He replaced the phone on its cradle and climbed the stairs. "We're all set, kid," he said to Joey. "We do it Friday."

chapter 18

". . . and seizing an opportune time"

"Thursday," Dibley said; "we'll do it Thursday." He breezed into the bedroom in his pajamas and gown. The gown was open, Dibley not yet having replaced the cord he'd sacrificed to Carol's costume. Carol, not yet ready to greet the morning, was lying in bed wearing even less than the costume.

"Ngruff," she said. Carol was one of those Rip Van Winkles who go to sleep for a hundred years every time they say goodnight and have to be brought slowly into the world again with lots of hot coffee. Dibley, on the other hand, was the type who can leap out of bed with all their cylinders ticking, instantly awake and ready to go.

"You're not paying attention," he said. "Look at this." He shoved a newspaper under Carol's closed eyes, and with the traditional non-understanding of the other type sleeper he demanded that she read it.

Carol could not have read the logo on the Goodyear blimp. "Mmph," she said and turned over exposing the kind of shape normally seen pinned to the inside of locker-room doors. Dibley, his head in the newspaper, didn't notice.

"Carol." He shook a pink shoulder with spectacular results a little lower down. "Look at this, will you? The mayor's cutting his vacation short. We can stop cooling our heels and go get him Thursday."

"Mmph," Carol said again.

"Wait a moment." Dibley had seen something further on in the news item. "He's hosting an out-of-state group the next day, Friday. Giving them lunch. That's much better. When he sees the gun he'll have his guests to think about as well as his own skin. Yeah, we'll do it Friday. O.K., Carol?"

Carol returned to her original line of thinking. "Ngruff," she said.

chapter 19

"Together they journeyed to another city . . ."

The bus hummed over the high suspension bridge spanning the bay that the Taunton River had helped shape a million years ago. A mile to the west Hog Island sat like a whale on the water, a sailboat beyond it beating its way south towards Homestead or Sandy Point.

They stopped briefly at a town five minutes later, then rode for another fifteen minutes and got off.

"Hello there," Austin said. "Good trip?"

Mira said, "I could think of better ways of spending five hours." He didn't bother with introductions, and Austin just nodded at the others.

138

"Everything going O.K.?"

Austin made a circle with his thumb and forefinger. "Like clockwork. Come on, I'm over here." He led the way to the car, opened the trunk for their overnight bags and stowed them.

"You get us rooms?" Mira asked.

"Sure, at the motel where I'm staying."

"Let's go then."

"No," McNally said. "We'll take a look at the house first."

Austin had never met McNally before, but he'd known the moment he'd seen him what he'd been hired for. But he was working for Mira and he waited, ready to ignore the other man if Mira said so. But Mira didn't say a thing, just glared at the big man and clamped his mouth tight.

Mira got into the front seat and his brother followed him, leaving the rear seat to McNally and Cahill. Cahill sat stiffly, not looking at McNally at all but very much aware of him. Cahill hadn't said much on the bus coming up and wasn't saying anything now. McNally didn't seem to know that Cahill was even there.

Austin drove them to the house he'd visited two days before. "Eighty-nine," he said, rolling the car slowly by it, "the red one."

McNally studied the house and the ones next door and the houses opposite. "What time in the morning?" he asked Austin. On the way up, Mira had told McNally what they were planning. If McNally had been impressed he hadn't shown it.

"Eight."

"How far is it from here?"

"Ten, fifteen-minute drive."

"How far's the motel from here?"

"About the same."

"If he's leaving at eight what time will he leave home?"

"Probably no later than seven," Austin replied.

"We'll get here at six," McNally said. "Let's get out of here."

Austin drove towards the motel, and nobody said anything till McNally spoke again. "You find a place to stash them?"

"No." He watched McNally in the rear-view mirror. "It's your neck, I thought you'd feel better if you picked the spot."

McNally nodded at that. "We'll check in, then you and me will go look."

When they reached the motel Austin waited in the car while the others went in and registered. McNally came out again and they drove off.

"You looking for any kind of place in particular?" Austin asked.

"Just give me the ten-cent tour. I'll tell you when to stop."

Except for the fact that it tapered at its northern end the island resembled a miniature Italy, a boot with toe and heel. Austin drove down into the toe and through a downtown section that fed the bridge that leapt two miles to another island in the middle of the bay. They came out at a small harbor, the sun angling down through gray clouds, spotlighting sailboats and cabin cruisers tugging at anchors. They continued down the tip of the toe past a lighthouse on a hill and round a point that turned them east. They drove past ponds and rocky inlets, then headed north through a section that was nothing but mansions and high-hedged drives.

They crossed a causeway, the bay on their right, then skirted a beach shaped like a boomerang with a white-steepled church and barn-colored summer houses set in the slope behind it. They followed the arch of the boot onto the heel, took a gravel road across a short promontory and came out at another beach. Austin was turning the car again when McNally stopped him. He got out and walked down the beach a little way and stopped opposite a bathhouse built on the sidewalk above the sand. It was brick up to the high narrow windows that ran around the four sides. On one side of the building was a wooden partition shaped like an L that hid garbage cans and outdoor showers. The front doors were held closed by an old-fashioned padlock that the salt air had peppered with rust.

"What kind of car she drive?" McNally asked Austin when he joined him.

"A VW."

McNally measured the partition with his eye, then looked around him. It was a long way to anything that resembled a house. They walked together to the car.

"You want to drive around some more?"

"No," McNally said.

chapter 20

". . . and set out for the river palace . . ."

All in all Dibley reckoned it was the most disorganized Friday morning of his life. And it was his fault: To ensure an early start he'd asked Walter and Swaboda to stay the night, assuming that they'd simply sleep on the two sofas in the living room. But just as everybody was preparing to go to bed Kitty had taken over and refused to share a room with a man. They'd sat around waiting for Rocky to replace Kitty and so solve their problem. But when that had happened half an hour later they found they had a brand new snag. Swaboda said that his mother was afraid she'd get her throat cut if she slept in the same room with a gangster. To make matters worse for Dibley, Carol took her part.

"Honestly, darling," she'd said, "we can't expect her to share the same room with two men."

Peeved, Dibley said, "We'll put up a blanket."

"James, don't be silly. Go and tell Charlie his mother's welcome to bunk in with me."

"Hell, that means I have to sleep on the sofa. My knees dangle over that thing."

Carol moved closer to him. "It'll only be for a little while. You can come in later."

"Carol!" Dibley was shocked. "I'm not going to roll in the hay with Mrs. Swaboda lying in the same bed."

Carol kissed his nose. "We'll wait till she's asleep."

Dibley wouldn't hear of it. He and Walter and Swaboda slept on sofas and chairs in the living room, and Carol and Mrs. Swaboda shared the bedroom. Carol didn't see Dibley till six the next morning, and not too well even then. Although Carol was getting the breakfast, she wasn't seeing too much. A somnambulist at seven-thirty, she was a zombie at six and should never have attempted to cook. Dibley came out into the kitchen to find her holding a pan over the stove.

"Damn it," he said, "Mrs. Swaboda's been in the bathroom for twenty minutes."

He peeked into the fry pan. "Well, what do you know, fry-in-the-bag bacon. They think of everything, don't they?"

He got a soft snore for an answer. He gently took the pan out of her hand and leaned her against the refrigerator.

Swaboda came in. "We're in luck. Walter just woke up and he's Walter."

Dibley ran a spatula round the pan. "What a guy," he said. "Anybody else waking up in a strange place might say 'Where am I?' But Walter says, 'Who am I?'"

Swaboda said, "I was only thinking the other day that he's tailor-made for a coat of arms: a mailed fist holding a cigaret rampant on a box of pablum."

"I've got the motto for it," Dibley said. "United we stand."

Swaboda noticed Carol against the refrigerator. "Hey, what's Carol doing?"

"Practicing sleeping. Come on, this is ready."

They sat down and Walter joined them and they started on the meal.

Walter and Swaboda stopped chewing at the same time. "This is a cunning recipe," Swaboda said.

"Different, isn't it?" Dibley replied, forking up some cardboard. "This is a test-market area; we get a lot of new things."

They left thirty minutes later, leaving Mrs. Swaboda still in the bathroom. It was cold on the sidewalk and dark, and they walked bunched together towards the parking lot. Dibley felt great. "It's all happening," he said. "Today's our last day as pedestrians."

Swaboda said, "We'll have the money by lunchtime and a new car before dinner."

Dibley felt something sharp in his coat pocket and took it out. "Well, that's appropriate—the spare key to the Studebaker." Ahead of them a garbage truck was gulping trash on Hudson Street. As they passed it Dibley tossed the key into its churning maw. "Thank you and goodnight," he said.

They turned into Greenwich Street and Dibley conducted a final run-through of the plan he'd put together over the last few days. "Right, we tow the gun over to the boat basin. We say good morning to the night watchman, who should be the only guy around at this time, and lock him in his cubby hole. We pick out a suitable cabin cruiser. We take the siderails down if we have to, put down planks and back the gun onto the deck. We unhitch it and secure it. We hot-wire the boat and sail it round to the Newtown Creek while it's still pretty dark and hide there till noon. Then we make a dash for it to Gracie Mansion and throw down on the mayor in the middle of his shrimp cocktail. We take the money, make a fast getaway to a nearby dock and get a cab back to the apartment. We call the cops, tell them where to find the boat and the car, then have lunch and a little wine to celebrate. Then we go out and get ourselves another automobile. Any questions?" They'd reached the parking lot and had stopped outside the gate.

Swaboda said, "It's perfect. Let's do it."

"O.K.!" Dibley jammed his hand into his pocket, pulled out

a key and thrust it into the padlock. He struggled with it for a moment, took it out and tried again.

Something was wrong. He brought the key up to his face and peered at it. In the dim yellow of the corner streetlight he made out the word, "Studebaker."

He'd thrown their only key to the parking lot into the garbage truck.

chapter 21

". . . where, by loathsome means, they too acquired a dhow . . ."

They glided the car to a stop diagonally opposite the house and parked in a patch of darkness. They waited in the car, the windows rolled up against the early morning chill. A house down the block showed a single lighted window, but the rest were asleep except for the one they were watching.

The street was still and quiet and it was twenty minutes before anything changed on it. The front door of the house opened, and a man and a woman were momentarily framed there. The door closed and a porch light clicked on and lit up the man moving down the path. They heard a garage door slide up and a car door open and close, then the long whir of a cold engine starting. The car was revved for a minute, then the white beams of reverse lights stabbed out onto the drive and two red rear lights appeared. A white Electra backed out onto the roadway and faced away from them. The driver took it forward, down to the end of the street and round the corner. The porch light winked out and the street was still again.

Mira reached for the door handle. "Let's go."

"Wait," McNally said from the rear seat.

Mira hadn't had much sleep; he'd lain there in the dark of his room going over every step, figuring possible snags. Up till now it had all been just an idea, but now things were starting for real, and he was wound up like a clockwork spring. He turned and said sharply, "You're working for me, McNally, not the other way around. Yesterday you had a lot to say and I let you. But not today. This is my job, my idea. I set it up, I call the shots."

Cahill shot a fast glance at McNally, waiting to see what he'd do. Austin was staying out of it and, like Joey, kept his eyes on the house.

McNally said, "You think you can handle things in there, do you?"

"As good as you," Mira said.

Cautious, Cahill said, "That's right, Frank."

McNally snickered. "A couple of shoplifters. All right, go ahead. You'll be screaming for me in two minutes."

Mira and Cahill got out of the car, crossed the street to the house and rang the bell.

The woman opened it and put a hand to the front of her dressing gown. "Excuse me, I thought it was my husband."

"We're friends of his," Mira said. "He gave us a message for you."

"A message?" She looked back and forth between the two men. "I don't understand. Cal just left here a minute ago."

"He just gave it to us."

A child of about four, a little girl, appeared sleepily at her mother's side. The woman dropped an arm around her and held her close. She spoke firmly. "What's the message, please?"

"We'll tell you inside."

With a fast movement the woman tried to shut the door, but Cahill was too quick for her. He shoved his body against it and

145

Mira slipped past the woman into the hall, Cahill following. The woman stepped back against the stair rail, her eyes wide, clutching the child with both arms now, hugging her to her body.

"The message is this," Mira said. "You and the kid are going to spend the day with a friend of ours. We want your husband to do us a favor and we want to make sure he does it. Behave and you'll be all right. So will your husband. End of the day you'll be back here."

Cahill moved towards her, a loose smile weighing down one side of his mouth. "Go get dressed and don't try nothing fancy. I'll keep the kid here with me to make sure."

He made a move towards the child, and the woman's hand flashed out. It was more of a stab than a blow, her nails catching him under the eye and taking out a tiny piece of flesh.

It stopped Cahill cold. "Jesus!" His hand leapt to his face.

She blazed at him, although her voice shook. "Stay away! Get out of this house! Both of you get out!" Her breath came in small fast sobs and she crumbled the last word. The child whimpered. The woman's face was starting to lose its fire and her eyes began to show tears.

Mira said, "I told you what to do. Now leave the kid and get—" He stopped his forward movement. The woman had swept the child behind her and snatched up a heavy glass ashtray off a hall table. She held it high above her head like a club. "Don't touch her. Just don't touch her." Her voice had broken and the tears were starting down her face, her body quivering.

Mira took the gun out of his belt and held it by his side. "You're making it tough."

The front door slammed. Mira spun and saw McNally standing there. He wasn't looking at Mira or Cahill—he was looking at the woman. He spoke to her, slowly and heavily: "Take the kid upstairs and get her dressed. You get dressed. Real warm. Then come back down here. You try to phone somebody and you'd better know how to talk fast. Now put the glassware down and do it."

146

The woman stayed where she was, watching him, sucking air in shuddering gasps.

McNally said, "If I have to take it away from you, lady . . ." his eyes flicked for the briefest second to the child behind her ". . . things could get rough."

The woman didn't move for a moment, then her upper body seemed to fold down on itself and she lowered the ashtray in stages. She placed it carefully back onto the table, took her daughter's hand and went up the stairs.

During the exchange Mira and Cahill had been standing rigid, as if McNally had been including them in his orders.

McNally looked down at the gun in Mira's hand. He said, "I thought the bank job was this afternoon."

Mira's head snapped up, the gun coming up with it.

McNally looked away from him. "The last guy that pointed a gun at me got it shoved up his nose." He waited a second, then looked back.

Mira rammed the gun into his belt and strode into the living room. He crossed to a table that was set up as a bar, snatched up a glass decanter, pulled the stopper and sloshed some whiskey into a glass. He raised the glass to his mouth, then slapped it back onto the table untouched. He went over to the window and stared sullenly through a division in the drapes.

Five minutes later the woman came down the stairs tucking a sweater into the little girl's slacks. She'd got her breathing under control and her eyes were dry and she'd got the child calmed down too; she was carrying a floppy teddy bear and whispering to it. She pulled coats from a hall closet and zipped her daughter into a parka. Except for the pasty color of her face and the fine trembling in her hands she could have been getting ready to go to the store.

Mira came over and spoke to Cahill, the words addressed to McNally. "I need something from her to prove to Burgess we got her."

McNally ran his eyes over her; she was busy with the buttons on her coat. He caught the dull flash of a gold ring on her finger. "You got writing inside that ring?"

She put a protective hand over it. "It's my wedding ring."

McNally told her to get it off. When she hesitated he said, "Want me to help you?" The woman brought her hand up to her mouth, wet her finger and twisted the ring off. Mira took it from her.

"Lights out upstairs?" McNally asked.

The woman nodded.

He held out his hand. "Car keys."

She rummaged in her pocketbook and took out some keys. He took them from her and relieved her of the purse as well. "You bring anything you shouldn't?" He dipped his hand into it, moved things about, then handed it back. "We're going to get on fine," he said.

Mira hated the man but he had to admit he didn't miss a trick.

McNally led the way to the door, switched off the lights and ushered everybody out. He shut the door after him and guided the woman and her daughter over to the garage, opened the Volkswagen, pushed the seat forward and settled them into the back. Then he got in behind the wheel, started the car, warmed it for a moment and took it down the drive and up the street.

Mira and Cahill crossed to the car.

Austin said, "All rightee?"

Mira told him to get going.

Austin drove west through the residential section until it petered out and the stores of the downtown area started to appear. There was a pick-up truck making an early delivery and a road sweeper whirring brushes along the gutter. The lights were on in a coffee shop, and in a store opposite, a man was folding newspapers.

They came out of the built-up area, getting nearer the water, and the dark shape of Conanicut Island sprang up behind the bridge across the bay.

Mira tucked the woman's ring next to the note in an envelope. He sealed it and handed it to Austin. Austin slipped it into the glove compartment and slowed the car. Ahead Mira made out a high perimeter fence broken by a gatehouse, the lights over it burning with a white magnesium brightness. It reminded him of his first glimpse of the penitentiary the night they'd taken him there.

Austin pulled up alongside the gate and took out the envelope. It was a different gate from the one he'd used before. "They said this was urgent," he said.

The gate man took the envelope and told him to park just inside. They watched the man go into the office and pass the envelope to his senior, who nodded over it and passed it back. The gate man came out and handed it to a messenger who dropped it into a pouch, straddled a motor bike and zoomed off.

They sat in the car for a long, stomach-fluttering ten minutes waiting for the cycle to come back. But it was a car that arrived, coming up very fast and slamming to a stop. The driver didn't waste any time getting into the office. They saw the senior man read the note the messenger handed him, then say something to the gate man, who came out and started towards them. He asked them to step inside and they let him lead the way.

"Four of you, right?" the man in charge asked. "You're going in on Burgess' say-so." He pointed to a visitors' book lying open on a table. "If you'd just sign here, please."

Austin signed first, then Mira. Then Joey scribbled a name and handed the pen to Cahill, who took it and dropped it. It hit the floor with a loud sound in the early morning office.

"Sorry," he said quickly, "cold fingers." He stood blinking nervously. Joey bent quickly and scooped the pen up for him.

"The driver will take you," the senior man said.

They went out and got into the car. The driver made a fast U-turn and headed back down the road. They sped past rows of low, lighted buildings, across an enormous square, a salt breeze lifting what was left of a predawn fog, and on by baseball diamonds and tennis courts. Ahead of them masts popped up against a slowly brightening sky. They raced down a road of jetties and wharves, the ships, a firmer addition to the darkness, slotted into them like fingers into a glove. The car slowed, turned down a jetty and stopped opposite a gangway that slanted up to the deck of a ship.

The ship was a four-thousand-ton Knox Class destroyer.

There were two sailors and an officer at the bottom of the gangway and a similar group at the top. Halfway down it a man stood by himself, a letter in his hand, waiting.

Austin went first, the others following, and started up the gangway towards him. The man was back-lit from the lights rigged over the deck and it was hard to see his face. He could see theirs clearly and he looked from one to the other as if half expecting to spot the face of a friend playing a lousy joke.

Austin said pleasantly, "Good morning, skipper."

"Follow me," the man said curtly. He turned and climbed the gangway to the deck, walked towards the bow and went into the ship. They followed him up steep narrow stairs and through a cabin door. He closed it and locked it, went past them to his desk and faced them.

"Where is my family?" There was no emotion in his voice; the question was asked flatly and directly by a man used to getting fast answers. Burgess was lightly built and of medium height, but his straight stance made him look taller and broader than he was. He had neat sandy hair cut in an old-fashioned back and sides, a slim, strong-boned face, a thin mouth. There was a stern firmness in the set of his jaw and the strong unswerving gaze; his whole bearing seemed to be one of brisk executive confidence till you got to the hands tightly clenched at his sides, his right thumb worrying a fingernail.

Mira said, "Play ball and you'll see them at the end of the day."

"Where are they now?"

"A friend's looking after them."

Burgess' expression didn't change, nor did he shift his stiff stance. But the breath he took before he spoke again went down unevenly. "I want your assurance that they won't be harmed in any way."

Mira shrugged. "That's up to you. You do us a favor and you'll get them back good as new."

"What do you want?"

They were standing in a one-two-two formation, Burgess at the desk, Mira and Austin in front of him and Cahill and Joey against the door.

"We want to borrow your boat for a little cruise south."

Burgess ran his eyes over them before coming back to Mira. "If it's Cuba you mean, you can forget it."

"Not Cuba. This isn't a hijack."

"We ain't traitors," Cahill said.

Mira said, "New York's where we want to go." He didn't complete the explanation; he wanted the navy man to come to him for it. Burgess obliged.

"Why New York?"

"Because we're going to take a bank for five million and we need a gun. We figured we'd borrow yours."

Burgess didn't give him the reaction he'd expected. His face remained stony. "You can still forget it." He let that sink in, then said, "Did you seriously think I'd turn my ship over to a gang of thieves?"

Mira said, "I thought you'd care what happened to your family."

"You're not taking this ship." He glared at Mira, who went on acting as though he'd miscalculated and appeared surprised that the captain held his family in such little regard.

Austin recognized the impasse and spoke up. "We're not asking you to give up the ship, skipper, just to lend it out for a couple of hours. We'll be out of your hair late this afternoon."

"Mister," Burgess said, "the United States Navy doesn't lend ships."

"What's the navy got to do with it?" Mira asked. "We're not holding the navy's family, we're holding yours."

Austin kept on at him. "Look at it this way, Captain, we're all Americans here so it's not like you'd be turning the ship over to the Enemy. We're forcing you to by threatening you personally. They won't court martial you, not for protecting your family. They'd like to maybe, but they wouldn't dare, so you don't have to worry on that score."

Burgess took no notice of him. He was still watching Mira and Mira knew it.

"You've got too much to lose, Burgess," he said.

"If I lose, you lose too. You'll go to jail forever."

"We'll go to jail, sure. But I'll see daylight long before you see your wife and kid again."

"Daylight?" Burgess said. "Listen to me. In seeking to take control of this ship you are stopping me at this present moment from exercising my command. So in effect you're already guilty of piracy. This country's very sensitive about things like that today, maybe you've heard. And if you think they'd ever commute a sentence for a charge like that, you've miscalculated. You're facing a lifetime in the brig, all of you, and I seriously doubt that you came here today with that possibility in mind."

He paused, watching the effect his words had had. He sensed the first stirrings of doubt in the men in front of him. The big fellow against the door shuffled uneasily, and the man next to him was looking worriedly at the leader. But he wasn't concerned with them; the leader was the man he had to beat. He shut the image of his family out of his mind and concentrated on keeping his voice in a hard straight line. "I'm going to make you a proposition. You take me to my family, just me alone, and you can walk off this ship and off this base free men. I've never seen you before, I haven't heard anything you've said to me in this cabin, you've never been in this cabin."

In the moments that followed, the metallic ticking of a brass chronometer sounded, as if it just that moment had started. The slight throbbing that reached their feet through the deck seemed new too, although it had been there from the start. And they became aware for the first time of the faint reek of diesel oil that seemed to be driving the air out of the cabin.

In a low shaky voice Cahill started to say something. "Frank, maybe we'd—"

"Shut up." Mira said it almost as an aside, but Cahill burbled to a stop. Mira moved to the side of the captain's desk and was a long time replying. "O.K.," he said.

"You accept?" Burgess asked quickly.

"No."

Four pairs of eyes stared at him. Mira picked up something from the desk, an oblong silver frame hinged in the middle to hold two facing pictures. On one side a dark-haired woman smiled across at the little girl on the other. Mira looked closely at it and said, "Call your men, Burgess." He handed it to the captain. "Then find a safe place for this."

Up till now, by forcing his mind to it, Burgess had been able to abstract the situation he was in; the family of a captain of a United States warship had been kidnapped in order to coerce him. He'd reacted quickly, intelligently, using the only weapon he had at his disposal, his wits. And now that it was put up or shut up, the correct course would have been to arrest these men and bank on getting the hostages back safe and sound; probably a better than even chance. But when he'd let himself look at the photos Mira had put into his hands, it wasn't the family of some nameless officer he was gambling with: it was *his* family, Marion and Lisa. It made it impossible for him to go by the book.

When he didn't look up from the photographs Mira knew that they had themselves a gun.

Austin knew it, too. He said, quietly and respectfully, "Commander Burgess, sir, according to my information you're due to up anchor for Norfolk round about now. What do you say we get underway?"

Very gently and very carefully, Burgess put the silver frame back onto his desk.

The ship moved out into Narragansett Bay and slid under the high center span of the bridge. The harbor appeared on their left, the lights on Thames Street giving way to a muddy daylight, the rest of Newport just beginning to stir. They rounded the Rams Head, picked up speed and charged out into Rhode Island Sound. On their portside the Brenton Reef light tower rose out of the water like a drowning hand, then ten minutes later Sandy Point, the tip of Block Island's teardrop, came up ahead. They passed its eastern edge, leapt the gap to Montauk, turned the corner and pounded down the Long Island coast. The ship pushed a white wall of water through a sea blown smooth in the night and built its speed up to twenty-eight knots. New York was a little over a hundred miles away.

Burgess had taken the ship out himself, leaving the four men in his cabin. He came back to them now and told them that he'd have to tell his officers what was happening. Mira said to go ahead and get them together and, after checking with Austin, told him to make sure the radioman, the gunnery chief and the helicopter pilot were present.

They assembled in the wardroom: Burgess, his executive officer, fourteen other officers and two enlisted men. Mira and the others stood behind Burgess, who faced his crew. Without any preliminaries Burgess said, "Gentlemen, I have something to tell you that you're going to find hard to believe. I'm still finding it hard to believe myself. This ship is no longer under my command. These men here are in command." He paused for a second watching the puzzled faces. Some of the men chuckled.

Burgess said, "I'm not joking. I wish to God I were." The way he said it and the way he looked saying it, there wasn't a man in the room who didn't believe him.

Burgess told them what had happened. He spoke steadily, choosing his words with a lawyer's caution. When he'd finished there wasn't a sound or flicker of life in the cabin. The men had been shocked into an iron stillness.

Burgess coughed behind his fist and started talking again. "As its captain, the fate of this ship is decided solely by me, so no blame will attach to any of you. And I'd like you to bear in mind that I am still its captain and have only been relieved of my command by these men who have no authority to do so. Therefore I am ordering you to accept my decision regarding the temporary command of this ship and warning you not to try to interfere with these men or to attempt to contact shore. You'll tell the crew nothing about this of course. I'll pipe them later and tell them we've been ordered to New York on a special training operation. It might be an idea to let them know that there are civilian technicians on board, which should explain the presence of these men. That's all, gentlemen. I thank you for your attention. I'd like the gunnery chief to stay, please."

Nobody moved. The men's eyes switched from Burgess to the group behind him, then came back to Burgess again. They seemed to be waiting for something more.

The captain relaxed imperceptibly and sounded a touch less severe when he spoke. "You're all good officers, and I know I'll have your obedience." His voice softened. "I'd like to think I have your understanding as well." He nodded to his executive officer, who dismissed the men. They filed out silently, believing what their skipper had told them but still dazed by it.

When the door had closed on them Austin started talking to the gunnery chief. "I want the five-inch laid, chief, high-ex contacts, the whole mag except the lead-off round. I want a starshell there. And I'll need the key to the battery plot."

Burgess looked appalled. "You're not going to fire that gun? We'll call it quits right here and now. I'm not going to trade my family's lives for other people's."

"You've got it wrong, skipper. The starshell's only to prove we mean business. We'll give the bank plenty of warning, plenty of time to get everybody out."

"Then why the high explosives?"

"Captain, this is something you wouldn't know about, but if you go into a bank waving a gun it'd better be loaded. If it isn't they're going to know it. We have to talk to the bank, so we have to sound like we can do what we're going to threaten to do."

"A lot of bank robbers have shot people and claimed later they'd never intended to."

"That's true," Austin said. "But that's because somebody went for an alarm or a guard went for his gun. That's not going to happen here. The bank can hardly start firing at us, and the Coast Guard or the navy wouldn't dare. Not while we've got the five-inch trained."

"I still don't like it," Burgess said.

"Look," Mira broke in, "like he says, nobody's going to get shot or killed. But we're only going to get one try at this. It'll either work or it won't. And we've got a lot better chance if we do it right. If things go wrong for us," he pointed a finger at Burgess, "things go wrong for you."

The chief looked at Burgess, who spent a long time with it before he nodded. Later, standing together at the bow, Mira said to Austin, "What was all that crap you were feeding that guy? I backed you up in there, but I don't see what you want with real shells. The bank isn't going to know from a mile away whether or not the thing's loaded."

Austin said, "The way I see it, this is the biggest bluff anyone ever pulled. I've been in enough poker games to know that the best bluff is one you can back up if you're called."

"They're not going to call us; they can't take the chance."

"Maybe not, but I really believe what I told Burgess. We'll sound more like we're ready to blow them away if we've got our finger on the trigger."

Mira, unconvinced but not knowing what else to say, watched the bow wave climbing the sides of the ship and streaming back to lose itself in the boiling wake.

chapter 22

". . . they loaded the sword upon a dhow"

There had been no other way of getting into the lot for another three hours, so everybody had dispersed and gone their separate ways. Carol had gone back to bed, an easy transition for her. Swaboda had gone back, picked up his mother and taken her to be first in line at a sale at Gimbel's. And Kitty, who had arrived on the scene at the last moment, had hauled Walter off to see if there was anybody left at Sardi's.

That left Dibley on his own, which was exactly where he wanted to be. He was infuriated, frustrated, embarrassed and bitterly disappointed. He jammed his hands into his pockets and set off down Greenwich Street planning to walk to the Battery and into the bay. It wasn't being shut out of the lot that made him so angry; it was the realization that even if they had got in, his plan wouldn't have worked anyway. Everything was wrong with it: He'd assumed that a boat of just the right size would be waiting for him all greased up and ready to go on a trailer. He'd assumed that they could steal something like that without the slightest trouble. And he'd assumed that they could get a two-ton gun onto it as if it were a golf buggy, then hotwire the boat and just tootle off. Ridiculous. He'd let boyish enthusiasm get the better of sound judgment.

He crossed Spring Street and turned east on Canal, skipping out of the way of some early traffic pouring into the Holland Tunnel. He walked towards Broadway, pausing now and then to look moodily into store windows full of electronic innards—condensers and circuits, tubes, oscillators, generators, gauges and jack plugs—and drew a sad satisfaction from the knowledge that people actually bought these things; people who clicked things neatly and correctly into place, not jumbled them in a hat and hoped they'd come out right like he'd done. Hot-wire a boat . . . hell, he couldn't even hot-wire a flashlight.

He turned south at the western fringes of Chinatown, one or two of the restaurants still burning their colossal neons, and passed by the back of the criminal courts. It was a sleazy street given over to a couple of bars and a group of store fronts offering to arrange bail bonds. Morosely Dibley wondered how long it would have been before he'd have been a customer had they got into the parking lot. The proximity to the law bothered him, and he got off the street and walked into Foley Square, only to find himself outside the imposing steps and pillared arcade of the courthouse. It reminded him that he still had a gun and a car that weren't his. He'd probably be walking up those steps any day now.

He ducked his head into his collar and hurried by into the no-man's-land of the Brooklyn Bridge approach. The wind channeled across it like an express train and lowered the temperature another degree. The geography of the city was making it impossible for Dibley to forget his ill-founded plan; he'd arrived at City Hall Park. He reflected miserably that City Hall was the reason he was standing outside it getting cold. It was one of the oldest maxims in New York: You can't fight City Hall. He should have had sense enough not to try. It was like a fox terrier taking on a crocodile. He walked down Nassau Street, brushing through the crowd that the subway was pumping up at Fulton. He reached Liberty Street and paused at the plaza that opened up on his left, the bank the plaza had been named for a monumental slab in the sky. Money, Dibley thought; that was the real reason all this had come about. A hundred fifty dollars, that's all. That bank there, wasn't that the one that had a billion dollars cash in its vault? They probably used a sum like a hundred and fifty to straighten shaky tables in the cafeteria.

He went on by the Stock Exchange, past Bowling Green and down to South Ferry till he couldn't walk any farther. As if to prove the point, the Staten Island ferry unloaded and a wall of commuters came at him. He stepped out of their way and was honked back off the road by the cars coming off the lower deck. A man driving a Jeepster with a high luggage trailer on tow yelled something as he went by. It completed Dibley's morning; New York, its government and its populace were all against him.

He went down into the subway and rode back uptown trying to think of something to cheer himself up. The plan hadn't been all that bad; pretty good in its way. In fact, if there'd been a fast easy way to get the gun onto a boat and then steal the boat it would have been a brilliant plan. But there were no fast easy ways of getting a cannon onto a boat.

It didn't occur to him till he was walking up the steps at Christopher Street that he'd just seen one.

He stopped, staggered by the realization. He swung a hand up; nine o'clock—Walter and Swaboda would be back by eleven—they had plenty of time.

He ran up the rest of the steps and shot out onto the street. He felt marvelous, exhilarated, on top of the world. His plan wasn't a dud, it was a winner. He marched down West Fourth as if he were leading a parade. They were going to be interrupting the mayor's lunch after all.

To anybody who'd seen them crossing Greenwich Street earlier that day, four major differences would have been immediately apparent: The tall one was carrying a flat brown paper parcel, the small one was dressed like a hood, the fat one was holding his arm out as if he were supporting somebody's elbow, and the girl was now awake. Dibley was in the middle of rehashing his early morning sojourn.

159

"I walked clear down to the Battery and I was so depressed I wasn't even looking where I was going, and some guy driving a trailer off the ferry nearly collected me. I got almost home before I realized that we didn't have to futz around looking for unguarded Chris-Crafts when we can simply drive the gun onto the ferry and steal the ferry. I don't know why I didn't think of it before."

"I don't know why you've thought of it now," Carol said. "I thought we were through with all this, then you go and pull me away from my job and here I am again. I've lost so much time on this silly idea they're sure to fire me."

Walter squashed a possible blow-up between Carol and Dibley by having a genuine coughing fit. "Oh dear," he said, wiping at his eyes, "I wish Kitty would smoke filters."

They reached the parking lot and went over to the Land Rover; the lot attendant was busy parking cars. They stripped the tarpaulin off the gun, and Dibley pulled the paper away from the package he was carrying and revealed a big piece of lettered poster board. It had a cord through two holes at the top which Dibley attached to the barrel.

"I thought the best disguise would be no disguise," he said, stepping back to give them a look.

The sign read, GUNS OF NAVARONE. RIALTO. NOW.

"He's a genius," Swaboda said. "A walking, talking, five-star whiz kid." They waited for Carol's customary bucket of cold water, but she was apparently saving it.

They climbed into the car. Dibley warmed it up, then took it out of the gate and headed uptown. When Swaboda told him that South Ferry was the other way he explained that they needed some props for what he had in mind, so nobody was surprised when they pulled up in front of the costume rental company. Carol, who was getting almost as quiet as Walter, elected to remain in the car.

"Hello again," Dibley said to the clerk behind the counter. "Do you think you could fix the three of us up with navy uniforms?"

The clerk eyed them sleepily. "You guys get thrown out of the army?"

"Three navy uniforms, huh?"

The clerk went out back, rummaged around and returned with some uniforms over his arm. In the changing room Dibley told the other two exactly how the new outfits fitted in with his plan. They loved the idea.

The clerk packed their regular clothes into boxes, and they went outside to the car.

"Hey, Carol," Dibley called, "the fleet's in."

Carol looked at them. The navy uniforms didn't fit any better than the army uniforms had. Walter's drooped on him, Swaboda's jacket showed his undershirt around the middle, while Dibley's sleeves barely covered his elbows. It was then that Carol threw the bucket of cold water.

"That's it. That is it." She climbed out of the Land Rover. "It's all over."

Dibley didn't get it. "What do you mean?"

"I mean I've been sitting in that car wondering what on earth I was doing sitting in that car. I'm little Carol Mars from Kew Gardens, Queens, formerly a law-abiding citizen with a good steady job. But look what's happened to me in the last week—I've helped swindle a dealer out of a car. All right, maybe they practically gave it to us and we're going to give it back anyway, so that didn't bother me too much. Then I did a bump and grind in the middle of the East River to steal a gun from the army. O.K., maybe I'm not crazy about armies and we were going to give the gun back, too. But when my lover comes on wearing a little-boy sailor suit in which I'm supposed to help him pinch a Staten Island ferry, that bothers me, that really does. So I'm out of it. You go ahead. Nothing I could say would stop you anyway, so the best thing I can do right now is go back to the apartment and start baking a rope pie to bring you in Sing Sing."

Dibley was taken aback by the outburst. "Carol, why didn't you tell me you felt this way?"

Quietly and carefully, Carol screamed. Then she said, "If I don't get out of here within sixty seconds steam will come out of my ears."

Dibley didn't argue. He walked a block, flagged down a cab and rode back in it. He changed places with Carol, who had cooled down a little.

"James, darling—"

He stopped her. "Carol, you're doing the right thing. This way if we do run into trouble we'll have somebody to come down and bail us out."

She put a hand on his arm. "Promise me the moment things look bad you'll get out of it."

Dibley promised. "Now go home and forget about the rope pie. Make lasagne instead. We'll have it tonight." He kissed her quickly and shut the door and the cab moved off. He watched it go, then turned to Swaboda. "This doesn't look like a little-boy sailor suit, does it?"

"Nah," Swaboda answered. "Not really."

They started towards the Land Rover, but the sight of Walter stopped them. It was nothing special, just Walter standing there wearing a vacant expression and a uniform three sizes too big for him. The hat rested on his ears, and the cuffs of the pants lay like a puddle over his shoes.

"Hollywood goes to war," Swaboda said.

They drove downtown.

They had one anxious moment when two policemen in a cruiser gave them a long look. "GUNS OF NAVARONE. RIALTO. NOW," one of the policemen read out.

"That was a damn good movie," his partner replied.

When they reached South Ferry they joined the line of cars waiting for the ferry to dock. This was the hard part, but Dibley managed it beautifully. When the boat arrived and the line inched forward, Dibley waited till it was their turn to drive on, cut the engine and got out and waved the other cars around him. He lifted the hood to make it look authentic. The ferry loaded and left, leaving the Land Rover right where Dibley wanted it, at the head of the line.

Dibley went over it for them. "As soon as we drive on we'll stop right there so nobody else can follow. Walter, you rush over and slide the rail across. Charlie, you get upstairs and make sure they don't let any pedestrians on. I'll tackle the captain."

And that was more or less what happened. Dibley drove the car and the gun down the ramp and onto the deck, jammed the brakes on, effectively blocking the entrance, and ran for the stairway. Swaboda wasn't far behind him. Walter was last out and went over to the deckhand standing at the rail.

"We must slide the rail across now," Walter said to him. His thin reedy voice didn't carry far in the hangarlike deck.

"What?" the deckhand said.

"We must slide the rail across now."

The deckhand dismissed him as a drunken sailor wearing somebody else's uniform. "Get outa here, will ya?"

Upstairs Swaboda was doing a little better. The man up there was giving him an argument but hadn't yet released the passenger rail. "I don't care what you say, Mac, I get paid for letting the customers on. I can't not let them on 'less the captain tells me."

"He's about to," Swaboda answered. "Just hold them for a minute. This is an emergency."

By this time Dibley was charging into the wheelhouse. "Captain," he yelled. The captain had his head out of the window trying to spot the hold-up. He banged it on the sill and came close to swallowing the cigar stub in his mouth.

"My God," he said, rubbing his head, "you're likely to give a man a heart attack jumping in like that."

Dibley threw him a fast salute. "Coast Guard, Captain. Don't let those passengers on."

The captain checked his cigar. "Why? What have they done?"

"It's an emergency, Captain. Give the order. Please."

The captain picked up a loud hailer, poked it through the window and told his crew to hold things up a minute. Then he turned back to Dibley. "Now what's this all about?"

"Captain, have you just come from Staten Island?"

"No, Europe." The captain rubbed his head again. "Of course Staten Island. I haven't come from any other place in twenty years."

"Captain," Dibley said, "we just got word there's been an outbreak of yellow fever in Saint George. We got here too late to stop your passengers, but we'll have to quarantine the boat."

The captain, who had brought his ship safely through a thousand blizzards and had once coolly navigated round a mine that had got loose in the harbor, didn't panic now. "Impossible," he declared. "We got meatloaf tonight."

"What?" Dibley said, faintly.

"It's Friday. My old lady makes meatloaf Fridays. If I don't go home tonight she'll kill me."

Dibley had expected an argument and had prepared himself with several different responses, but nothing in his preparations had included meatloaf. He decided to get dramatic. "Captain, if you make another trip to and from Saint George you might well be responsible for exposing thousands, perhaps millions, of New Yorkers to a hideous epidemic."

"Hell," the captain replied, "with all the troubles they got, pollution, crime in the streets, alligators in the sewers, they ain't even going to notice a thing like that."

"I'm sorry, sir, but the Coast Guard has ordered you to the quarantine station."

The ferry man sighed. "It's her mother's recipe. She'll kill me."

Down on the lower deck Walter was still at it. "We must slide the rail across now."

"Will ya beat it?" the deckhand shouted. "I've taken all I'm gonna take from you." He shoved Walter away and Walter sat down hard on the deck. It must have jogged the switch inside his brain because when he got up Rocky had taken over.

164

"So," he said, setting his feet and hitching. "You thought I'd be easy meat, eh, sonny? Think you're pretty handy with your dukes, huh? Well, I'll tell you something. My mother could lick you." He stabbed two fingers forward. "Her mother could lick you. Come on, you wall-eyed stumblebum, let's see what they taught you at the convent." And so saying, Rocky left.

The deckhand rushed at Walter, who said reedily, "There has been a misunder—" The deckhand hit him in the eye and Walter collapsed like a deck of cards.

In the terminal building the blocked cars had set up an insane honking, and the stalled pedestrians above them were developing into a fist-shaking mob. Swaboda burst into the wheelhouse. "Let's get out of here—they're getting up a boarding party."

The captain reluctantly picked up the loud hailer, ordered the ropes cast off and reached for the telegraph. "Why couldn't we get yellow fever Wednesday?" he said through his cigar. "We have stuffed cabbage Wednesday."

The engines shuddered and the ferry drew away from the dock amid a furious roar from the terminal.

"Er, Captain," Dibley began matter-of-factly, "there's just one thing. The mayor is naturally very worried about the epidemic threat to the city and wants to see the ferry personally."

"My wife will want to see it personally," the captain said.

"However, he's holding an official luncheon right now and can't get away. So before we sail out to the quarantine station," Dibley paused to pick a piece of lint off the captain's jacket, "would you mind if we just popped up the river to Gracie Mansion?"

The mayor got a nice hand for his little speech of official welcome and sat down smiling. At the other end of the table the mayor of Omaha got to his feet, and on behalf of the group, the mayors from Nebraska and Kansas, he thanked his host for the excellent lunch and for the hospitality that had been extended them during their stay in the city. He got a nice hand too, and then the table applied itself to cordials and cigars.

The mayor of New York had the mayor of Wichita seated on his right, and as a nice gesture and to sort of even things up the mayor of Peabody Bluffs was on his left. Throughout most of the meal he'd been deep in conversation with the Wichita man discussing the state of that city's aircraft industry and the Kansas winter wheat harvest. Now he turned to the man on his left. "Well," he said, expansively, "and how's everything out in, where is it you're from again, Moscow Corners, isn't it?"

"Peabody Bluffs," the Nebraskan answered. "Not bad, not bad at all, Mr. Mayor. Of course, our town isn't as big as New York, not nearly."

"Uh huh," said the mayor, in a way that said he was always open for a new statistic.

"But on Saturday nights it gets pretty wild."

"Lots to do, is there?" the New Yorker asked.

"Oh sure," said the Nebraskan. "And anyway, if it ever gets dull it's only twenty miles to Beaver Flats."

"How are you liking New York? There's lots to do here, too."

"Oh, I know that, Mr. Mayor, but so far I've only been doing one thing."

The mayor ashed his cigar. "What's that?"

"Getting mugged," said the man from Nebraska.

The mayor seemed surprised. "What, here in New York?"

"Yes, sir. When our plane landed and I went to the washroom I was mugged there. A man stole my watch. Then when I got to our hotel a man in the elevator pulled a knife and I had to give him my wallet."

"Why, that's terrible," the mayor of New York said.

"Then when I got into my room a man stepped out of the closet and held me up for my shoes and my Remington razor."

"But nothing's happened since then?" the mayor asked.

"No, I've stuck pretty close to the group since then."

The mayor took a thoughtful puff and frowned at his cigar. "Well, I would say you've been awfully unlucky. It's true we do have a few petty thefts now and then—we had one last Tuesday if my memory serves me right—but nothing like you describe."

"I sure am glad to hear that, Mr. Mayor. I was beginning to think everybody in this city was a mugger."

"No, no, no." The mayor was emphatic. "Why, I'll bet New York isn't any more dangerous than your town of, Turkey Crossing, is it?"

"Peabody Bluffs."

Their conversation was interrupted by an aide hurrying into the room and whispering something in the mayor's ear. The mayor excused himself and followed the man out of the dining room.

The aide started gabbling before the door was even closed. "You must come to safety, sir, immediately. There's a man on the Staten Island ferry threatening you with a gun."

"I see," the mayor said evenly. "Simpson, I thank you for your concern but I don't think there's any need for immediate panic if I am here and the man is on the Staten Island ferry."

The aide jumped up and down. "You don't understand, sir. He's on the phone now. He's calling on the ferry's ship-to-shore. The ferry's anchored in the river just off the back lawn. And they've got an army cannon."

The mayor took a moment replying. "Simpson, if somebody had told me that a few years ago, I would have said they'd been working too hard. But not today. Let's go take a look."

They moved through a series of rooms to the back of the house and came out into a small drawing room with long French windows fronting the lawn. The aide pushed binoculars into the mayor's hands—not that he needed them.

"Right there, sir, see?"

The mayor saw. "What will they think of next?" There was a note of admiration there somewhere.

His aide was a lot more worried. He hopped from foot to

foot and wrung his hands. "I don't know who they are, sir. Although I thought I could see some kind of sign on that gun."

The mayor adjusted the focus. "I can't quite . . . there it is, RIALTO. NOW."

"Cubans!" his aide cried.

"What did they want, did they say?"

"They said something about money, sir."

The mayor handed back the binoculars. "We'd better go talk to them."

They retraced their steps and entered an inner office where a phone was lying off its cradle on a desk.

"Tell them it's impossible for us to raise more than a hundred thousand," the mayor said. "Wait, I'd better tell them myself." He picked up the phone and spoke into it crisply. "This is the mayor speaking. How much do you want?" There was a pause and then the mayor slowly took the phone down from his ear.

"How much?" his aide asked fearfully.

"One hundred and fifty dollars," the mayor replied. He brought the phone up again.

"Would you hold the line, please? We may be a little while." He placed it gingerly on his desk and turned to his aide. "How much do you have on you?"

The aide checked his wallet. "About forty dollars, Mr. Mayor."

The mayor checked his. "I've got three. Better get the rest of the staff in here."

Five minutes later the cook, the butler, the chauffeur, a maid and two security men were in the room digging into billfolds and pocketbooks. The aide went up the line collecting the money and counting it out as he went.

"Seventy, eighty-five, ninety-five, one hundred seven, one hundred twenty-two, one hundred thirty-four. We're sixteen dollars short, Mr. Mayor."

The mayor coughed, a little embarrassed. "I appreciate this, everybody, and I hate to push, but we need another sixteen dollars."

"Come on, everybody," his aide said. "I want to see a sea of green."

The cook and the maid turned away and dug into their necklines and the chauffeur took off his right boot. Everybody else jingled change out of their pockets.

The aide made another collection. "Four fifty, five twenty-five, five ninety-five," he found a nickel in the lining of his jacket, "six dollars. We're still ten bucks short, Mr. Mayor."

One of the security men unholstered his gun and handed it to the mayor. "This is worth about eighty dollars, sir."

The mayor took it and examined it. "Thanks, O'Neil, but I think the people we're collecting for have all the guns they need." He sighed. "There's nothing else to do. I'll just have to borrow it from one of the guests inside."

He reentered the dining room and peered through the cigar smoke. He went over to the only person he could see who wasn't talking to anybody and drew him aside. "I'm awfully sorry to bother you with a thing like this, but I wonder if I could ask you a big favor."

"Ask away," the man replied.

The mayor brought a hand up to rub at a nonexistent itch on his cheek. He was too preoccupied to notice that he was still carrying the security man's gun. "You couldn't let me have ten dollars, could you?"

The other man dived for his pocket. "Sure. Of course. More if you want it."

"No, just the ten," the mayor said, accepting the bill. "You're very kind."

He left the room quickly.

The mayor of Peabody Bluffs let out a long breath. "Gee willikers," he said. "Even the mayor!"

In the outer office the aide had dismissed the staff and was holding the telephone out. The mayor took it. "Hello? Are you still there?"

"Still here," Dibley answered.

"We've done as you requested. We have the money for you now."

"Is it in small bills?" Dibley asked.

The mayor confirmed it. "Yes. Some of it's even in small change."

"Right. Here's what you do: Have somebody bring it out to us in a boat. And I want you to promise me something, Mr. Mayor."

"Yes?"

"When we take this ferry back to the terminal I want you to promise nobody will try to arrest us."

"You're taking it back to the terminal?"

"Right, and I want your word that there won't be a single cop within half a mile of the Battery."

"Very well," the mayor said, "you have it." He slammed his hand over the mouthpiece and said to his aide, "Get every cop in the city down to the Battery."

Dibley was speaking again. "I hope there are no hard feelings, Mr. Mayor. We're not hold-up artists, you know. This money was owed to us."

"I see."

"I wouldn't want you to think it was anything personal. I think you're doing a darn good job. I voted for you last election, and I'm going to vote for you this time too. We all are."

"Really?" The mayor held the phone a little closer. "Just how many are you?"

"Counting my girl," Dibley told him, "and my partner's mother and my other partner's two very close friends, I guess you could say there are seven of us."

"Seven," the mayor repeated.

"Well, goodbye, Mr. Mayor. And remember, you gave your word."

170

The mayor replaced the phone. He seemed miles away. "Simpson, forget what I said about the police." ,

"Forget it? You're not going to let them get away with it, sir?"

The mayor straightened his tie and smoothed his hair. "This is an election year, Simpson. We can't afford to alienate the criminal vote."

chapter 23

"They dealt the treasure house a dreadful blow . . ."

The spume of water at the bow died like a fountain being shut off, and the ship turned in a wide sweep and slowed for the Sandy Hook cutter coming towards them. Cahill puffed up the ladder to the flying bridge. "Hey, that boat . . ."

Mira told him to relax.

"The pilot," Austin said. "He won't spot us if we stay up here. He'll stick with the helmsman."

The cutter came alongside, then went away again and the destroyer picked up speed and slid past Sea Gate into the Lower Bay. The Verrazano came up fast and soared over them like an arrow and they moved into the Narrows. A stone's throw away on their left, ships worked the docks at Rosebank and Clifton, and opposite, cars zipped round the bend of Bay Ridge. The land curved away on both sides and the Upper Bay stretched in front of them six miles to the tip of Manhattan.

In the hazy distance the Wall Street buildings swept up from the water like a mountain in the sea. The ship nosed through the harbor getting closer, the buildings starting to separate and define themselves. On the Hudson side the twin towers of the Trade Center rocketed into the sky, breaking up the mountain's triangular shape and giving it a lopsided look. In the middle of the central group of buildings, surrounded by tall, slimspired structures, the thick slab of the bank reared up like a monument in a forest.

"How about it," Mira asked, "now that you see it, it's still O.K., isn't it? You can hit it O.K.?"

"No problem," Austin said. "With a gun like we've got it'll be like hitting a barn with a baseball."

They looked down at the gun mount on the bow. It squatted there like a heavy army tank, its sides smooth and rounded, twin bubbles like frog eyes on the top, the slim, tapered barrel extending fifteen feet over the deck.

Joey flicked his eyes at his brother, then ventured a question. "How do you aim a thing like that?"

Austin pointed up behind him. "You see that big steel box up there, underneath that thing that looks like a dish? That's the director. I get in there and take a fix on the building, then go back to the battery plot and press buttons. The computer does the rest. Elevates the gun, trains it, loads and fires it all automatically. That's the best ship's gun in the world." He looked back at Manhattan, very close now. "It could make a real hole in this town."

The ship had slowed to a crawl to drop the pilot, and Austin said it was time to talk to Burgess. He and Mira went down the ladder to the bridge. The captain was leaning over the wing, seeing the pilot away. When he saw the two men he dismissed the helmsman, and an officer took the wheel.

Austin said, "Skipper, I want the lieutenant to take her in slow and easy and weigh anchor just ahead of that island there, I'll tell him exactly where. And we're going to need an anchor crew ready."

Burgess okayed the instructions and went back out onto the

wing. His movements and commands were still crisp and efficient but there was a stretched grayness around his mouth and his eyes looked dead. Except for orders to do with the running of the ship he hadn't said a word to any of his officers since he'd dismissed them in the wardroom.

The destroyer approached the flat pancake of Governors Island and slid into Buttermilk Channel. When they cleared the island they were almost level with the tip of the Wall Street complex and less than a mile away. As the ship inched forward Austin watched the angle changing on the bank. The buildings around it threw up a high fence which effectively screened all but its top floors. Austin knew that the only spot where he could get a clear shot at the building was where there was a gap in the fence on the eastern side.

There was a break in the height of the buildings there between the ornamental peak of Forty Wall Street and the slim candle of the Cities Service Building. But he had to have the ship anchored in the exact spot.

"Easy now." Austin's hand moved up and down in a patting motion. "Easy . . . when I give you the word, cut the engine and get that hook down fast."

He watched the buildings sliding by the bank, high palings of glass and stone. The ship nudged through the water and the fence continued, then suddenly the top half of it was no longer there.

"Now!"

The man at the wheel shoved the telegraph and barked an order into a tube. A metallic roar lifted from the bow as the anchor splashed down into the bay. It dragged for a moment, then bit and held. The chain tightened and the capstan reversed and the ship settled rock steady in the water. It had come to rest at the entrance to the East River just off the end of Atlantic Avenue. On the Manhattan side Pier Four lay about thirteen hundred yards away. Above it, at something like a forty five-degree angle to them, the upper half of the bank stood out against the sky.

It was a fine clear day with practically no wind. A slow flowing current coming down the river moved the ship around its anchor slightly. Austin waited till the ship had stopped swinging, then spoke to the helmsman.

"Lieutenant, I'm going to let you in on a little secret. I'm going to put a shell into one of those buildings over there. Now before you get excited, let me tell you that nobody's going to get blown away, that is, as long as you keep this ship pointing right where she's pointing now. Do you think you can do that?"

The officer said he could.

"Fine. I don't want this ship swinging one degree till we up anchor again."

Austin left the bridge and descended to the main deck, hurried aft, went through a doorway and down another deck. The crewmen he passed didn't take any notice of him. He fished out the key the chief had given him and let himself into the battery plot. It was a small room stuffed full of computer banks with a central console. He sat down at it, clicked switches and brought the room to life. Dials glowed and needles flickered and a soft electric humming filled the air. He left the room, locked it behind him and went back up to the bridge. He passed the silent captain still standing on the wing and climbed one more ladder to the flying bridge. He said nothing to Mira or the other two but moved by them and started up the rungs that were set into the side of the steel box. He went up them quickly, opened the tiny hatch at the top and disappeared inside.

He settled himself in the seat and put his eye to the telescope and pressed a button. The director slowly revolved and the image of the buildings moved in front of his eyes like a strip of film. When the bank appeared he released the button, jabbed it once to center the building and increased the magnification. The bank zoomed at him, filled his vision, the telescope seeming to press against the high glass windows, picking out shapes moving behind them. He elevated slightly, took a quick look without the scope, then went back to the eyepiece. He adjusted it a touch, then locked on, read off wind speed and direction, corrected for parallax and punched a button.

A radar beam leapt across the water, bounced off the bank and sped back again. A miracle clock timed the trip and flashed the figures to an electronic brain. Circuits closed and relays clicked and the range was computed.

Austin climbed out of the box and clambered down the rungs, ignored the three men again and made his way back to the battery plot.

The room was full of whirs and clicks and smelled of electricity and magnetic tape. He went to the console and fed in information: initial velocity, dead time, wind speed and direction, negative ship/target, speed and course. He closed a row of switches and waited while the computer figured train and elevation and parallax angle. A red light blinked, and out on deck the gun mount began to move.

A warning bell clanged as it shifted on its oiled track and revolved ponderously to its left. The black gaping mouth of the barrel rose towards the sky and seemed to sniff the air like a blind animal searching for something. It came to a halt simultaneously with the turret, and the ringing stopped.

On the console the red light turned green.

Austin, very carefully, set the gun for single action, turned a key in the console and left the room, double locking it behind him.

He found Mira on deck. "O.K.," he said, "let's go talk to the radioman."

"Chase Manhattan . . ."
"I want to talk to a vice-president fast."
"Anybody in particular, sir?"
"Somebody with an office who can see the harbor."
"I'll try, sir, but most of our executives are on the sixteenth." The operator held the call and checked with a supervisor who gave her a number. Mira heard a phone being picked up, then a different woman's voice, a sharper one.

"Mr. Peterson's desk."

"Put him on."

"Who is this, please?"

"Never mind, just put him on."

A phone buzzed in an office and a slim thirty-year-old man pushed at the horn rims on his nose and picked up the handpiece.

"Mr. Peterson, there's a man on the line who won't give his name but insists on speaking with you. He sounds angry."

"Thanks, Millie. Put him through."

"Mr. Peterson for you."

"Hello, can I help you?"

"Listen and listen good. I'm not kidding and I'm not playing games. This is a stickup. A real live stickup. Just look out your window and you'll see what I mean."

"Who is this?"

"Who cares? All you need to know is that right now you got a five-inch navy gun pointing right at you."

"I see."

"No you don't. You think I'm a nut. You can see down the bay from your office, right?"

"Yes I can."

"Well, take a look off Governors Island and tell me if you don't see a destroyer there."

"Oh yes, I see it," Peterson said, his back to the window.

"You don't believe a word I'm saying but you're going to. I'll call back in five minutes. You talk to your boss. Tell him to get ready to clear a few floors. And tell him to make sure the vault's open for business."

Peterson listened to the caller hang up and replaced the phone himself. He swiveled in his chair and squinted through the window down the bay. He turned back, drummed his fingers on the desk for a moment, then reached for the phone.

"Millie, get Jack Ekman for me, would you?" He took another look while he waited.

"Hello, Jack? I've got a new one for you. I just got a call from a guy who's threatening to bombard us from a destroyer in the harbor. How about that?"

"Not bad. I don't think we've ever had one of those. Can you see a destroyer?"

"Sure, in the East River. Some kind of navy ship anyway."

"What did this man say?"

"Something about keeping the vault open and clearing the place. He said he'd call back in a few minutes."

"I doubt you'll hear from him. These people usually get their jollies from one phone call. That's one good thing about them, they don't pester you all day."

"I thought I'd better report it anyway, Jack. If nothing else it's good for a laugh in the bar car tonight."

"You did the right thing. Don't forget, we've got that meeting at four."

Peterson told him he'd see him then and replaced the phone. He went back to the memo he was drafting, taking some care with it.

The phone buzzed again.

"That man's on the phone again, Mr. Peterson. The one who called before and wouldn't give his name."

"Put him through, Millie."

"Peterson?"

"Yes."

"You had a chance to talk it up yet?"

"Look, fella, I'm going to hang up now. Don't call again because you won't get through."

"I want to tell you something, Peterson. I figured you'd take me for a nut, so I got a little demonstration lined up for you. Clear everybody out of the fortieth floor and a couple above and below. Twenty minutes from now you're going to get a shell through one of your windows up there, so if you end up with ambulances outside don't say I didn't warn you."

"Wait a second . . ."

"Twenty minutes."

"Hello . . . ?" The bank man hung up, opened a bottom drawer, took out some binoculars and went to the window. He took a long hard look at what he saw, then got his secretary to get Ekman for him.

"Jack, that guy called again. Do you think you could come up here? I want you to take a look at this." He hung up and went back to the window. He was still standing there when the door opened and a man walked in. He was a big man, a good ten pounds overweight, which the cut of his suit did a lot to hide. His hair was gray at the sides and beginning to patch on top. He was speaking as he came through the door.

"So much for my predictions. What did he say this time?"

"He claimed he was going to put a shell in the fortieth floor to show us they mean business. He said in twenty minutes." He handed Ekman the binoculars. "You see it there, just in front of the island?" Ekman took the glasses. "I may be wrong, but it strikes me that whenever I've seen a warship the guns have been pointing where the ship's pointing. That gun's pointing right down our throats." Ekman turned back from the window. "The things people notice. Somebody over in Brooklyn saw where that gun was pointing and decided to have a little fun." He handed back the binoculars. "It's the wildest thing I've ever heard of, but with that gun positioned the way it is we'll have to treat it as a genuine threat. We'll have to clear some floors. It's ridiculous, but we'll have to do it."

"How about calling the Coast Guard and getting them to check on the ship?"

"We'd still have to clear the floors while we were doing it. He said twenty minutes?"

Peterson looked at his watch. "Fifteen now."

"Call Security and get them to handle it. Get them to tell the staff we've had another bomb threat. Hell, we may as well go the whole hog; get our fire department to stand by too." Peterson picked up a phone. "Damn it," Ekman said, "these

178

people cost us a fortune. Why can't they ever call on a Sunday?"

The red sweep hand circled the bottom of the clock and started its climb again. It appeared to accelerate as it passed the nine and seemed to Mira to take a lot less than fifteen seconds to reach the twelve.

"Bingo," Austin said and moved his hand.

Mira said, "Maybe we'd better give them a little more time."

"Why? We gave them fair warning."

"A couple more minutes couldn't hurt."

"I'm not so sure. We said twenty minutes, we should be on the dot. We're going to have to bargain with those people. We have to show them we mean what we say."

"They'll know it when that shell hits them. It's just going to be easier all round if nobody gets hurt."

"I can't guarantee that."

Mira stiffened. "What do you mean? You told me you could put a shell in there right where you wanted it."

"I can," Austin said. "But there are always variables that can affect a shot. A last minute puff of breeze, a slight drift of the ship, the projectile itself . . . no two shells are exactly the same; you never really know what kind of shot you've got till it hits."

"Are you telling me you're going to be lucky to hit that bank?"

"I'll hit it, don't worry about that." Austin glanced up at the clock. "I'm just saying you shouldn't be surprised if there's maybe a casualty or two."

"Look, what we're doing, hijacking a navy ship, firing on the city and everything, they're going to come after us in droves. But if we knock off people while we're doing it they'll never go away. Ever. There are a lot of guys who robbed banks sitting in the sun in Florida. Not that many killers."

The thought didn't bother the gunner; he remained as casual and as genial as he'd been the first day Mira had met him. "I just wanted you to get the picture," he said. "I just checked the wind and there's hardly a breath of air. And the helmsman's holding it steady. If they've cleared four floors that should give me plenty of latitude as long as we don't have a wild shell. But I'll tell you this, if we wait much longer they may decide it's safe to go back in again."

When Mira didn't answer Austin faced the console again. "Why don't you go out on deck and enjoy the fireworks?"

It was a vast room running clear around the top floor of the building, private dining rooms on the western side, the board dining room splitting them up, kitchen and serving areas hidden at the back, and on the eastern side, where the men were standing, black leather Eames chairs were set in ordered groups around marble-topped tables.

Ekman, in front of the glass wall that faced the harbor, took the binoculars away from his eyes to look at his watch. Peterson was checking his too.

"They're three minutes late," Peterson said.

Ekman brought the binoculars up again. "What a surprise. How about it, John," he was speaking to the security man next to him, "shall we give it another ten— *My God!*"

Everybody else had seen it too, a black cloud exploding out of the gun.

Moments later they heard the boom, dulled by distance and the heavy plate glass.

"They did it," Peterson said. "They fired that thing."

Ekman said, "But did they hit us?"

A jangling phone answered his question even before the security man snatched it up. The man listened a moment, then burst into speech. "Forty-one. The fire panel's going crazy."

The three of them jumped for the elevator. They lost time

waiting for it to rise and more time switching elevators on forty-seven.

The acrid reek hit them as the doors opened on forty-one. They dashed down a corridor, a smell like hot needles in their nostrils, the heat already reaching for them. They ran round a corner into a chaos of noise and flame and boiling smoke. The place was awash in a roaring, flaming surf that broke against the walls and over the ceiling. The shell had smashed through a window, ripped through an interior wall and exploded in an open office area. The flare that had starred from the shell had sent a dozen rockets of white-hot phosphorus smashing into desks and cabinets and glass partitions. The phosphorus dripped in thick flaming globular balls, slid down walls and moved on the carpet like a river of lava. Claws of violent heat scratched at them, tried to peel their skins away, the incandescent brightness too harsh for their uncovered eyes. A stifling amalgam of cordite, chemical fumes, melting metal and burning plastic and fiber grabbed for the backs of their throats, drove them choking back up the corridor. Security firemen tumbled by them, ran out hoses, shouted to each other, tried to get in close. The hoses filled and swelled and gushed water that was sucked dry by the flames. The flare was a giant firework whose chemical fire would have burned on an iceberg. But like a firework it had its climax and it roared to it, flaming hotter and brighter than ever, then it eased off and started to die. A man in a fire suit spraying foam ahead of him got a wall under control, then another. A third wall spluttered under the weight of water battering at it. The heat lessened, the roaring dropped and the blue-white glare began to dull. The phosphorus burned itself out and the fire beneath it was quickly killed by the hoses.

The noise and the frantic action was replaced by a hot sizzling silence. A thin drizzle rained down from the ceiling like the aftermath of a squall, the water hissing angrily where it fell. The entire area was a charred and flooded wreck. Steel desks lay blackened and twisted out of shape, the typewriters that had rested on them warped and burned, their keys a dark green jelly. Partitions leaned in and out crumpled like tissues, the glass in them melted or littered over the floor. The carpet was all but gone, tiny islands of it smoldering here and there. The acoustic insulation on the ceiling had disappeared completely, leaving a scorched tangle of wires dangling down. Against a wall a filing cabinet drawer hung out crazily, blown open by the explosion, its twisted metal divisions separating nothing but soggy black ashes.

Ekman pulled out a handkerchief and wiped at something at the corner of his mouth. He said as steadily as he could to the security man at his side, "Get everybody out of the building. Then call the police department and tell them we have an emergency on our hands."

The man ran off looking for a usable phone. Ekman grabbed Peterson's elbow and they hurried together back down the corridor and into an elevator. "I want all senior V.P.'s in my office in five minutes. No, better make it your office. I want to be there when that guy calls back. When's that supposed to be?"

"He didn't say any special time."

Ekman said, "I'll tell the chief myself. Christ, I wouldn't have believed this could happen in a million years. Not in a million years."

When they reached Peterson's office his secretary came flapping up to them. "It's that same man calling again, Mr. Peterson. He's being very rude to me and I didn't know—"

"Put him through, Millie." They went by her into the office and Peterson jumped for the phone. "Hello?"

"Peterson? Do you believe me now?"

"Hold on, please, I'm putting you through to a senior officer."

Ekman took the phone and spoke into it hard and sharp. "What do you want?"

"I'll tell you what I want. I want you to go down into your vault and get five million dollars."

"Five *million* . . . ?"

"I want you to pack the money into three suitcases. Then I want you to take them up onto the roof and put them into the helicopter that's coming over."

"You're crazy. We can't take a loss like that."

"You're in for a lot bigger loss if you don't."

"What you're asking's impossible. Our vault's closed. It's on time locks. We couldn't open it even if we wanted to."

"Don't hand me that crap."

"It's the truth. The only money we have is what's in the cashiers' drawers. It's not peanuts, two hundred thousand, maybe more. That's all we've got to give you."

"Nice try," Mira said. "Now I'm going to tell you this just once. You've got thirty minutes to get five million up onto the roof. And it had better all be there. If you're short you won't get just another starshell through your window, you'll get the whole magazine, high explosives this time."

"Listen to me—"

"Twenty-nine and a half minutes now."

They had twenty-six minutes left when the police arrived—three detectives and a group of patrolmen. Ekman briefed the senior lieutenant, who sent one of his men upstairs to check on the damage. His partner stood at the window with binoculars and read off the number painted on the destroyer's bow. He reached for a phone. The lieutenant gave him a fast string of orders. "I want to know everything about it: its name, where it came from, its captain. But call in first and get hold of Underhill and fill him in. Tell him to call Floyd Bennett Field for a couple of choppers. I want the Coast Guard, the harbor master, the harbor precinct in, too. And tell everybody I want a tight lid on this thing. There are a dozen other people who should know about this, and they're going to scream, but the fewer in on it the better."

The other detective was dialing. "How about the Bureau?"

The lieutenant made a face. "Yeah, I guess so. No way to keep them out."

Peterson's secretary bustled in, a young man in tow. She said to Ekman, "This is Mr. Garelli, sir, from Accounts. Personnel sent him."

"I thought I'd see if we had anybody on the staff who knew something about destroyers," Ekman told the lieutenant.

"Good thought."

"Thanks for coming," Ekman said to the man. "You probably heard we had a bomb go off on forty-one, which is why we're clearing the building. We'll only keep you a minute."

Garelli, short and dark haired, said he wasn't worried.

The detective asked him if he'd been in the navy.

"Yes, sir. I served eighteen months on destroyers with the Sixth Fleet. Weapons Officer."

"Then we can use you," the policeman said. He handed over binoculars and picked up a pair for himself. "Would you take a look at that ship on the river down there and tell us what you know about it?"

The man stepped to the window and brought the glasses up. "Oh sure, that's a Ten-Fifty-Two Destroyer Escort."

"You're sure about that . . . ?"

"Yes, sir, you can't miss them. The clean look, straight up and down. And the mack structure amidships. The other class DD's have mostly twin stacks raked back fast. After gun mounts too."

"They carry a helicopter, right?"

"Yes, sir, they do. An SH ThreeD most likely. You can see the pad, that flat deck near the stern. That's the hangar forward of it."

"What about the ship's armaments?"

"I can tell you," Garelli said, "a new Knox boat like that's got the works. The five-inch, torpedo tubes, ASROC and Sea Sparrow as well."

"What are they exactly?"

"ASROC's an anti-sub defense. See that pepper box back of the gun mount? That's it. It's an eight-tube launcher. Fires a missile that carries a depth charge or a torpedo to the target area. It drops into the water near the sub and it's all over."

184

"And the other one?"

"Sea Sparrow? That's an anti-aircraft missile system. It uses two tubes of the ASROC box."

"Anti-aircraft," Ekman broke in. "Could it be used against a target on shore?"

"Surface-to-surface, surface-to-shore, anything you like," Garelli replied.

"What kind of warhead?"

"Conventional or nuclear. All the torpedos and missiles on that ship can carry both."

Ekman glanced at the detective but he was already asking the navy man another question. "What about that gun, that five-inch? What can you tell me about that?"

"Mark forty-two," Garelli said. "One-twenty-seven mil, fifty-four caliber linked with a Mark fifty-six radar system. It's dual purpose, automatic and rapid firing, and it can hit anything on the nose within a ten-mile range. It's a gold-plated wonder."

"What's its rate of fire?"

"Forty rounds a minute."

"Forty . . ." Ekman barely said the word.

The lieutenant thanked Garelli for his help, and Ekman told him to keep the meeting confidential. When the door had closed behind him Ekman sat down in a chair.

"Forty rounds a minute. . . . One flare ripped the hell out of us. You can imagine what thirty or forty high explosive shells would do."

From the window Peterson said, "Just our records alone. In sixty seconds those people could set us back a couple of years."

The lieutenant checked the time. "Mr. Ekman, there's not much we can do. We have one hell of a threat sitting down there on the river, and to remove it we'd have to bring up another navy ship or call in an airstrike. And we can't do that because we'd never clear the harbor in time and that ship's too close to Brooklyn anyway. For another thing, we don't know who's on board. And there's a bigger problem," the detective said. "Normally it'd be your decision whether to pay or not if you were held up. But in this case there are a lot of other people to be considered. They've fired one shell and hit you, but that's no guarantee they might not hit somebody else if they unloaded the lot on you. So while the bank can decide on its own to say yes and pay the money, it can't decide on its own to say no. It's a very unfair situation you're in."

"I know it," Ekman said.

"As I see it, Mr. Ekman, all you can do is give them the money now and we'll bust a gut to get it back later. Believe me, whoever they are they can't get away with something this big. That ship's obviously going to wait till dark, then make a run for it. Once it's out of the harbor things will be different."

Ekman walked to the window. He smoothed his hair back as if he were looking at his reflection rather than the ship on the river. He seemed a long way away. "You know, a British ship did this once, when they saw Seventeen Seventy-Six coming. Anchored off the city just like that destroyer's doing, a man-o'-war. They didn't want money, just wanted to show the folks who was boss. The city was all wood then, of course, and would have gone up just like that. O.K., it's steel and concrete now, but it's just as vulnerable as it was then. I never realized how vulnerable. Look at us, perched on the very edge of the coast, wide open to the ocean. Our business headquarters, our banks, the stock exchanges, all the things that make America hum sitting on the water like ducks on a pond." He turned back to the room. "What if that ship decided to take it out on the city itself, turn its gun on the Brooklyn Bridge or lob a missile into Times Square or drop a depth charge on the Lincoln Tunnel? Nuclear stuff. How do you put a price tag on a couple of million people? The enemy isn't a foreign country anymore. It's small groups of desperate people, like the one I suspect has taken over that destroyer. And whether they're motivated by politics or madness or sheer greed, if they can turn our own weapons on us they can make us dance."

The lieutenant was looking at his watch. "I'll have to ask you to make a decision, Mr. Ekman."

Ekman turned back to the window. "It's already been made. They made it for us when they fired that gun."

chapter 24

". . . a brave but foolish person"

Harvey Baden was the switchboard operator at the Fiftieth precinct in the West Forties, which was not what Harvey wanted to be. Harvey wanted to be a detective. Since he was sixteen he'd wanted to be a detective. He couldn't imagine anything more exciting than stealing up to a hideout in silent unmarked cars, surrounding the place and with his men in position, guns peeking over car hoods and spotlights ready, raising a bull horn to his mouth and saying, "Give up now, Mad Dog, you'll never make it," like they did on the TV shows. Harvey had practiced this line for years using a thick cardboard mailing tube that echoed nicely and gave his rather high voice a deep manly tone. There was a stage, the year the Mets won the Series, when he had switched to, "Now batting, number fourteen, Harvey . . . Baden." But that didn't last long and he soon went back to making predictions about Mad Dog's chances.

Harvey figured that his path to detective status would be a simple straight line: He'd join the force, make patrolman, do something heroic and be promoted to the plain-clothes division. The force took him happily enough; he was well over the required height even if he was a little slimmer than they liked them, and he got on well with everybody. He was a pleasant young man with a mop of red hair, not too red, and a nice open face dotted with freckles left over from childhood. He graduated from the police academy and went from rookie to patrolman with an unblemished record. But then his plan seemed to have bogged down. Nothing heroic happened. He did have one chance but he flubbed it miserably. As he passed by an apartment house on Madison a doorman had rushed out and grabbed him and told him that they had a thief cornered on the ninth floor. Harvey had raced up there in time to see a man fleeing down the corridor and disappearing into an apartment. Harvey had bolted after him and arrived outside the wrong door. Behind that door a very good friend of a powerful man in local government was in bed with his much younger wife. He was getting on in years and not the man he once had been, and he was huffing and puffing and trying his best for her. Harvey had thumped on the door and delivered the line he'd waited years to say: "Give up now, Mad Dog, you'll never make it." The thief got away, but they caught Harvey, and he was transferred to the switchboard, where he could do no more harm.

However, this hadn't cooled Harvey's ambition, and he figured that at the very least his new job made him party to inside information—information he could use to his advantage when the time came. He was going to make detective yet. When the call came through for the precinct captain that Friday afternoon, Harvey put it through and listened in as he always did.

The captain's name was Ralph E. Marble, known as Shazam by the entire New York City Police Department. The nickname was a fairly recent acquisition. When he'd been Officer Marble and Sergeant Marble and Lieutenant Marble, everybody had just called him Ralphie. But when he'd made Captain, things had changed. His rank and name were too natural an association to resist. Even strangers couldn't resist it. At a police party or a bowling night or at a PBA meeting somebody would introduce him to a cop from out of town.

"Lieutenant Branigan, Captain Marble."

"Shazam!" the stranger would say.

The captain had once thought about getting a new name and had gone to see a lawyer about it. The lawyer had told him that you had to have a pretty good reason to change your name in New York and asked him what his was.

"The unfortunate combination of my name and rank in the Police Department," he'd replied.

"What's that?" the lawyer asked.

"Captain Marble."

"Shazam!" the lawyer had cried.

The captain had kept his name and, by doing so, his nickname too. It was a little unfair, because the captain couldn't have looked less like his comic strip namesake. Instead of Captain Marvel's giant frame, bulging muscles, black wavy hair and beetle brows, Ralph Marble was a bald and paunchy fifty-three. He came bouncing out of his office, the phone call still fresh in his ears.

"Baden," he yelled. "Baden, get my wife on the phone, then get everybody in here on the double. On the double."

He bounced back into his office, a plump rubber ball, too excited to sit down. "By golly," he said aloud, "the biggest thing to hit the Fiftieth in years." He snatched up the phone that buzzed on his desk. "Hello, May? Listen, May, something big's come up, I mean really big. A colossal robbery down in Wall Street. Just about every precinct in the city's involved. . . . Yes, the Fiftieth too. It's finally happening, May, something I've waited years for. Go out and buy a new dress. If one of my men can make the arrest, the Commissioner's going to have to invite us to dinner."

Out at the switchboard Harvey was still trying to recover from the first phone call. A heist of staggering proportions and it was going on now, so there was still time for him to play a part. Captain Marble's words came back to him; If one of his men made the arrest . . . He was one of his men, wasn't he?

Another young officer, a friend of Harvey's, came through the door and checked in.

"Fred," Harvey said, "I won't be wearing this uniform much longer."

"You joining the Boy Scouts?" his friend asked.

"Fred, the only way I'm going to get out from behind this board is to get out from behind it and do something." He took off the headpiece and held it out. "Take over for me, will you? If Shazam asks for me tell him I've gone home sick."

The other man accepted the headphone. "O.K., you owe me a favor."

Harvey went to the locker room, changed, tucked his gun carefully into his belt holster, went out onto the sidewalk and was confronted by his first problem: transportation. Harvey didn't own a car and had no access to one. And no detective ever operated without a car. He could rent one, but it wouldn't have a police radio and he'd be lost without that. What he needed was a squad car, but he couldn't get one without the captain's signature. He decided to go down to the garage and take a look around anyway. There were always a couple of cars being serviced down there; maybe he could borrow one unofficially.

Still thinking it was a good idea he walked briskly to his left and down a long ramp into the basement. There were three green and white cruisers there, and a mechanic was deep inside one of them. He wasn't too crazy about borrowing a cruiser: too easy to spot. He was beginning to wonder if he'd have to walk when he saw the solution parked near the entrance: Captain Marble's Plymouth. The captain drove in from Jersey every day and parked in the precinct garage. Being a keen hunter he had a big station wagon equipped with everything including, Harvey knew, a police radio. It was perfect. The captain would be at his desk till all hours; Harvey could take it and bring it back, and the captain would never know. Even better, he could take it and bring it back with those bank robbers bound hand and foot. Harvey could see it clearly—it was almost a premonition—that's exactly what was going to happen. And to give weight to his conviction he saw that the key was in the ignition.

Harvey got into the captain's car, started it, drove unnoticed up the ramp onto West Forty-seventh and headed for the Battery.

chapter 25

"... returning from the palace of the vizier"

Dibley opened the paper bag again and took another delighted peek inside. "Look at it, real money. Who said you can't fight City Hall?"

"They're a pushover," Swaboda said.

Dibley sealed the bag again. "A hundred and a half, enough to buy a car and a steak for Walter's eye. How would you like that, Walter?"

Walter, holding one hand over his eye like a man taking a reading test, said, "I'd like it."

They were standing on the stern of the ferry enjoying the view and the euphoric feeling of having successfully gouged their pound of flesh from the city. Swaboda said he'd never had so much fun. "I had a ball working that cannon, raising and lowering it, sighting it, pulling the trigger. It must have looked like the real McCoy. Incidentally," he said to Dibley, "how did you get the captain out of the way to use the ship-to-shore?"

"I used the one in the other wheelhouse. I unplugged his before we left. I didn't want the terminal asking him what he was doing on the river. He would have told them."

Swaboda tapped a finger against his temple. "Dibley, you've got it up here."

Dibley returned the compliment. "You did O.K. yourself, Charlie. Whatever reason you gave the captain for that guy rowing out to us, it must have been a good one."

Swaboda modestly looked down at his shoes. "It was nothing. I simply told him that the mayor was crazy about the Staten Island ferry hot dogs."

"I thought I saw you hand that man something," Dibley said. He thought back on it. "I only hope the mayor didn't take it the wrong way."

They turned their attention back to the river scene. In the bright, windless afternoon the city looked great. Even Welfare Island, which normally reminded Dibley of a burned-out liner, lost a little of its drabness. They slipped in and out of the thundering shadow of the Queensborough Bridge and waved cheerfully to the maids walking their big English prams in the little cement park at Sutton Place. The UN came up, the sun flaring through its green glass walls, then the Newtown Creek on the opposite bank, a cesspool of beached junk and floating oil. It too looked a little more respectable on such a fine day.

They slid under the Williamsburg Bridge and turned the corner of the Lower East Side. Ahead of them the Manhattan and Brooklyn Bridges formed a double cat's cradle over the river.

"Yikes!" The placid smile on Swaboda's face vanished. "I've just thought of something. The quarantine station."

Dibley sounded as though he'd been stabbed. "The quarantine station. We're going there . . . we'll have to get out of it. Maybe we can tell the captain that the guy who rowed out to us said the yellow fever scare is over."

"He'd never buy it. We've already got him convinced they're going round Staten Island burning people's underwear."

They fell into a moody silence, their brilliant triumph and the fine weather forgotten. Dibley watched the traffic running up and down the elevated highway back of the Fulton Street wharves. He was thinking hard but something was bothering him, pinging away at the edges of his brain trying to get his attention. Then he realized that it was the traffic itself that was flagging him down.

"Hey," he said, "do you guys see anything funny about that traffic over there?" The other two looked hard, Swaboda through two eyes, Walter through one.

Dibley said, "Am I seeing things or is there a predominance of police cruisers?"

"A very big predominance," Swaboda said. "And they're all heading in the same direction."

"South," Walter said.

"Towards the Battery," Dibley said. He thumped the rail. "I knew it. I knew the mayor would take it the wrong way. He thinks we charged him a hundred and fifty bucks for a hot dog."

Swaboda looked bitter. "Whatever the reason, it's all over. There's no place we can land where they won't be waiting to grab us. We're doomed to sail the harbor forever."

"No we're not," Dibley said, his face expanding like a sunrise. "Look at us, what are we wearing?"

The other two checked their clothes. "Navy uniforms," Swaboda answered.

"And what do you see ahead of us there?" They followed Dibley's pointing finger.

"Well, what do you know," Swaboda said, getting the message. "A destroyer."

chapter 26

". . . although their plan, upon examination . . ."

When nobody answered the door the two men walked round the back to a wide, deep lawn hedged in on three sides, a child's swing set and a covered sandbox in one corner. There was nobody there, either. Next door a woman was raking leaves under an elm tree. They went over to the hedge and spoke to the woman, showed their badges and started asking questions. The woman couldn't help them. "She could be at the store. Or she might have left early to pick up Lisa from school. That's her little girl."

"Which school is that?"

"Saint Michael's Kindergarten. It's not far."

"Do you know if she goes anywhere special on a Friday, bridge or bowling, anything like that?"

The woman thought about it. "Now wait a minute, I think it was last Friday Marion came over for coffee, so if she does go to any of those things you mentioned I don't think it's anything regular."

One of the men flipped through a notebook. "Could you tell us if she's still driving a white Volkswagen?"

"Far as I know. It was parked out front yesterday. As a matter of fact she might have driven it up to Providence today. I know she goes up there now and then to the department stores. She could be up there."

The men asked her to get in touch with them if her neighbor turned up. The woman leaned on her rake and watched them walk away across the lawn, worried by their questions.

One of the men, the younger one, said, "Think we should look inside?"

"Definitely."

He produced a bunch of keys and fiddled at the front-door lock till he found one that worked. They walked into a quiet that seemed to be more than just an echo of emptiness, that kind of dead silence that follows a sudden loud noise. The younger man went upstairs and his senior took the ground floor. He went through the living and dining rooms and out into the kitchen and the laundry, pausing in each room, checking things like a man come to give an estimate.

His partner came down the stairs and joined him in the kitchen. "The little girl wasn't at school today. They phoned here about ten-thirty but got no answer." He looked around him. "Maybe she went to Providence like her neighbor says."

"I doubt they'd go all that way without breakfast."

"Somebody had breakfast, there are dishes in the sink."

"That's breakfast for one. So it was probably Burgess."

"She could have stopped for something on the way."

"Not with a kid. Wait till you're a father, Mannie, you'll find out. I've never known one yet who didn't get out of bed hungry as a horse, or a mother who'll let her child go out on a cold morning without eating. Find anything upstairs?"

"Pajamas and gown on the bed, a drawer left open. Same thing in the kid's room. The beds are unmade."

"It doesn't add up, Mannie. Look at this place, neat as a pin. Clean ashtrays, cushions plumped up—she's a good housekeeper, this lady. But then you've got clothes lying around, drawers left open, a glass of booze over there, some of it spilled. And the dishes half done, that's what bothers me most. She fixes breakfast for her husband and being the kind of woman she is washes up as she goes. So you've got a juice glass and a plate in the drying rack. But why leave a cup and saucer and a knife unwashed? A little thing, I know, but it doesn't gel."

"You're thinking she was interrupted."

"It would make sense. Four men drive into the base with a message for an officer, a fifteen-year man with a perfect record. Six hours later his ship is holding up a bank in New York. It must have been some message they handed him."

The younger man started to reply but stopped when he saw the change coming over his partner's face. He watched, surprised, as the man turned and bolted through the door and down the path. He ran after him and saw him jump into the car and start talking to the radio mike.

"George, buzz Wagner out at the navy base, quick. Tell him to put the gate messenger on, you got that? The gate messenger." He looked up as the other man reached him. "I should turn in my badge, I really should."

"What's up?"

"Tell you in a minute."

The radio crackled and a voice said, "Lieutenant, I've got him right here. Hold on." Then a different voice spoke. "Hello?"

"This is Lieutenant Kas; I was talking to you a little while ago. Now listen, that envelope that guy gave you for Commander Burgess, you said you could feel something inside it, like a marble you said."

"Yes sir, that's right."

"Could it have been a piece of jewelry, a pin or an earring, say?"

"A piece of jewelry? Well, it was small and hard like that. Yes sir, I guess it could have been. Sure."

"Thanks, that's all." The policeman thumbed the button on the mike. "George, get me Carlson, quick." He looked up at his partner. "You got a date tonight?"

"Uh huh."

"Cancel it."

The radio spoke. "Lieutenant?"

196

"John, get out an all-points on a white VW, license number"—he clicked his fingers and his partner leaned over to the mike and supplied it. "Then call Captain Wheaton, that's Wheaton, at the navy base and get a description of Burgess' wife and child and get that out. Statewide, Massachusetts, too. I want every hotel, motel, rooming house, you name it, checked and a run down on every couple with a little girl who've checked in since this morning. Start in the immediate area and work outwards."

"Lieutenant," the voice said, "this is going to take forever."

"It'd better not. I don't think that family's got forever."

chapter 27

". . . and, mounting a winged horse, stole a king's ransom . . ."

Joey shaded his eyes and looked up at the helicopters. There were two of them in the sky flying in wide circles above them, hovering from time to time, then flitting off for another circuit. In the water, one on either side of them, one ahead, three police launches moved at a much slower rate, their engines barely ticking over, the long fast-looking boats built for speed, slightly nose down at the bow. A quarter mile away a Coast Guard cutter steamed nervously back and forth.

Austin said, "What with the choppers and the police boats and the Coast Guard spotted round the harbor I'll bet there must be fifty pairs of binoculars on us right now."

Joey said, "I guess they can see us up here, huh?"

"Sure, they know what we look like. They'll have photographed us nine ways to Sunday by now."

"We should've stayed out of sight," Cahill said. "Mira was dumb not to think of it."

Joey said mildly, "Frank figures there's no need. Five million's going to get us so far away they can't touch us."

"How far? He saying we got to leave the country?"

"I guess."

Cahill scowled at the news. "First I heard of it. Maybe I don't want to leave the country."

Joey held his reply when he saw his brother coming up on deck.

"What's holding the helicopter up?" he snapped at Austin. "We're cutting it too close."

"They're getting it out now. Just wait a moment."

Mira was too edgy to wait. "I'm going to see what's holding them up."

"Hold it." Austin said fast. "You're supposed to be a technician, remember. Don't go talking to the air crew."

Mira leveled an angry finger at him. "Don't tell me what to do. I'm running this thing. Your part's over, mine isn't. So stay out of my way. Come on, Joey." Mira went down the ladder and his brother followed him.

Austin said to Cahill, "He's not going to choke, is he?"

Cahill's mouth turned sour. "The guy don't have it. I had to nurse him through every job we ever done." He looked at Austin, uneasy. "What do we do if the crew tumbles?"

"The crew only knows what they're told."

"What about when you fired the gun, what did they tell them about that?"

"They thought that was a salute."

"They didn't see the shell hit the bank?"

"Not unless they were watching for it. Incidentally," Austin said smiling, "how about that shot? Right through the window."

Cahill wasn't impressed. "You had a lot to aim at."

"I would've had more to aim at if we'd been going after a

bank in that building." He indicated the Trade Center Towers. "How many windows would you say are in those things?"

"Christ knows."

"Have a guess."

"I don't know, ten thousand, twenty thousand."

"Near enough forty-four thousand. Quarter-inch tempered plate glass."

"How do you know a thing like that?"

"I know a lot about those buildings," Austin said. "Thirteen-fifty feet high, one hundred and ten stories, two hundred thousand tons of steel, six hundred thousand square feet of glass. Load-bearing exterior walls tied to horizontal spandrel beams. They built them to last."

Cahill looked at him. "What are you, a building freak?"

Austin turned in Cahill's direction, his eyes still focused for distance. "Yes, that's right. Let's go aft and see how they're doing."

They went down to the main deck and walked through to the stern. The ship was roughly divided into three parts; the multitiered bridge structure towards the bow, the rectangular missile launcher and the gun mount in front of it; the clean, neat clutter of the midships section, with its black-painted radar rigs perched on top of the high cylinder that hid the engine exhausts; and the double-decked open space of the flight pad and the fantail at the stern.

The helicopter, a Sea King, was being wheeled out of the hangar when they got there, its tail assembly hinged back on itself and its rotor blades folded together along the fuselage like an insect's wings that had stuck together.

Cahill regarded it, uncertain. "Those things safe? I ain't ever been in a plane before, let alone one of those."

"Safe enough," Austin said.

Mira hurried up to them. "That's the pilot, the guy putting the helmet on, right?"

"That's him."

Mira crossed to him. "You flying this thing?"

199

"Yes." He was a young lieutenant and he was scared. He'd been scared over in Nam with the shore batteries coming close sometimes, but that had been a different kind of fear, a shared fear; what happened to him happened to the ship. But in a few minutes he'd be on his own with these hoods, and if things didn't go right he'd be within easy reach.

Mira could see that he was frightened and laid it on thick.

"All right, you heard it all in that meeting, so you know what happens if you screw up. You see that building, the big square one? You're going to land on the roof. We're going to be there just long enough to take on a couple of suitcases, then we'll get off of there fast. You take it nice and slow coming back, you got it?"

The pilot gulped and nodded.

"When you land us here you stay in your seat because we'll be coming back. Soon as we're on board again you take off and drop us midtown; I'll tell you where. You don't look right or left if you don't have to, and you don't look back at us ever. And if I see you touch anything that looks like a radio you're a dead pilot." Mira paused to give the threat its full weight. "You know this town?"

"Pretty well."

"You're going to need to, because, sonny, you're going to do some fancy flying. Let's go."

The pilot didn't wait to be told a second time. He ran to the helicopter, climbed in and went through a quick preflight check. There was the high rising whine of a starter motor and the rotors began to turn. The engines fired and held and filled the air with jet noise.

Mira and Joey ran bent over for the door. Cahill was hanging back and Mira waved for him to come on. He lumbered after them and climbed up awkwardly into the craft. The twin turbines sucked air, screamed harder as the rotor blades dissolved into a thin sheet of movement. The long silver machine stretched itself and began to lift its twenty-thousand-pound weight off the deck of the ship.

On the roof of the bank a walkie-talkie crackled in a policeman's hand. "Three of them getting into the chopper, one of them carrying an overnight bag. The fourth's staying on board."

"Tell him to stay with it," the lieutenant said. "Both choppers every step of the way. Get those launches underneath it, too. I want them to feel the whole world's wearing a badge."

Without binoculars the helicopter looked like a grasshopper rising from a stick in the water. It climbed into the sky, pivoting on itself, the police helicopters, Bell 47G's, riding the sky above and behind it.

They heard the burr of the engines, faint at first, then growing in volume, the roaring whine of the Sea King's jets drowning the piston engine thump of the other two craft.

The Sea King angled up towards them, higher and bigger every second. It rose up and over the building, and their heads craned back to follow its flight. It stopped a hundred feet above them and circled the roof, taking a look. The roof was recessed thirty feet below the top of its facade and was dominated by three giant cooling towers that stretched across the entire depth of the building. There was a washing rig on the western side and near it a small group of men. Between the cooling units two flat-topped elevator towers jutted up like building blocks and on one of them three uniformed bank guards stood, each with a suitcase by his side.

The helicopter began a slow cautious descent. Twenty feet above them, the downdraft from its rotors whipping across the roof, it hovered uncertainly as if expecting a giant flyswatter to smash down from the clouds. It dropped the rest of the way and its main wheel unit touched the top of the elevator block.

The bank guards hurried towards it and heaved the suitcases in through the loading door that had slid open on the starboard side. The door slid shut again as the helicopter went up and over the side of the building and blared away towards the river.

Inside, the three men worked quickly. Joey unzipped the overnight bag he'd carried on board and grabbed up the three sea bags that lay rolled up inside. He passed them round, and they shook them out and snapped open the suitcases. They were high, big-ribbed aluminum cases the size of small trunks, and the money was packed tightly inside them in neat stiff bundles, large-denomination bills smelling of fresh ink and new paper. The sight of it stopped the three men. Mira reached for a bundle and held it like a jewel in front of him, then snapped out of it and began taking out bundles six at a time and stacking them efficiently into the sea bags.

When they'd finished they were just able to hook them closed. They stowed them in some rear seats and closed and picked up the suitcases and got ready as the helicopter lowered over the destroyer.

From the moment they'd lifted off the flight deck and moved towards Manhattan every man on board had had his eyes glued to them.

Except Austin.

Thirty seconds after the take off, he'd gone back to the flying bridge and climbed up into the director.

Then he'd taken another visual fix a few degrees to his left.

chapter 28

"...and recovered the treasure ..."

They went up to the ferry's wheelhouse where the captain was sucking the flame into a new cigar. He flicked the match away and puffed out an initial stream of smoke, clearly getting little enjoyment from it.

Dibley approached him with a certain amount of trepidation. Now that he'd got his own back from the city his earlier devil-may-care, Don Quixote attitude had faded somewhat.

"Afternoon, skipper." He threw a semisalute.

The captain took another puff.

"Captain," Dibley began, "our work here is finished." He wondered if that hadn't sounded too noble and came down a peg. "What I mean is we've alerted you to the danger and shown the mayor the ferry, and frankly there's not much else we can do."

The cigar wagged up and down in the captain's mouth. "Damn right. You already got me in schtook with my old lady."

Dibley ploughed on. "So instead of us coming all the way out to the quarantine station would you mind dropping us off at our cutter out there?"

The captain squinted ahead at the Coast Guard cutter. "It'll have to slow down like twenty knots."

"Not that one," Dibley said, pointing. "That one."

"That ship off the island there? That don't look like no cutter I ever saw. That looks like a navy destroyer."

Swaboda said, "It's on loan."

The captain chewed his cigar suspiciously. "Wait a second. If I been exposed to yellow fever, you been exposed too. So how come you don't have to go into quarantine like me?"

Swaboda had the answer all wrapped up and ready to go. "We had it when we were kids."

The captain wasn't crazy about the explanation but accepted it, although he threw up a final weak barrier. "I don't like it. What do I do when I get to the quarantine station?"

"Just tell them you're the fever ferry."

"She'll kill me," the captain said.

With a great deal of cursing, but with a great deal of skill, he brought the ferry up to the ship's starboard side, the Brooklyn side. And as the crew was lining the Manhattan side watching, like everybody else in the harbor, the helicopter landing on the bank, nobody noticed the ferry or the three sailors who stepped off it onto the destroyer's deck. That was all they had to do, the upper deck of the ferry being only a few feet above the warship's rail.

"What do we do now?" Swaboda asked.

Dibley told him. "Look as though we belong."

Walter produced a Kleenex and began rubbing at a bulkhead. Swaboda started to whistle "Anchors Aweigh." A moment later the whistling died, killed by a fast intake of breath.

"Oh no!"

Dibley got ready to run. "What? What?"

Swaboda turned to look after the departing ferry. "I left Mom in the Ladies' Lounge." They watched the ferry heading up the harbor until a noise in the sky drew their attention. A big silver helicopter was coming right for them.

In fact, the sky seemed to be full of helicopters.

"It's coming in . . . closer . . . it's down. They're getting out with the suitcases . . . the same guy's carrying the overnight bag. They're moving along the deck . . . going inside. No sign of the fourth man. Hold it, I see him on the bridge . . . yeah, it's him. He's coming down now, down the ladder to the main deck . . . he's walking aft . . . he's gone inside."

"Have you tried that chopper again?"

"He won't answer, Lieutenant. Ship won't answer either. Any luck with the visuals?"

"No, they're blind too. Stay with it."

"Roger."

"What do you make of that?" Swaboda asked.

"Only that we're home and dry," Dibley answered, happy. Swaboda didn't understand so Dibley helped him out. "Three guys come out of a helicopter wearing civilian clothes and carrying suitcases and go into the ship. Now what kind of a helicopter would you say that was?"

The dawn broke over Swaboda's face. "The liberty helicopter."

"What else."

"What a super unbelievable piece of luck."

"What a sensational piece of timing."

Walter turned a verbal handspring too. "Good."

Swaboda observed that the pilot was still in there. "Maybe he's waiting to make another trip."

"Fellas," Dibley said, "I think we're about due for shore leave."

They started towards the flight deck and got as far as the hangar before they spotted an officer coming towards them. As one man, they wheeled in their tracks and started walking the other way. They went through a door and kept going towards the bow, Dibley leading, Swaboda bringing up the rear. The officer was right behind them and gaining. Dibley knew that a ship this size probably had a crew of something like two hundred men, and he doubted that one officer would know them all by sight. But there was no sense putting it to the test. He risked a glance behind and was just in time to spot Swaboda scampering up to the next deck, the officer on his tail. Dibley hurried Walter through a door and they emerged onto the bow. He looked above and saw Swaboda framed against the sky at the side of the bridge, then watched as he climbed one more deck to the open space above it. The officer was making for the same spot, too. He lost sight of Swaboda then but could see that he'd run out of decks and wondered with a sinking heart if everything was going to end for them in the next few moments. But he got a nice surprise: The officer was just standing at the rail training binoculars on the city—he'd climbed up there just for a look-see. But he took his time; it was a good ten minutes before he came down again during which Dibley and Walter busied themselves checking the anchor chain for breaks, Walter buffing it up with his Kleenex. Sixty seconds after the officer had descended Swaboda joined them on deck and the three started aft again.

"I didn't think you were ever going to lose that guy," Dibley said.

Swaboda agreed. "I was beginning to think I owed him money."

Their confidence had been badly shaken and Dibley knew that it was mainly this that had kept them alive so far. Not wanting to lose it at this point, he held a little pep talk as they hurried down the ship.

"This time we don't turn back for anybody. This time it's up, up and away. If they want our names or a pass or anything we'll fake it through. We're three sailors going in to tear up the town."

"The Copacabana," Swaboda said, catching the mood.

"Jimmy Ryan's," Dibley countered.

"P.J. Clarke's, Charlie O's."

"Yellowfinger, Maxwell's Plum."

"The Frick Collection," Walter said.

Their spirits restored they reached the flight deck unimpeded, strode across it and climbed through the open door of the helicopter.

The pilot heard them enter and, not daring to turn his head, got a vague impression of three men behind him. He jumped to the obvious conclusion and took the helicopter into the air.

Dibley sank down into a seat and made a thumbs up sign at the other two; it was all working like a charm.

"Three crew members getting into the chopper. It's lifting off."

"Crew? This could be something. They look like they're running?"

"Hard to tell, Lieutenant. They got into it normal enough but that chopper sure got up in a hurry."

"Is it coming this way?"

"Looks like it. Yep, it's turning now."

"One of you stay with it. I want its position every step of the way. If it tries a landing we should be able to get there, so stay on its tail."

"Will do."

The navy pilot didn't have much more of an idea where they were going than the police did. Midtown was all they'd told him, but that was a big place. And if he didn't find out soon he'd overfly it and maybe that hood might do something crazy. He took a deep breath and called over his shoulder, "Where to?"

Swaboda was closest to him and passed the question on to Dibley. "He wants to know where we're going," he yelled in his ear.

"Make it sound good," Dibley yelled back.

Swaboda looked lost. "Where do I tell him?"

"One of those bars we were talking about it."

Under pressure all Swaboda could remember was The Frick Collection. "Name one."

"Kilroy's," Dibley replied. "Sixth and Forty-second." It was the first he thought of. Swaboda relayed the information and the pilot's helmet went up and down.

They were well over the city now, this part of it between Wall Street and Midtown looking as if it had been bombed flat in comparison. They zipped over the bottom of the Bowery and sped uptown.

The sight of the city so close sobered Dibley and he knew that they weren't quite out of the woods yet. Those two helicopters above the ship . . . they'd looked like traffic helicopters from a radio station, but he hadn't paid them much attention . . . could they have been the police? What if the cops had seen them getting onto the destroyer and into the helicopter and were waiting for them to land? It was a definite possibility. He voiced his fears to Swaboda, who was more optimistic.

"I doubt it. Still," he said, "we'd better make it look good getting out."

He looked round the cabin and spotted the sea bags. "They look authentic. Why don't we borrow them?"

"Good idea," Dibley said.

They told Walter and the three of them pulled the bags out of the seats and set them down beside the door. A moment later Dibley felt his stomach somersault and his ears pop as the helicopter dropped fast.

He wondered where the pilot was headed; till they'd passed it he'd assumed they'd been going to the Midtown Skyport.

But there was no doubt in the pilot's mind; they'd told him they wanted Sixth and Forty-second, and they'd also told him he'd be doing some fancy flying, so there was only one possible place they could mean. He brought the helicopter zooming in over the public library and put it down with a bounce in Bryant Park, Sixth and Forty-second exactly. Except for the resident winos sitting on the benches the place was deserted.

"How's that for service?" Swaboda said.

They slid open the door, hopped down, hoisted the bags onto their shoulders and dog-trotted to the sidewalk thirty feet away. The helicopter had come down too fast to give a crowd

208

a chance to gather, but a bunch of people stopped to watch it take off again.

The three men pushed through them and dodged across Forty-second Street up Sixth Avenue. Nobody was shouting at them, nobody was chasing them, no wailing sirens polluted the air.

"We did it," Dibley said. "We pulled it off."

Across the street Kilroy's neon congratulated them.

"Come on," Swaboda said, "I'm buying."

"It's coming up out of Bryant Park. I think it landed there."

"You think. Didn't you see?"

"Not for sure, Lieutenant."

"But did those sailors get out?"

"I don't see anybody."

"Goddamn it, I told you to stay close."

"Impossible, Lieutenant. That Sea King'll do a hundred and fifty. I'm flying an egg beater up here."

"Well, where's it headed now, for crissake?"

"Back to the ship, it looks like."

"O.K. Stay midtown. If it comes back pick it up again. And stay awake up there. I could do a better job myself on the top of the Empire State."

"Yes, sir."

chapter 29

". . . was not without surprise . . ."

Austin knew how much a uniform could change a person's appearance; when he'd worn one himself more than one person had told him how much different he'd looked. But he was still a touch surprised at the change in the three men in front of him. Joey looked all right, he had the same build and was about the same age as most of the other members of the crew. And Cahill might have passed in a petty officer's khakis—a double-breasted jacket would have taken a few pounds off his figure—he was too weighty for the regular white hat uniform. But it was Mira who was the odd man out; he looked no more like a seaman than he would have looked like a doctor had he put on a surgeon's gown. Austin had seen it before, the first day their intake had been issued uniforms. Some of the men looked like they'd never worn anything else all their lives; some of them looked as though they might grow into it. The rest, a handful at the most, looked very badly miscast.

"You have any trouble getting them?"

"We busted open some lockers," Cahill said. "Here's yours."

Austin was still seated in front of the console. He reached out a hand and took the uniform and placed it on the chair next to him. There was a moment when nobody said anything, then Cahill spoke again.

"So, don't you want to know how we did?"

"Sure," Austin said. "How did you do?"

Cahill looked at Joey. "We pull off the biggest heist ever and the guy just sits there. I mean they paid up," he said to Austin. "Three suitcases jammed with the stuff. You never even seen a picture of so much dough. You're rich, buddy, you're lousy with it. You're not happy?"

"Sure I'm happy." Austin's voice was flat and lifeless.

"Get into the uniform and we'll split," Mira said.

Austin didn't look at it. "The radioman cooperate?"

"Called the cops nice and polite," Mira answered, impatient.

"What did he tell them?"

Mira frowned. "What we said we'd tell them." It was clear to him that Austin was just keeping the conversation ticking over. He was like a man holding a trump card who wanted to choose his own moment to play it. Mira shut up to give him an opportunity, but it was Cahill who forced the issue. He picked up the jacket of the uniform and tossed it into Austin's lap.

"What do you say we haul ass, huh?"

Austin very carefully placed the jacket back on the chair. "You guys go along. I've got something to do here first." Then he said into the hushed silence, "A message I have to deliver."

"Who to?"

Austin's mouth stretched into a short smile. "New York."

Cahill looked at Mira, baffled by the answer. He hadn't the vaguest idea of what Austin was talking about, and neither had Joey. But Mira knew, and his stomach twisted into hard icy knots.

Austin saw that he knew. "I've got to fire that gun, man. It's all ready to go."

"You already fired it."

"I fired a flare, that's all."

"It got us what we wanted. The other shells are just a bluff. You told me."

Austin spread his hands. "I lied to you."

Mira's voice rose a little, wavered a bit. "But we already got what we went after."

"You did. I'm about to."

"I don't get it," Cahill said. His forehead glistened and he wiped a hand over it. "We got five million bucks. What more do you want?"

"You think losing five million's going to hurt them? They'll make that back in a week. The money's insured anyway. But it'll take a year to fix the hole I'm going to put in their shiny new Trade Center."

The words pinged around the room, bounced off the shocked stillness. Austin went on talking in his calm, casual manner, the smile still etched onto his face.

"Five million's nothing alongside that. Those buildings cost six hundred and fifty million. And if one of them gets blown in half by a destroyer I'd call that an act of war, wouldn't you? Let's see them try to collect on that."

Joey looked at his brother, but Mira wasn't taking his eyes off Austin. Joey said, "There are a lot of people in that building."

"That's right, Joey. All of them solid, upright citizens, too. Just like the ones who grabbed me off my dad's orchard and sent me overseas to get shot at. Let's see how they like it."

"This is why you came in, isn't it?" Mira said.

"That's right. I've been looking for a long time for a way to get back. You showed me a beauty."

Mira swallowed tightly. "I figured you for a spook, but nothing like this."

Austin said, "We're trading fair. I lived up to my end of the deal. You're all rich men."

"We're all dead men if you fire that gun."

"With five million you could hide on the moon. You told me that yourself."

"You unload on the city and Fort Knox wouldn't do us much good. You can't do it, Austin."

Mira made his move then, but Austin was waiting for it. His hand flew back to the console and his other arm shot out straight ahead of him.

Mira checked his rush an inch away from Austin's fingers. "If I hit this trigger the whole mag goes."

Mira stayed where he was and Austin lowered his arm, although his hand still hovered over a switch.

"Get it through your heads. I'm going to fire this gun. The only choice you guys have is whether you're on or off the ship when I do it."

Cahill started for the door. "I don't want no part of this."

"You've got plenty of time. I want to make the city sweat awhile longer yet."

Mira took a step backwards and put a hand on his brother's arm. "Come on. The guy's crazy."

The word seemed to amuse Austin. "No, not crazy, friend. Just polite. They spent a lot of money to teach me to fire a gun. I just want to show them how good I learned."

They left him smiling at them, went out of the door and up through the ship towards the stern. They stopped at a door that led out onto the flight deck.

"I knew it," Cahill said. He was puffing hard and sweating and his big frame moved up and down between breaths. "I said it was too big for us from the start."

Joey asked his brother what they were going to do.

"Same as we planned. We run. Only we run faster and farther. New names, new faces maybe, whatever it takes. Let's get out there."

They pulled out the stretcher and the blanket they'd stashed behind some downpipes fifteen minutes before. Joey lay down on it and Mira covered him with the blanket, obscuring most of his face.

"Get your hat down over your head," he told Cahill. He adjusted his own. "And don't look up."

They picked up the stretcher and went out onto the deck and carried Joey round past the hangar. Mira spotted one of the police launches close in, but it was off the bow and at too sharp an angle to the ship to get a good look at them. That was a break; the launches had been his main concern. He wasn't too worried about the helicopter above—it would only get a limited view of them. They were expecting a wounded sailor; they might not be looking that hard at them anyway. He hoped that the uniforms would be all the disguise they needed.

They moved across the flight deck. The ship's helicopter was where Mira expected it to be, although he had no way of knowing that it had just that minute landed after its second trip to Manhattan. They ducked under the slowing rotor blades and slid the stretcher in through the loading door, then got in themselves.

Mira didn't notice the expression of dumb amazement on the pilot's face. He was staring at the empty rear seats.

He reached the pilot on the run. "Where are they?"

The pilot was shaking his head. "I don't—"

Mira grabbed the man with both hands. "The bags," he screamed into his face. "Where are the bags?"

"The other guys . . . I thought it was you . . ."

Mira shook him like a rag doll. "What guys? What guys?"

Terrified, the pilot gabbled an answer. "I flew three guys into town. They took the bags."

Mira jerked the man up against his seat belt and lashed out at him with the back of his hand. It was a wild, clumsy blow and the pilot's helmet took most of it.

"You dumb bastard!" Mira yelled. "You idiot dumb bastard! Where'd they go?"

"A bar. Kilroy's. Sixth and Forty-second."

Mira thumped the man back against his seat. "Get this thing into the air."

"Two crew men carrying a guy on a stretcher. They're moving towards the chopper . . . they're loading him in now."

"All right. This time we don't lose him. We know where he's coming down and I want him staying down. Ram his tail rotor if you have to, anything so long as he stays put."

214

"Lieutenant, that tail rotor's a five-blader. It'd go through me like a buzz saw."

"So he's bigger than you, you're two against one. Is your buddy getting all this?"

"Loud and clear, Lieutenant."

"Where are you now?"

"Over the hospital."

"Stay there. Fountain, you there?"

"Go ahead, Lieutenant."

"What's the score?"

"I've got the place roped off and a dozen men on the roof."

"Good. Get a guard on the wounded man and let me know his condition as soon as pos. If I can talk to him right away let me know that. And, Fountain, I want that pilot, understand?"

"Roger, Lieutenant."

On the wing bridge Burgess watched the helicopter rise into the sky. The officer who came up to him saluted and started talking without waiting for his nod.

"Three of them on it, sir. The fourth's still on board."

"The gunner?"

"Yes sir. They carried the young one on in a stretcher. They were wearing uniforms."

"Uniforms?"

"They broke open some lockers, sir."

"Was that man hurt?"

"No sir, they were faking the whole thing. They made the radioman tell the police that one of the crew had tried to be a hero and got himself shot and they were sending him over to hospital. Bellevue, I think it was."

Burgess' second in command, standing just behind him, asked about the suitcases. "They're still below where they left them, sir."

"Then they're coming back," he said to Burgess. "They

wouldn't leave without those. Or the gunner either, I guess."

Burgess didn't comment and his officer spoke again. "Did you get a chance to get to the pilot?"

"No sir. When I saw them coming I didn't want to interfere."

The executive said, "I'd give a couple of stripes to know why he made that second trip."

"Sir, one of the air crew says he saw some crew getting into the copter just before it lifted. But I called a muster and there's nobody adrift."

Both men looked at Burgess, who swung his eyes back to the helicopter.

He watched it climbing up the sky, beating through the air towards the city.

Down on the main deck Austin watched it too before he lowered his gaze to the skyline. Because of the ship's position, and because the two buildings were staggered one behind the other, the south tower of the Trade Center partly hid its twin and looked taller and broader. Beyond it, low over the Jersey Meadows, puffs of cumulus clouds moved like zeppelins, making the towers appear to be toppling.

He noticed that the breeze that had come and gone a little while ago had left the harbor unruffled, the air still, and that the ship sat solidly in the water pointing like an arrow towards the same spot in Manhattan.

He left the rail and went into the ship and back to the battery plot.

He'd been bluffing Mira a little; the gun was still trained on the bank. He'd been about to reprogram it when they'd walked in on him with the uniform. He wondered idly if Mira would have jumped him if he'd known.

He sat at the console and moved switches, listening to the computer click and hum as new target information was fed in from the director.

He did everything slowly, savoring the moment, drawing

216

each little operation out. He was never going to be in a position like this again.

He wanted the feeling to last.

chapter 30

". . . or unforeseen events . . ."

"Police . . ."

"Hello? My name's Gibbs. I'm calling from Third Beach."

"Yes, sir?"

"I fish off the beach out here. I'm retired now and I've been coming here, oh, maybe five years and—"

"What's the problem, sir?"

"I think there's something funny going on. Like I say I fish off the beach out here and I got into the habit of washing the catch down at those outside showers at the old bathhouse. If I've got a catch that is, somedays you do better than others, you know?"

"Could you be specific, sir?"

"I'm being specific. Today I noticed right away something was different. There was a car parked in where the showers are, behind the partition, so then I walked round to the front to have me a look. Well, sir, I swear that lock was busted on the front door. I didn't go in 'cause I figured they might still be in there, the people who broke in, I mean."

"Thank you, sir, we'll have a man check it."

"I know it wasn't the fella who looks after the place because it wasn't his car . . . Hello?"

On the other end of the line the officer had terminated the call and was commenting on it to another man.

"The busiest day we've had in two years and we're supposed to worry about some kids breaking into a bathhouse."

"Always the way," the other officer said.

The man in the phone box hung up the phone and looked angrily at it. Nobody even said goodbye anymore. He went out onto the sidewalk and gathered up his gear; the wicker basket, the floppy brown hessian sack, the big surf rod broken down into two lengths. He squinted at the bathhouse a hundred yards away; when the police arrived he'd tell them that it was he, Tom Gibbs, who'd reported it. Not for any pats on the back or anything like that, but because in his day you saw a thing through. Not like now; the slapdash seventies he called them. Even worse than the sloppy sixties. He began to walk towards the building, his nylon windbreaker flapping back over the thick Irish-knit sweater and the chamois leather shirt underneath. He wore dungarees and tennis sneakers and a peaked cap on his head.

He wouldn't go too near it, just take another look maybe, see if the car was still there. He approached it from the rear stepping lightly, his sneakers making little sound on the sandy concrete. Yep, there it was all right, one of those foreign beetles. That meant the people were still in there, although what could they steal from an out-of-season bath house? He crept around to the front to take another look at the lock. When he got there the door was open and a man with a gun was standing in it.

"Inside," McNally said.

With more surprise than fear Gibbs said, "What?"

"Come on, pop, move." McNally stepped aside and waved the man forward with his gun. Gibbs got his legs going and went through the door and McNally slammed it shut behind him.

The room was a long narrow rectangle, wooden slats on the floor, with a fixed bench running round all four walls, coat hooks stuck at intervals above it. At the far end of the bench a woman and a child huddled against the gray cement wall.

"What's going on here?"

"Anybody with you?" McNally asked.

The old man shook his head.

"Get comfortable. You'll be here for a couple of hours."

Gibbs walked down the room and sat next to the woman. He put the basket on the floor and leaned the rod between his knees.

"He hurt you?"

"No."

McNally sat down a few feet from them on the opposite bench. He'd put his gun away and seemed to have lost interest.

Gibbs looked at the scared face of the little girl peeking out from under her mother's arm. She had a teddy bear tightly clutched in her arms.

"What's this all about?"

The woman did a pretty good job of keeping the waver out of her voice. "He came for us early this morning. He's holding us hostage."

"What for?"

"Can the chat," McNally said.

"Now listen, young fella—"

"You listen. Just sit tight and say nothing. Both of you."

Gibbs breathed out hard through his nose and got a fresh grip on the fishing rod. "A woman, a little kiddie and an old man. You scared of us, mister?"

"Pop, I get paid to make people behave, and if they don't I persuade them real hard. Young or old, it's all in the job. Now shut up."

She knew she had to make a decision. The arrival of the fisherman had given her an option. Up till now the gun that she was carrying had been useless to her. She didn't have it in her to kill somebody, and short of just walking up to him and pulling the trigger she didn't see any way out of it. She'd have to get too close to him to take his gun herself and if she ordered him to take it out and drop it he'd kill her with it. She'd seen the way he handled guns when they'd heard the fisherman snooping round the first time; his arm had swept up, and although she hadn't seen his hand go into his jacket, at the end of the movement he'd been holding a gun. But now she could cover him while the old man took his gun. The only other consideration was Lisa. God knew how much this thing was going to scar her; it might stay with her for years or she might forget it in a week. But she might never forget the sight of her mother threatening a man with a pistol. She bent down to her and whispered in her ear, then straightened and spoke to McNally.

"She has to go to the bathroom."

"Take her."

She stood up with the little girl, putting the bear down on the bench. "We'll leave Teddy here," she said to her. She took her hand and led her halfway up the room to a door that led off to some toilets. She guided her into a cubicle and talked to her. She shut the door on her daughter and came back into the room and sat down on the bench again. Trying to do it casually she picked up the bear. It had big fluffy ears and glass button eyes and a flat body that could be zipped open to take pajamas or toys.

Her hand went to the zipper and moved it along its slide, then crept into the quilted pouch inside.

Whether it showed in her eyes or the furtive way her hands moved, or whether McNally just sensed the gun, he stopped her with a sharp command.

"Hold it!"

The woman froze. Then she started speaking. She formed her words quietly and precisely as if she were talking into a tape recorder.

"My husband is away a lot. He bought me a gun. When I was upstairs this morning I took it from my bureau drawer. I thought you might look in my pocketbook so I hid it in here. It's pointing at you now."

220

Gibbs, the old man, was sitting forward. His eyes went to the bear in the woman's lap.

McNally's eyes stayed on the woman, then looked back at the wall. Apart from the brief turn of his head he hadn't moved. He said, "Lady, you and your husband have a lot to learn."

He sounded different, speaking in a softer, more natural manner she hadn't heard before.

"One, if you do have a gun in there and you keep it in the bureau like you say, it's probably a ladies' bedside twenty-two. Two . . ." he very carefully got to his feet ". . . if it is a twenty-two . . ." he started walking slowly down the room ". . . you'd either have to be lucky or know what you're doing to hit me where it hurts. The heart or the head, say. Or the lungs. And three," he turned at the far wall, "what your husband should have got you . . ." he reached for his gun as casually as if he were going after a cigaret ". . . is a thirty-eight, like this. Something that would do you some good."

She couldn't believe it; a moment ago he'd been sitting a few feet from her with his hands by his sides and she'd had a gun on him. Now he was standing at the other end of the room, his body side-on to her, a much smaller target at a far greater distance, and he had that big gun out and was pointing it squarely at her body. She knew she should have stopped him. She'd been going to. But the way he spoke . . . and what he said . . . He'd been too smart for her.

"Take your hand out slow and easy."

She brought the gun out and let it droop towards the floor, her head doing likewise. It had been no more use against him than the teddy bear she'd hid it in.

"You're too cute, lady." The hard sharpness was back in his voice and his face had gone stiff. He started angrily towards her and for the rest of her life she was unclear on exactly what had happened next.

At the same moment McNally had moved for her she caught a sudden glimpse of her daughter at the door looking as if she were going to rush right into his path. She got a vivid visual

221

association of her little girl and the advancing gun in McNally's hand and she cried out, "Lisa!"

Her whole body had jerked upright and her fingers had clenched instinctively. McNally had been right about the gun and her chances. It was a twenty-two and she was lucky.

The bullet smashed into his left kneecap, hitting him in mid-stride as his weight was coming down on it. His leg went from under him as if he'd tried to step up onto a paper bag, and he sprawled forward onto the floor, the gun bouncing out of his hand. But the man was a pro, and like a good ball player who bobbles a grounder but keeps the ball in front of him, he kept the gun within reach. It was only a foot away, but the time it took him to haul himself to it was enough time for Gibbs to stop McNally from killing her.

He'd reacted amazingly fast, almost as if he'd known what was going to happen. Instead of the shot surprising him it had acted on him like a starter's pistol and he'd jumped to his feet, snatched up the rod and knocked McNally cold.

It was an old rod, built the way they used to make them, and the heavy steel and wood reel thumped down on McNally's head like a weighted pipe.

It ruined the reel. And as Gibbs later told the police there was a time when he could have found a man who would have been willing to fix a thing like that. But not these days.

chapter 31

". . . or unbargained for-occurrences . . ."

When the warning bell started clanging Burgess immediately assumed that they were removing the threat from the bank and facing the gun away.

Then he saw how wrong he was.

The mount was moving left not right, and the barrel was elevating into firing position again.

With a fine river of fear running through him he saw where the gun was pointing. He didn't have to be dead in line with the gun to know for sure; there was only one possible target and everybody on the bridge knew it.

With a kind of numb fascination he said aloud what all of them were thinking. "They're going to try it a second time."

The buzz of a bridge telephone startled them.

Somebody snatched it up. "Message from shore, sir."

"From shore?" Burgess reached for the phone. "If he's broken silence . . ." He spoke into it. "Captain."

He listened, then jerked the phone closer. Then his shoulders fell and he squinched his eyes shut and let out a breath like a man coming up from a deep dive.

It lasted only a second. He twisted and yelled at his officer. "Jimmy! The director . . ."

The man didn't wait for an explanation. He raced out onto the wing and jumped for the ladder to the flying bridge. He wasn't even halfway up it when, back in the battery plot, Austin closed a switch.

Deep inside the ship, in the magazine beneath the mount, twin horizontal drums revolved, the shells and casings that lay in them clicked forward a notch and were sucked up two by two, shooting through separate tubes to slap together in the gun breech. The gun bucked and fired and went on firing every second and a half, the crashing detonations swelling in the air, each explosion folding into the previous one like an unending clap of thunder. The concussions washed back over the ship, staggering it, massive tremors shuddering through the decks. The gun was like a monster gone crazily out of control, roaring and spewing great blasts of black smoke, as if it were tearing itself apart.

Austin was running for the door. He climbed up through the ship, the hammering slam of the gun shaking the ladders as he scurried up them.

He burst out onto the foredeck, and although the air was curtained with roiling black smoke he saw enough to stop him dead: Instead of the shells smashing into the tower, blowing it apart, they were passing way to the left of it, exploding harmlessly in the river off the Jersey City docks, the water shooting up in high thick columns.

He was stunned; it was point-blank range, he couldn't have missed. The ship was still dead on course and he'd set the director himself.

He swiveled his head and looked up at it as the last round pounded out of the gun and it stopped firing. The silence that followed the crashing wall of noise seemed almost as shattering, and Austin, temporarily deafened by the blasts, might not have heard the men who came running down at him. But even when they grabbed him and pinned his arms back he took no notice. He just stood there staring unbelievingly at the director.

He didn't take his eyes off it till they bundled him below.

chapter 32

". . . and delivered the robbers . . . to the captain of the vizier's guard"

Kilroy's was teeming with its usual mixture of regular customers and passing Sixth Avenue trade, all of them getting along very nicely on a variety of subjects. A man on crutches, who'd wandered in to drink up his compensation check, was describing his accident to a retired developer who came in every day to work on a quart of Bell's. Next to him an elevator starter was talking politics to two hard hats who'd been sent an hour ago for a couple of six-packs. In the middle of the bar an architect was buying the sweeper a drink and explaining why he was getting an early start on the evening's drinking. At the end of the bar a group from the big ad agency on Forty-third Street was putting in a late finish to their lunchtime drinking. They were swapping movie stars' real names. One of them, a balding man with a Gabby Hayes beard, came up with Robert Taylor's. His friend, chubby face, sweptback hair and glasses, claimed that Trigger had been born Elliott Schranz.

The group at the opposite end of the bar weren't so cheerful. They were half a dozen college ball players who'd just been beaten in a preseason game and had come in to take the sting out of the defeat.

Dibley, Walter and Swaboda, sitting in a booth just behind them, were, on the other hand, celebrating victory.

Dibley raised his Martini. "Gentlemen, I'd like to drink a toast to you. You backed me up every inch of the way. You were both terrific. And Walter, you can pass that on to Rocky and Kitty when you see them, too."

"Hold it," Swaboda said. "If anybody gets toasted it's going to be you." He picked up his draft beer. "To our leader without who, wait, whom, we'd still be getting thrown off the Penn Central. I give you James Dibley."

"James Dibley," Walter repeated, raising his Singapore Sling. They all drank.

Dibley said, "Now let's drink to the ferry boat captain."

"I've been wondering about him," Swaboda said. "What's going to happen when he gets to the quarantine station?"

Dibley speared an olive—Kilroy's had got a jar in specially for the advertising crowd. "He'll be doing us another favor. They'll find out soon enough who the gun and the Land Rover belong to and return them. That's the nice thing about all this: Nobody's going to be out who doesn't deserve to be. The Port Authority's bound to be insured against loss of revenue for the ferry, and the mayor will claim against the city, now that I think about it. And as for these," he patted the sea bag next to him, "we'll leave them on the USO's doorstep with a note."

"A perfect result," Swaboda said. "Although for a while there, back on the ship, I thought it was all going to end in the mud."

"So did I. When that officer came after you . . . Incidentally, did he or didn't he spot you?"

"He missed me. I found a fantastic hiding place." Swaboda dragged on his beer. "I spotted some rungs going up a kind of box underneath one of those things that look like a big soup bowl. I thought it must lead somewhere and I was right. There was a little door in the box and I got inside and hid."

"What was it?"

"I don't know; the crow's nest, I guess. There was this fantastic telescope in there. I could see the whole city like it was a couple of feet away. I could even pick out our old apartment in Jersey City. I had a ball in that thing."

"But you didn't touch anything in there, did you?"

"You're kidding," Swaboda said. "I pressed every button in sight. I love stuff like that."

Dibley frowned. "You shouldn't monkey around with navy equipment. You could have started World War III."

"Naw," Swaboda said. "Nothing happened, did it?"

Officer Harvey Baden wasn't doing so well. He was no closer to capturing those criminals than he had been back behind the switchboard. He'd toyed with the idea of getting up onto the roof of the bank, sneaking onto the helicopter somehow and riding it back to the ship. But his mother had made him promise he'd never fly, so that was out. He was pretty sure a frogman could have got onto the ship unobserved but that ruled him out, too. His mother had a pathological fear of his drowning and had never let him near any sizeable body of water. He thought he'd had it solved when he'd come home one day and told her that she didn't have to worry anymore because he was going to take swimming lessons at the Y. "Don't take them, you'll drown," she'd screamed. His mother had had a very vivid dream years ago of her son's demise. He'd crashed into the sea in an airliner while choking on a chicken mayonnaise sandwich. Harvey had also promised to stay away from chicken mayonnaise sandwiches.

He'd been following everything on Captain Marble's police radio so he knew about the helicopter landing midtown. Parked at the Battery, close to the action, he'd just had to sit there like everybody else and watch it fly over. But he didn't figure to be caught napping this time. He knew that it was coming over again, this time with an injured sailor for Bellevue. But was it? Harvey had a hunch that it was just a blind. That was why instead of heading up First Avenue to Bellevue, he was driving up Sixth on his way to Fiftieth Street. Harvey was convinced that the navy plane was going to try another midtown landing. It had worked once, why not twice? From his years on the switchboard he knew how thieves operated: When they knocked over a house or an apartment and got away with it, nine out of ten times they came back and tried the same place again. So midtown made sense. And he was certain he knew where. These people had imagination and daring—look at the caper they'd pulled; and look at the way they'd come down practically in Times Square. So it stood to reason that their second landing would be equally spectacular. There was only one place. It was obvious—the skating rink at Rockefeller Plaza.

He tried to think whether they'd started skating there yet or whether the outdoor cafe umbrellas were still up. Either way there was nothing to stop a helicopter from dropping down between the buildings like an express elevator and letting someone out. It was ideal—Rockefeller Center would be tough to seal off—a person could disappear in those underground concourses; they were like rabbit warrens. Heck, they could even run down into the IND and be over in Queens before you could turn around. Sure they were going to land there, and all he had to do was be on hand when they came. Of course, the radio report said that there were just three sailors, one wounded. But what if they were the bandits? Wouldn't that be a smart way of getting off the ship? And what if he, Harvey Baden, was the one who arrested them?

With his heart thumping he stopped for a red light on Twenty-third. Detective Harvey Baden, dark suit, snap brim hat, flashing the badge. "You'll never make it, Mad Dog . . ." He was waiting impatiently for the light to change when he heard a sound that couldn't possibly be coming from the cab next to him or the truck behind him. It sounded like . . . Harvey thrust his head out of the window and peered above him. The navy helicopter was coming down fast. It looked to be making for the roof of an apartment building not thirty feet away.

228

Harvey couldn't believe it. He'd been right! Not the skating rink but not Bellevue either. His chance to get off the switchboard was practically landing in his lap.

He gunned the car and belted it over to the curb. He had his gun in his hand and was out and running into the building in three seconds flat. The elevator was waiting for him—it was his day. He jabbed number Fourteen and the doors closed and he was whisked upwards.

He was reminded briefly of the last time he'd run into an apartment house with a drawn gun. But there was no chance of making that mistake again; this time he couldn't pick the wrong apartment.

The doors slid back and he charged down the hall, jerked open the door at the end, tore up the stairs and burst out onto the roof.

"Give up now, Mad Dog, you'll never—" The command died in his throat. He'd expected to see a helicopter and sure enough he was seeing one. But it was on the next roof.

He'd run into the wrong apartment house.

The shock of his discovery rooted him to the spot. He was dimly aware of the helicopter lifting off the roof and of the police helicopters, coming up fast from two sides, that were going to be too late to stop it. Then he saw something that galvanized him back into action: Three sailors disappearing through the roof door. There was still time!

Harvey turned and bolted down the stairs and back down the hall to the elevator. The floor indicator showed a clear bright B and the letter remained unblinkingly bright—the elevator was mired in the basement as if the cables had snapped. Harvey groaned; some woman doing her laundry probably and making sure of the elevator. It figured—now that things had started to go downhill everything would be against him. He got a fast mental picture of himself, old and gray and due for his pension, "Pop" Baden still taking down details of lost wallets and jammed automobile horns. No! He'd taken down his last jammed automobile horn. He was going to get those guys, those sailors, whoever they were. He was going to get somebody.

He ran for the stairs, body leaning forward, knees pumping high, the way they'd taught him at the Police Academy. He took them four at a time, thundering down them faster and faster, building up speed like a stone dropped from a window. He counted off fourteen floors, forgetting that most New York apartment houses, with a bow to tenant superstition, eliminate the thirteenth floor and call it the fourteenth, and belted through the door into the basement.

The woman who had the elevator door propped open with her laundry gave him a shocked look of terror and delight. It was finally happening: She was finally going to be raped in the laundry. And by a red-headed man with a gun, would you believe?

Harvey disappointed her. He bounced off a Bendix and went out almost as fast as he'd come in, thus causing the woman, a plump forty-five, to go back onto her diet for three hours. He raced up the stairs, through the lobby, past a bored-looking doorman and out onto the sidewalk.

For the second time in a few minutes he came to an astonished halt.

The car wasn't where he'd left it against the curb. It was fast disappearing up the avenue. And the worst part of it was he was pretty sure that the three people in it were wearing navy uniforms.

It was clear what had happened, painfully, agonizingly clear: Those three guys had beaten him down to the street, probably intending to escape the helicopters by running into the subway entrance ten yards farther up the sidewalk. But when they'd spotted the car at the curb, its door open, its engine running and nobody in it . . .

When he realized the full import of his action Harvey caught his breath and held it for so long he almost damaged his brain. He, Officer Harvey Baden, had not only failed to apprehend three suspects in the city's biggest robbery, but had supplied the means for their getaway—a Plymouth Fury station wagon with police radio and power windows that belonged to his own precinct captain.

Harvey looked down at the gun in his hand and was bringing it up to his temple when he heard the sirens. He put the gun away and walked off like a dead man. They were too late to catch that car anyway, and Harvey wasn't about to tell them he'd seen them go. He'd have to explain what he was doing there, why he was out of uniform and how he'd borrowed Captain Marble's car and how he'd run into the wrong . . . He brought the gun out again. No, not with his own gun. He knew a better way.

He went into a phone box, checked a number, dug out a coin and dialed.

"Calypso Airlines, may I help you?"

"Do you have a flight tonight?"

"Yes, sir, our nine o'clock. May I reserve you a seat?"

"Please," Harvey replied. "And listen," he said in a voice from the crypt, "I'd also like to reserve a chicken mayonnaise sandwich."

Mira had taken it easy pulling away, wanting to look like any other car just melting into the traffic. Two blocks north, with no sign of any chase, he put his foot down and sped up the avenue, weaving in and out, running red lights when he could and barreling through the greens. When they made the light at Forty-second he slammed the car over to the curb and screeched to a stop outside Kilroy's. They piled out of the car and ran inside and right away spotted the sailors and the sea bags.

"There they are," Cahill yelled.

Everybody in the bar looked up including Dibley. He got a glimpse of three angry sailors starting towards them and made the correct assumption.

"Heads up," he said, "somebody's come for their property."

231

Swaboda had seen them too. "That pilot—he finked on us."

With the money almost within their grasp the three men weren't too careful about the way they shouldered through the crowd at the bar.

They should have been.

Joey barged into one of the ball players and spilled his drink. The college boy grabbed Joey's arm. "Who you shoving, sailor?"

Mira knocked his hand away. "Leave the kid alone," he snarled at him.

He went to move by him, but the ball player wasn't going to let it go at that. He'd been humbled on the field a few hours ago and was still sore about it, and he wasn't going to let any half-pint runt push him around with the fellas watching. He shot an arm out and caught Mira's elbow, spun him and pulled him into a looping overhand right. It was a good punch, most of his two hundred pounds behind it, and it caught Mira on the hinge of the jaw. His head snapped back and his knees buckled and he went down hard, out of it.

Joey had hit the man twice before another member of the ball team threw a punch at him. Somebody else thumped Cahill who, although no fighter, started swinging in self-defense.

For a brief moment one end of the bar became a maelstrom of fists and elbows, then the bartenders went into action. They had their orders about fights; a New York State liquor license isn't that easy to hold on to and a blemished record doesn't help when renewal time comes around. Consequently, in the less plush bars of New York, belligerents are dealt with swiftly and mercilessly.

The two barmen snatched up long wooden billies, vaulted the bar and went after the newcomers. Joey was poleaxed from behind and Cahill went under to a hard glancing blow on the side of the head, and the fight was over.

The head barman, working at the steam table in the front window, shouted over at Dibley. "Hey, sailor. Get your buddies back into that wagon out there and piss off." Dibley, like Walter and Swaboda, had been an open-mouthed spectator to the brawl and was still trying to figure out how it had started.

"You heard me," the bartender said, "get them outta here. You guys," he said to the college boys, "bunch of trouble-makers. Give 'em a hand."

The college men, cocky after the fight, were happy to help.

"Give the sailors a hand," they cried.

Frank and Joey were picked up bodily, hefted onto shoulders and carted out of the door. It took two of them to carry Cahill.

"They need air," somebody shouted. "Let's put them on top."

The suggestion was loudly approved, and the three men were hoisted up onto the roof rack of the wagon and laid out full length side by side.

Cahill was too groggy to understand what was happening and the brothers were both still out.

One of the ball players called to the man who'd hit Mira. "Hey, Bobbie, you should tie yours across the hood."

"Better tie them down anyway," Bobbie replied.

They dug out some rope from the back of the wagon and went to work.

By the time Dibley and his partners had struggled out with the sea bags the college boys were just tying the last knots.

"Aw, fellas," Dibley said. "Come on now, you can't do a thing like this."

"No trouble," they said. "All part of the service." The team rolled back into the bar extremely pleased with themselves.

Swaboda said, "Poor guys, they didn't deserve this."

"Come on," Dibley said, "let's get them down."

They stepped towards the car and reached up to the roof rack.

Their hands froze on the ropes.

Sirens were filling the air.

Normally Dibley wouldn't have even noticed the sound, sirens being as natural to New Yorkers as air conditioning, but there was something about the sound of these that worried him. Walter and Swaboda felt it too.

"You know," Swaboda said, "if the cops did spot us getting on the helicopter that pilot would have finked to them, too."

"Exactly what I was thinking," Dibley said.

The sirens stopped.

Dibley looked at the other two. "Well, that's a break."

They looked back at him, uncertain. Nobody was convinced.

The sirens wailed into life again very close.

They hurled the sea bags into the back of the car, tumbled into the front and slid down out of sight. They heard the sound of warped tires squealing into the avenue and the screech of brakes behind them. They didn't have to look to know that policemen were pouring into Kilroy's.

As Dibley rocketed the car away and swung it into the cross street, he assumed that they hadn't spotted the three sailors on the roof because they hadn't been looking for three sailors in that position. He didn't give it much thought, being involved in passing cars on the wrong side and honking pedestrians out of the way. The pros say you can't make a getaway in a car in New York City on account of the congestion, but Dibley was proving them wrong. He zoomed down Forty-third and across Broadway.

"How are they doing upstairs?" he yelled.

Swaboda stuck his head out and took a look. The rush of air in their faces had brought the three men on the roof to a bleary level of consciousness. They could see where they were but were gropingly trying to fathom how they'd come to be there. They held on tight and kept wondering.

"They're still there," Swaboda called back.

Dibley swerved into Eighth Avenue. "Can you see any cops?" he hollered.

"Not yet."

"We'll get them down when we're sure we're safe." Dibley flicked his head sideways. "This doesn't look like a rental car, so they probably live in town. See if you can find their address."

Walter sprung open the glove compartment and came up

with a letter. He passed it to Swaboda, who read off the address.

"Captain Ralph Marble, Four Twenty-two West Forty-seventh. They must be staying with their skipper."

"That's only a few blocks away. Any sign of the police?"

"Nothing."

"We'll drop them off now." Dibley swung the car carefully into Forty-seventh. "How are we doing on numbers?"

"Next block," Swaboda said.

They crossed Ninth and Swaboda began to count off. "Four fourteen, four sixteen, four eighteen, it's two more to go."

They were concentrating on the numbers, not the houses, and the buildings looked pretty much the same anyway.

"Good," Dibley said, "they've got a garage."

He turned into the entrance, drove down the ramp, swung around a pillar and tried to stand up behind the wheel. He hit the brake so hard the car stalled.

For a brief moment life as they knew it on the planet Earth stopped for them and they gaped in wonder at what looked like a basement full of police cruisers.

"It's a trap," Dibley cried.

Then a couple of things dawned on them: For a start there were no policemen in the cars or crouched beside them holding guns. In fact the only policemen in sight were two patrolmen at the far end who had their backs to them and were taking no notice. For another thing one of the cruisers had its hood raised and another was up on a hoist.

Dibley changed his opinion. "This isn't a trap . . ."

Swaboda finished the sentence. "It's a police garage."

Walter said, "I think we should leave."

They didn't take a vote on it.

They eased themselves out of the car and started for the door.

From the top of the car where he was lying Cahill saw something move in front of his eyes. "Hey," he said weakly.

"Sorry, buddy," Dibley whispered to him as he went by, "this is the best we can do for you."

Captain Marble was thinking about going down to the Battery himself, although he knew Headquarters wouldn't like that. Damn it, it was this not knowing he couldn't stand. A horrible thought struck him: What if Ellicott over at the Sixty-seventh brought it off? Or Borman at the Ninety-second? That would be worse. He remembered Borman at the last police party saying something to the commissioner and they'd both looked over in his direction and laughed. Please, anybody but Borman's men. But what was he worrying about? The Fiftieth was the equal of any precinct in the city—he'd trained his men himself, hadn't he? Of course, in a case like this there was always a chance the FBI would make the arrest. He tried to remember the last time the FBI had made a criminal arrest and was immediately comforted. But he'd still like to know what was happening down there.

He picked up the phone. "Baden?"

"He's gone home with a headache, Captain."

"A headache? My God, the biggest thing to hit the Fiftieth in years and one of my men goes home with a headache. Whatever happened to ambition?"

Bored, Harvey's friend said, "He went home too, Captain."

"What's that?"

"You say something, Captain?"

"Any news from Wall Street yet?"

"Not yet, sir."

"Well, buzz me the moment you hear anything, understand?"

"Yes, sir."

The captain hung up feeling that he'd at least done something. He was drumming his fingers on the desk and starting to worry about Borman again when two patrolmen came almost bashfully into his office.

"Yes, yes, what is it, men? I'm a very busy man."

"We got them, Captain," one of them mumbled.

"Got who? Speak up, I've got a precinct to run."

"The guys who pulled that job in Wall Street, sir."

"What job in Wall Street? I don't—" Captain Marble's voice congealed in his throat. "You don't mean the job in *Wall Street?*"

The men were nodding.

"*The* job in Wall Street?"

The men went on nodding.

It just couldn't be, the captain thought wildly. This was the Fiftieth Precinct: three jaywalkers and a barking dog convicted in the last two weeks.

"We got the money too, sir."

"The money as well?" It had to be a joke. But no, look at their faces: No twinkle-eyed dead-pan expression, no mouths clamped down tight on silent laughter, these men looked more embarrassed than anything.

With a blinding excitement building inside him Captain Marble realized that they were telling the truth.

He leaped to his feet. "Fantastic! Fan-tastic!" He snatched up the phone. "Baden, get me my wife, quick."

"Baden's gone home with a headache, Captain."

"Then whoever you are, get me my wife. Hurry." He clutched the phone to his chest. "I can't believe it, the Fiftieth pulling off the biggest arrest of the year. Wait till Borman hears about this. You men are in for a promotion. A big promotion."

"Thank you, Captain," the patrolmen said, not looking at him.

The phone sounded and he whipped it to his ear. "Hello, May? Have you bought that new dress yet . . . ? You have? Great! Because we did it, May. We caught those bank robbers . . . Yes! Where?" He took the phone down. "Where did you find them, men?"

One of the policemen coughed. "In the er, garage, Captain."

"In the garage," Captain Marble hollered into the phone. It

occurred to him what he'd just said and he took the phone down again. "What garage?"

It was the other policeman's turn. He coughed, too. "Our garage, Captain." The smile that had been creasing the captain's face sagged in the middle.

"You mean *our* garage? The *precinct* garage?"

The men scuffed their boots. "Yes, sir."

Captain Marble's mouth went from the horizontal to the vertical.

"Where . . ." He swallowed and took another crack at it. "Where in heaven's name were they?"

This was the moment they'd been dreading. They swapped a quick glance, each hoping the other would reply. Finally the senior of the two shouldered the burden. He tried to make it sound like the most natural thing in the world. "Lashed to the roof rack of your car."

Heads down they waited for the explosion, but there was none forthcoming.

They raised their eyes.

The captain seemed to have been struck by lightning and expertly embalmed. They were beginning to consider holding up a mirror to his mouth when a tiny sign of life showed in the flickering twitch of an eyelid. He subsided heavily into his chair and lifted the phone as if it were an iron dumbbell. He croaked into it in a glazed, glassy-eyed voice, "Take the dress back to the store, May. And, May," he spoke with the speed of a coffin being lowered into the ground, "see if they'll exchange it for a shotgun."

chapter 33

"And what has been is destined to be again"

"All right, you can look now," Dibley said.

Carol took her hands away from her eyes. "Wow. A convertible yet."

They were standing outside the apartment in front of the '56 De Soto that was parked at the curb.

"The guy wanted one fifty for it, but Charlie beat him down to one fifty-five."

"Ooh, what a fib," Swaboda said. He flicked a duster proudly over the fender. Walter was shining the tires with a Kleenex.

"Isn't it a honey?" Dibley said. He was carrying the navy uniforms in the costume company's box which he dusted off before putting it in the back seat. This car they were going to look after. "A few scratches here and there of course . . ."

Carol tried to sound enthusiastic. "It's terrific. Um, what are these things all over the body? They look like patches."

"I think they're rust spots," Swaboda said. "But otherwise it's in great condition. Only one previous owner."

It looked to Carol as if the owner were previous, too. She'd often wondered what the Mafia did with the cars they bombed. She searched for a compliment.

"It looks reliable. Certainly should be able to get you up to Westchester twice a week."

Dibley laughed. "You want to know a funny thing? This'll

kill you. After all we went through to get a car to take us up to the clinic we're not sure we need to go there anymore."

"What are you saying?"

"Just that, for some reason, our day on the harbor seems to have accomplished what Doctor Segal couldn't."

"He's right," Swaboda put in. "For me, anyway. When Mom sailed away to the quarantine station she sailed away for good. I haven't seen her since."

Carol kissed his cheek. "Why, that's wonderful, Charlie."

"Isn't it?" Swaboda went to get into the car, then stopped, stepped back and held the door open. "Oh sorry," he said. "After you, Dad."

"A miracle cure," Carol murmured to Dibley.

"Well, O.K.," he murmured back, "maybe Charlie needs another visit or two but not me or Walter." He raised his voice. "Right, Walter? We haven't heard a peep out of Rocky or Kitty for ages."

Walter left off polishing. "That's right."

Carol said, "I'm so glad, Walter. Frankly, I wasn't too wild about either of them." Walter's body suddenly went all limp and gangly as if he'd grown a foot in height. He looked down bashfully at the Kleenex he was holding and ran it through his hands as if it were a lariat. He said in Gary Cooper's slow drawl, "Cain't say I hankered after them any m'self, ma'am. Nope." He swung a leg up and climbed lazily over the car door and sat down, tall in the back seat.

Carol drew Dibley aside. "That double bill at the Roxy," she said, "the day Walter was born? They must have shown a trailer, too."

Dibley said, "Just as long as they didn't show a Donald Duck cartoon."

Carol took his hand. "That only leaves you and your problem, darling!"

"Don't joke, Carol. I mean it. I'm cured."

"Honestly?" Carol asked, hope springing eternal. "You're really cured?"

"I'm really cured," he said, smiling.

"Marvelous!" She came into his arms.

"Not one sneeze all day."

Carol sighed and untangled herself. "Come on, let's get the costumes back to the rental company."

They got into the front seat. Dibley turned the key and the engine started with a nice deep roar.

"How about that?" Dibley said.

"Sweet as pie," Swaboda said.

Dibley took it away from the curb. The car accelerated smoothly, purring along. He swung the wheel to take a right. The car cornered evenly with a minimum of sway.

"Smooth as silk," Dibley said.

The next moment there was a tremendous bone-jarring thump that shot them out of their seats, and the car ground to an agonized stop.

Astonished, the three men got out to take a look.

Both front wheels had collapsed and the car seemed to have broken in two.

They turned their heads and gazed at the enormous pothole they'd hit.

Their first reaction was one of horror and disbelief. Their second reaction was entirely different.

Grim-mouthed, eyes burning with vengeance, they looked back and forth at one another and nodded in consent to an unspoken suggestion. Then, starting to undress, they opened the rear door and reached into the box for the navy uniforms.